To
Fiona
With best wishes
from
Ina
01. 11. 2025

WANDERERS ALL

Stories from Emigrant Families

Iona Carroll.

IONA CARROLL

Foreword By

Gwen Chessell

Silver Quill Publishing

ALSO BY IONA CARROLL

The Story of Oisin Kelly Series:
Crying Through the Wind
Familiar Yet Far
Homecoming

Short Stories:
Other People's Lives

A CIP catalogue entry of this publication is available from the British Library.

Foreword © Gwen Chessell

ISBN: 978-1-80440-250-4

Typeset in Georgia

Front Cover image: *Timandra*
Ref: PAColl-2200-1 Alexander Turnbull Library, Wellington, New Zealand/records23107244

Back Cover Images: Family photographs

Back Cover Image of Author: Copyright © Zoe Meadows Photography

Cover Design and Artwork: Copyright ©Fiona Ruiz
www.ionacarroll.com

Silver Quill Publishing
www.silverquillpublishing.com

To

My Daughter

Isla

My Grandchildren

Ginny and Malcolm

And to the Ancestors

Who have been whispering in my dreams for years –

Don't Forget Us. We Existed. We're Part of You

Whether You Like It or Not

CONTENTS

Fuller Family

Price Family

ACKNOWLEDGEMENTS

This book would never have seen the light of day had it not been for the many people who have helped me over the last two years in gathering together the knowledge needed to write it.

First and foremost, I would like to extend a heartfelt thank you to Marie Livingstone whose painstaking research and enthusiasm for this project has helped me more than words can say.

The idea for my writing this book came from Anitra Balzer. Her inspirational and well written book about her pioneer family in America gave me the idea to record my own ancestral story.

I am indebted to Silver Quill Publishing and Wendy Leighton-Porter who agreed to publish the book.

Thanks to Gwen Chessell, writer and friend who wrote the Foreword and whose own biographies about colonial figures in Australia and New Zealand are well worth a read.

I would also like to express my appreciation and thanks to Oliver Eade who gave his time and effort in the formatting of the book and whose encouragement has always been appreciated.

Thank you to Fiona Ruiz. Her inspirational cover design illustrates the contents of the book so well.

I would like to thank the descendants of the Wills and Joll families in New Zealand who have helped me with the research needed for this book.

It was Kathryn Parsons of the Hamilton Library, NZ who provided one of the first clues about the Wills family for me.

I have a special thank you to Jeanette Clarkin-Phillips whose act of generosity in sending me the History of the Wills family helped me to get started.

Don Auckram's extensive knowledge of the Wills and Joll families was of great help. Thank you Don.

Athol and Betty Sowry in New Zealand. You helped me with Zaidee.

Wendy Slater, Carolyn Tweedie and Tom Cooke a big thank you. You three brought the Fuller family alive for me.

Anne Paddison, Phil Purcell, Dorothy Griffey, John McDonald and Barbara Jackson who gave me information about the Price family.

To Pam Brough and family I send a special thank you and hope this fills in a few of the gaps.

Librarians at the NZ Library Service. NZ Papers Past.

Librarians at National Library of Australia. Trove.

Of course none of this would have been possible without the Internet, Ancestry and the miracle of DNA.

Perhaps the biggest thank you has to go to my ancestors. I like to think they would enjoy the stories as much as I did writing them and forgive me for any inaccuracies of which I am sure they would say there are many!

FOREWORD BY GWEN CHESSELL

For Iona Carroll, learning about her emigrant ancestors to Australia and New Zealand has led her to weave in *Wanderers All* an unforgettable and colourful tapestry in words which depict her ancestors' varied lives. Using the outlines of their true experiences, she has researched and re-imagined the feelings and emotions of the brave adventurers who took the enormous step of unrooting all that was familiar to them to try their luck in a new and untried environment. Two of the five families depicted voyaged on the vessel, *Timandra*, a 382 ton barque that provides the link between their stories. *Timandra* is said to have been one of the best known and happiest emigrant ships and this is borne out by some of Iona's stories. But there were tensions on board too during that seemingly endless voyage, including misery, heartbreak and death. Iona tells us about the families' experiences on arrival, their trials and disappointments, their happinesses and sorrows as well as how they integrated into their new lives, and how they interacted with their fellow emigrants and the settlers already established in their communities. Neither are the encounters with the Indigenous peoples forgotten.

These narratives of the five families who have imprinted their lives indelibly on antipodean settler history are colourful and sometimes throw up unexpected outcomes. Several trades and occupations are described, including that of an occupation that is not usually highlighted as an emigrant calling but which went on to become a family dynasty. Divided into separate stories which depict different aspects of their experiences, she tells us about the good and the bad in the emigrants' lives, not sparing us from the more unedifying aspects of some of the protagonists, usually the men. She also chronicles the sufferings and forbearance of the women, those heroines who went through loss, disappointment, anguish, ill-health and heartbreak, often just to satisfy the ambitions of their men. With acumen, Iona has included, at the end of each of her tellings, the sources from which she has been inspired, as well as where possible, contemporary photographs which bring her subjects further to life.

Based on her ancestors' compelling histories, *Wanderers All* is a unique and vivid palimpsest of ordinary people who dared to launch themselves into the unknown. It is all the more valuable as an inspiring testament and memorial to Iona's forebears who worked to lay the foundations of a new and thriving world.

Gwen Chessell
Berwick-upon-Tweed, 2024

AUTHOR'S NOTE

This book has been a voyage of discovery for me. As I researched the trials and challenges that my ancestors faced it became clear to me that I, too, had embarked on much the same journey.

I had made the sea journey alone and in reverse. My voyage was undertaken with much more comfort than my emigrant ancestors had done. I am an Australian and at the age of thirty-three, I travelled from Australia and New Zealand on board the P & O liner, the *Canberra* bound for a new life in Britain.

My ancestors had travelled from Britain and Ireland, round the Cape of Good Hope as I was to do a hundred years later, to arrive on a foreign shore, and they must have been both bewildered and optimistic as they viewed what would have been for them, an alien landscape.

I, too, had much the same feelings for arriving on a freezing April day in Southampton, I did shiver with the cold and although I could speak the language, I did not know a soul in the country. The new world I had entered was as unfamiliar to me as it must have been for my ancestors when they first caught sight of a different land twelve thousand miles away.

In a way this book is a tribute to all those millions of souls who have made similar journeys, some by choice as both my journey and that of my ancestors was, but others less fortunate who left their place of birth through necessity, escaping war, famine and persecution.

Studies have been done about people who have emigrated and these passages from emigrant Germans to Australia gave me some understanding of my ancestors' migration and consequently my own particular journey.

"There is also evidence that it was not the very poorest people who took the opportunity to use subsidized fares to migrate." *Wegge, Simone A, Different Profiles, Different Choices; mid nineteenth century Hessians who emigrated to the Southern Hemisphere p.418*

This study of the personality of people willing to migrate brings a new perspective.

"...Modern psychologists working in Hamburg with potential emigrants have been able to demonstrate a spectrum of personality types, varying from *stay-at-home* (ocnophilic) to *migration-prone* (philobatic) with a range of behaviours in between. They found that *migration-prone* people are highly self-reliant and welcome 'the dissolution of attachments to objects (here defined as people and culture) at the place of origin and the establishment of object relations at the place of destination'. While these *migration-prone* people could give a plethora of reasons for their decision to migrate, the authors found that it was the person's innate, internal voice which dictated that they should emigrate, and not external factors such as poor socio-economic conditions."

Reynolds, Katharine Letters and diaries as useful tools in the construct of history: a case study of emigration from Frauenstein to Australia 1852-1854.

Mindful of the German studies about emigrants, I looked into my own ancestors and discovered that they, too, had left their place of birth bound for a new life and each and every one of them had done so voluntarily. This revelation led me to wonder what their lives had been once they were in a new environment, far from family and friends and all that had been familiar to them. I decided to write some stories about them based on true events but fictionalised.

I cannot help but wonder what the various 'memorable' characters would have made of one of their descendants writing these stories and how true to their actual personalities they were. Would the ancestors have been amused, dismayed, annoyed, we will never know?

For this reason, I have added a note at the end of each story with references. Given that we will never know how accurate the stories are I hope that the notes will provide some credibility. I have attempted as best I can to try to be true to the actual facts but records can be somewhat hazy at times given the time span. At times the newspaper reports and transcriptions of births, marriages, and deaths have thrown up discrepancies. Human error in recording is universal. So also, is memory. It is possible that the characters I have brought to life would have difficulty recalling the events described in the stories with precise detail. Certainly after time had passed recollection would be even more difficult. Every person, no doubt, would have a different version. I apologise for any inaccuracies.

It is out with the scope of this book to chronicle the whole lives of the descendants. The histories of the families have concentrated instead on giving factual evidence to the main characters with a brief history of their time.

There are heroes and villains in these stories. Social history may have changed in many ways since their time but human nature does not. The hopes, dreams and aspirations of our ancestors are the same as our own.

"We need to be charitable about the moral failings of our ancestors – not as an act of charity to them but as an act of charity to ourselves. Our own unconscious assumptions and cultural habits are doubtless just as impregnated with bias as theirs were. We should be kind to them, as we ask the future to be kind to us." *Adam Gopnik, American Prophet – The Gifts of Frederick Douglas, the New Yorker, Oct 15, 2018, p82.*

To me, this is proof of an indomitable human spirit which resides in greater and lesser degree in all of us. We have much to learn from our ancestors for without them none of us would be here.

THE WILLS FAMILY

Origin of the Family Name

The family name Wills is derived from the ancient Germanic personal name William, which itself comes from the roots will, meaning will or desire, and helm, meaning protection.

The Wills surname has been traced back more than 900 years to ancient times with the name first found on record in Saltash, Cornwall, England. From the beginning of the 11th century, the surname of Wills along with some other influential families were somewhat quite wealthy.

FIRST AND LAST LOVE

ALBERT'S STORY

I was eighteen and a half years of age when I boarded the *Timandra* in Plymouth Harbour bound for New Plymouth in the Colony of New Zealand. My parents lied about our ages to get the passage out. I was seventeen on the ship's register. Well, I don't blame them for the lie. There was nothing left in Cornwall for our family and this new beginning was within our reach. Nothing in Cornwall but high taxes, high rents and no chance of bettering oneself, at least in New Zealand the Plymouth Company were offering us land, our land. No chance of ever owning anything in Cornwall, just beholding to the master who thought nothing of evicting you if you couldn't pay the rent. I was the eldest in the family and I thought a lot.

I'll never forget the day we first saw the *Timandra*. Impressive indeed was the barque lying at anchor in the harbour with the sails yet to be unfurled. It was a chilly day that

November morning and I shivered, not knowing whether it was the cold or the excitement of the long journey ahead. We would be at least three or four months at sea. The sight of the *Timandra* was remarkable to me, a farmer's son, but would this wooden vessel and all on board survive the journey to the other side of the earth? None of us had ever been to sea nor had we seen the mighty oceans roar. It has to be said that all we had was faith and hope in equal measure.

This would be my last sight of Plymouth. Never again would my feet walk on English soil nor would I breathe in the Cornish air. Calstock and my life there would fade into a memory as sure as night follows day. I remember my mother's face was set hard for she hadn't wanted to leave but my father insisted, reassuring us all that we would find our fortune in New Zealand.

Our family huddled together like the other families in safe little groups. Next to us stood Samuel and Elizabeth Joll and their five children, the family looking slightly bewildered, all, that is bar Samuel who was built like an ox with a voice like thunder, when provoked. I was a little in awe of Samuel I must confess. 'His bark is worse than his bite,' my father had said. If the rumours were true Samuel had been the victim of his elder brother, Josiah's temper, and once his violent sibling had belted him with a bridle. 'Tails will wag about Samuel,' my mother told me. 'He's had a lot to put up with.' That was the end of the matter as far as she was concerned. But I kept my distance even so.

'This be the end of the home country for us. Say your goodbyes now. We'll not see these shores again, another world beckons us, a better world we sail to where we can own our farms, ain't that the truth to be told, James Wills?' roared Samuel to my father who was looking just a little apprehensive, I noted, what with the steerage passengers all jostling together and the crew doing their best to get the ship and the passengers, all two hundred and one free emigrants and ten cabin passengers, moving for Captain Skinner had said they sail at two pm.

We had arrived early to board the *Timanda* because Father had heard that for the steerage passengers, it was imperative to be amongst the first in the queue to secure the best bunks. I held little Betsy's hand, and we shuffled our way towards the nether regions of the ship. Betsy was frightened.

'Where are we, Albert?' She started to sob.

'We're going on a long journey, Betsy.'

I tried to reassure my little sister as best I could but I must confess at that moment I felt apprehensive, and my excitement of a few moments before diminished somewhat. What with all the jostling and the grumbling, we began to feel like driven cattle being forced into an enclosed space, not knowing what was ahead of us. And what was ahead of us in the dark and damp space that was to be our home for the next three or four months was three beds across, three feet deep with little space to do anything. A large brown rat appeared out of nowhere in the black space. It scuttled in front of us as we piled our possessions and bedding onto our chosen beds. Seeing the rat, Betsy let out a shriek.

'Now, Betsy, be quiet. It won't hurt you,' my mother admonished her youngest daughter but I thought Mother looked a trifle fearful as well.

Fortunately, the wily rat disappeared as fast as it had appeared but Betsy couldn't stop sobbing.

'I don't like this place,' her sobbing had turned to anger. 'Can we go home?' And she stamped her foot.

'No, Betsy, we can't. Now you have to help us. Where is your mug?' said big sister, Thirza, because all the steerage passengers had to bring their bedding, plates and cutlery along with their clothes.

It seemed like an age to find Betsy's mug but at last, we found it and arranged our bedding and clothing as best we could whilst all the time we could hear the wooden boards creak as the clipper swayed. It had been cold and windy when we arrived six hours ago. Now the wind had increased in ferocity. Even down below the decks, we could hear it howl. We wondered whether we would indeed be able to sail that day. In the darkness, I think all of us felt anxious but decisions had been made, and we were destined to leave a country that held no promise to venture to a new world where we hoped the promises would become real.

Our bunks were positioned close to the anchor closet and at two o'clock in the afternoon, or thereabouts, we heard the rattle of the chains and voices from above. The sails were set and the *Timandra* put out to sea. We made our way upwards to the lower deck, jostling past the other passengers to see Plymouth Harbour disappear before our eyes. The harbour was covered in a thick mist. None of us would ever see Plymouth again. The chattering and the grumbling ceased, and then we heard the unmistakable voice of Samuel Joll,

'We be free now, folks. I be gettin' a farm of our own out there in New Zealand, and 'tis a better place we go to, mark me words.'

Someone gave a cheer and talking started once again. I, for one, hoped that Samuel's optimism would prove to be true. Certainly, it was a venture into the unknown that might lead to new and exciting experiences for every one of us, and for me, that was reason enough to believe Samuel. Little did I know at that point how close my relationship would become with Samuel 'Growler' Joll.

We sailed right into a storm. Below decks, fearful passengers, cursed, cried, and vomited, not knowing what was happening above as the clipper swayed and ploughed through the choppy seas. The combination of human flesh so close together and the stench made it seem like we had indeed entered Hell.

The storm abated a day later, and the clipper sailed on.

Oftentimes, as we navigated along the coast of Africa we had no wind and that was the worst time for passengers and crew. Then the clipper drifted, not going anywhere, just rocking gently up and down on an empty sea devoid of any living thing bar sea birds and the occasional pod of dolphins, and both crew and passengers grew restless. Fights broke out and prayers were said for the return of the wind. To tell the truth I found the whole experience tedious beyond belief. Even though I knew a lot of the farmer families in Calstock by sight, never before had we been placed in such proximity to one another. The atmosphere was tense and nothing seemed to exist for us outside the *Timandra*. We felt trapped and the petty arguments were blown up out of all proportion. Had these same events occurred on land, nothing much would have been made of them and in a few days, the matter would have been settled. Not so, on board the ship. Grievances could last for days and tongues wagged with venom as people took sides, and the gossip grew and grew. When we crossed the Equator into the Southern Hemisphere, the weather turned warmer. It was stifling in the enclosed space below decks. Sickness and discontent prevailed, and I fear I began to feel much the same although mercifully, I was spared the sickness.

Rumours spread like wildfire. We sailed for days and saw nothing but the blue sea. It was as if the *Timandra* was forever trying to capture that tantalizing line of the horizon in front of us but never able to, and leaving a trail of white waves behind, for the sea just went on and on. In this monotonous space, anything could spark a rumour. People buzzed with excitement when another vessel was spied on. It gave us all some sort of solace that there were other living beings about, and we were not alone on the high seas. It was on the 16th day of November, however, that the rumours became real as twelve or thirteen vessels were sighted aft. The weather was calm that day. There wasn't a cloud in the sky. I have the date etched forever on my mind because along with the excitement of seeing these other ships, it was the day that I first spoke to Ann Joll, Samuel's eldest daughter.

My sister, Thirza and I often escaped from the dark space below decks to breathe in the fresh air above. These were fleeting moments because Thirza was engaged with the other women sewing up garments for the men whilst we men were put to work doing manual chores. We had heard the rumour of sightings of the vessels and we were eager to see them, even just for a few moments. The lower deck was crowded with chattering folk. We pushed our way through the crowd to stand at the railings and observe about twelve or so clippers in the distance. There was much cheering and waving but I was doubtful if there could have been much response from the other ships from that distance. But we were relieved there were other people in vessels like ourselves after all.

'You remember Ann Joll, Albert?' and Thirza nudged me playfully in my ribs. 'She's looking quite lost, don't you think? We should speak to her. Her father's nowhere to be seen. Looks like she's been left in charge of her siblings like we have to do.'

This was the first time I had noticed Ann Joll. She was a slightly built young girl with beautiful eyes. Those eyes seemed to look right into you, and I felt myself blushing. My shyness wasn't wasted on my ever-astute sister, Thirza for she giggled, and then gave me a push towards Ann so that Ann and I stood together at the railings whilst her young brother and sister looked on, both children oblivious to what was happening.

"Tis indeed a fine sight to behold so many sails afloat, don't ye not think so, Miss Joll?' I felt rather awkward so close to this beautiful young lady and I stuttered a little.

'I agree,' was the answer.

'Are you enjoying the journey?' I doubted whether that would be so, given our conditions below deck but I was at a loss as to what else to say.

‘I have to say that I will be glad when we arrive in New Zealand. The journey is tiresome, to say the least. My father keeps our hopes alive of a new life there... and a better one,’ she added.

For such a young woman I found her words refreshing. I was eager to speak further but at that moment, her young brother tugged at her skirt, wanting attention.

‘I’ll have to go,’ she said softly. ‘Mother needs me.’ She smiled at me then. I thought it was the most wonderful smile I had ever seen, and I truly think at that moment, I fell in love with Ann Joll.

****

ANN’S STORY

I was surprised that Albert Wills had noticed me. I knew his sister, Thirza but Albert had always seemed so much older than myself, but in truth, we were only seven years apart in age. My father was a blacksmith at Calstock, and Albert often brought horses to be shod there, but never once did he speak to me, so I was somewhat confused when he seemed pleased to see me that day as we watched the sailing ships. I was rather flattered to be the object of his desire for I knew in an instant that he liked me. I hoped we would meet again on this wretched ship for I had no liking to be on board. The days were long and the seas were so vast that I was fearful that we would never reach New Zealand even though my father was certain we would make our fortune in the colony. I wondered what thoughts were going through Albert’s head and whether he, too, expected to become a wealthy man with servants, something we could never have hoped for in Calstock.

I didn’t have long to wait until I met Albert again. A few days later, on Christmas Day, the *Timandra* reached Cape Town, the southerly town at the bottom of Africa and everyone, including both the steerage and cabin passengers were allowed to leave the ship. We were told that the *Timandra* would be anchored there for a few days to gather supplies for the next leg of the journey.

I thought Cape Town was magnificent. My first sight of the Lions Head and the mist covering the massive horizontal top of Table Mountain filled me with wonder for I had never imagined anything could exist in the world that was so awe-inspiring, and all so different from faraway Calstock. A few dozen sailing ships were anchored in the harbour and small boats ferried passengers and crew to the town. My brother, Samuel and myself had been given leave to go onshore and we clambered into one of these small boats. We were both eager to be free of the *Timandra* and I must confess, a few hours on dry land to explore this town and perhaps venture closer to the granite cliffs of Table Mountain was an intoxicating thought for me. Never before could I have imagined that a mountain could have such a vast surface. The mountain dominated the town which was hemmed in between the craggy cliffs and the sea. I think for the first time since boarding the clipper in Plymouth Harbour, I felt excitement rather than apprehension. So both Samuel and I were in good spirits. I was relieved to be on dry land again even though walking was difficult and my steps felt odd as if I was still on board the ship. It was hot in this southern town and my thick woollen stockings, petticoat and chemise were unsuited to the climate. Samuel, likewise, was feeling the heat but we were both so intrigued by the sights before us that our heavy garments didn't seem to bother us much.

The streets were dusty and the wooden buildings were so different from what we had ever known. But it was the colour and the bright sunshine that intrigued us the most. We saw a giant lizard basking in the sun on top of a granite rock. The creature was used to human traffic because it did not attempt to flee even when Samuel put out his hand to touch it. I loved the plants. Some were familiar to me, poppies, lilies and daisies, but there were unusual and beautiful ones there too. I later learned the name of the proteas and the strelitzias. This unusual and colourful flora would remain in my memory for the rest of my life.

A small group of about six black men stared at us as we passed. I was unsure of them as I had never seen dark skin before. The men looked to be as curious at the sight of our white skin as we were of their dark bodies. I hurried past and kept my head down. As we passed a tavern we heard shouts and revelry and two of the men from the *Timandra* staggered out into the street. Both the men were very drunk. They had to hold on to each other for support, and one of the men shouted out some lewd words to me. I felt myself blushing and quickened my pace but the man, perhaps seeing the fear in my eyes, pushed his companion aside and pinned my arms to my back, and tried to kiss me. Seeing this happening, Samuel attempted to kick the man in the shins but failed to land his foot in the right direction. The man laughed and took hold of the boy by the armpits and threw him to the ground. By now I was both frightened and furious. The other man lent on the railings for support whilst all the time he egged his companion on with more slurred and coarse language.

I don't think I realised for a moment that my rescuer had appeared out of nowhere, but Albert Wills had witnessed the whole unfortunate episode. When Albert saw the drunk toss poor Samuel to the ground and then try to molest me, he made a move. He grabbed hold of the man and hit him so hard on the chin that the drunk, now even more unsteady on his feet, fell face down on the dusty road, and remained there whilst his companion beat a shaky exit in the direction of the harbour.

'Are ye alright, Miss Joll?' asked Albert. 'That brute had what's coming to him, didn't he, young Samuel?'

Samuel nodded his head, and then he gave Albert such a look of adoration that I almost felt embarrassed. But I was trembling and Albert took my hand.

'We'll walk on now,' he said. 'Are you perhaps able to accompany me further along the road? I have a fancy to get closer to the mountain and away from the town. 'Tis such a magnificent sight to behold, don't you think?'

Table Mountain, ahead of us, had shaken off the early morning tablecloth of mist and its craggy sides and top were now visible.

I did not attempt to loosen my grip on Albert's hand. The three of us walked slowly towards the foothills of the mountain.

'Do you think New Zealand will be as beautiful as this?' I asked Albert.

He gave my hand a little squeeze and I felt as if something magical had happened to me. I blushed again but this time I was joyful.

'I believe so,' said Albert. 'With you by my side.' He added, and this time it was his turn to redden slightly.

****

Albert Frederick Williams Wills and Ann Joll were married on 26 December 1850 at the Weslyan Chapel, New Plymouth, New Zealand.

Grave of Albert and Ann Wills at the Mouteka Cemetery, Nelson, New Zealand.
Albert died 24th September 1896. Ann on 11th August 1898.

****

Both the Wills and Joll families sailed from Plymouth in England on 2nd November 1841 on board the Timandra and arrived in New Plymouth in New Zealand on 23rd February 1842. It is possible that Albert and Ann did meet on board and were attracted to each other. The incidents described are pure fiction, however. It is interesting that Albert and Ann did not marry for another eight years. Albert was then twenty-seven and Ann twenty years old. It is possible that Albert wanted to make a name for himself in the Colony before approaching Samuel and Elizabeth Joll to marry their eldest daughter.

THE BRAWL

It was no secret that Betsy Wills and Mary Ann Proust did not see eye to eye. Betsy thought Mary Ann exhibited airs and graces above her station, and Mary Ann had decided that Betsy, with her brood of six, was stubborn. The two women sometimes engaged in idle chit chat but when they did so, there was always underlying tension in the air. They did not like each other.

They had been at sea for a few months before this underlying tension came out in the open, and with surprising results. The women steerage passengers were required to sew up garments so that they were usefully employed, and not idle, so their days were spent sewing men's shirts and women's shifts. When the weather was fine the women were able to do their sewing on the lower deck and most times this was agreeable to them. However, one morning when there wasn't a cloud in the sky and enough wind to keep the *Timandra* ploughing through the waves at a steady pace, Mary Ann Proust set upon Betsy Wills and her daughter, Thirza with words that would have been heard in a bar room brawl,

'Ye are an effin' thievin' bitch. Give 'em back.'

And Mary Ann launched herself at Betsy's daughter. Thirza, at that moment, was sitting quite comfortably on a stool, and busily sewing away, and was startled beyond words when Mary Ann landed on top of her. She toppled off the stool and onto the wooden floor. The other women in the tight sewing circle looked on, astonished. No one was more startled than her mother, Betsy, however. She had just finished sewing one garment and was about to start on a man's blue shirt. When Mary Ann landed on her daughter, Betsy threw cloth and thread and needle into the air. Now Betsy was a tigress if one of her children were harmed in any way and the sight of her nemesis wrestling Thirza to the floor brought out strong maternal instincts. Mary

Ann tried to wrench Thirza's shoes from her feet. Mary Ann was a hefty woman and Thirza was a thin young girl. It was no contest.

'You thievein' whore. Them's me shoes ye got on,' Mary Ann screeched.

'How dare ye speak to my daughter like that, you filthy harridan. We all know ye for the lyin', connivin' piece of shit that ye are,' retorted Betsy.

Furious now, Betsy grabbed Thirza's upturned stool and walloped Mary Ann on her buttocks.

Mary Ann had on a thick woollen skirt, and not much harm was done, except perhaps to her dignity. She yelped and untangled herself from Thirza, who still had the offending shoes on her feet.

'Ye'll regret sayin' that to me, Betsy Wills. I'm goin' to kill ye.'

Mary Ann went for Betsy full on. She pulled Betsy's hair and scratched her face, drawing blood. Betsy wiped her face and seeing the blood on her hand, shouted,

'That does it! I'll teach ye to make accusations with no proof. Me daughter's a good girl an' no thief. It's ye who's the greedy one. Them ain't yer shoes she's got on her feet, it's you who's the liar, not my Thirza.'

The two women were locked together and may have remained so had not the *Timandra* hit a giant wave at that moment. The rocking movement caused both Mary Ann and Betsy to topple onto the floor, still clinging to each other. It was then that the fight got started. One of the women in the sewing circle cried out,

'Give it to her, Betsy. She deserves anything she gets.'

Mary Ann was the least popular member of the sewing circle and was disliked by all and sundry. She was also a lazy woman and didn't pull her weight as far as the sewing was concerned, or anything else for that matter. Betsy and her daughters, on the other hand, were meticulous needlewomen and had received praise from Captain Skinner for their endeavours. This praise had been given in front of Mary Ann and the other women. Mary Ann, always simpering towards those she considered her betters, may well have resented the praise heaped on Betsy. She was no match for Betsy's talent with the needle and was rather slovenly with her garments. Betsy could stitch up five men's shirts to Mary Ann's two. This had been noted by the astute Captain Skinner and perhaps he had made a point of praising Betsy in front of Mary Ann for that reason. Whatever it was, Mary Ann resented Betsy and her daughters even more after that.

Thirza and Maria, seeing their mother battling Mary Ann and looking as if she was being hurt in the process, decided to intervene. Betsy, by this stage, was pinned down by the weighty Mary Ann who continued with her raging insults. It looked as if Betsy was about to be wounded as Mary Ann began to thump her with ferocious intent. Blows landed on Betsy's face and shoulder. Betsy tried to kick her tormentor, and in the ensuing battle rolled over on top of Mary Ann so that Thirza and Maria who had been ready to pull Mary Ann off their mother had to stop. They had been about to tackle Mary Ann by one pulling her legs and the other grabbing hold of her shoulders. Now, they too had to watch as the battle got even fiercer.

The commotion had to bring an audience. A group of men, seeing what was happening, surrounded the fighting women. By now, the rolling motion of the ship caused Betsy and Mary Ann to roll as well, over and over on top of each other. The men looked on, amused and not a bit excited as the women had ripped each other's garments, and Betsy's right shoulder was now exposed, revealing part of her breast. What the men and the women witnessed was a flurry of petticoats, two panting women, and plenty of expletives between scratches and punches. It certainly livened up the day for all concerned.

'Best throw a bucket of water over 'em,' said one of the men.

'Ay. Sure is a catfight, lads. Let's give 'em a few more minutes. See who comes off the best,' and he smirked.

'I fancy the fat one.'

'That be John Proust's wife, mate. Best leave that one alone.'

'Right enough. Ye don't tangle with Proust, that's for sure. Guess the wifey is the same make.'

'Wonder what them's fightin' over?'

'Might be John Proust. He's well hung.'

This brought much chuckling.

By now the women from the sewing circle and the men had hemmed Betsy and Mary Ann into a smaller circle. The two women were contained in this area and it looked like both of them were tiring.

''Bout time ye finished this, lassies. Or it'll be a cold bucket 'o water over ye both.'

He was a heavily built man and he moved in fast, avoiding the kicks from Mary Ann. He dragged her off Betsy, and then he pinned her arms behind her back so that she was captive but she hissed like a trapped viper, cursing him, too. The women cheered. Thirza and Maria rushed to their mother.

'That be the end of it then,' said one of the men.

'It'll never be the end,' Mary Ann yelled. She spat in the direction of Betsy and her daughters as she tried unsuccessfully to free herself from her captor.

Thirza and Maria helped their mother to her feet. Maria took off her shawl and put it over Betsy's shoulders so that the torn chemise was no longer visible. Together the girls guided their mother to her stool. No one spoke. A few minutes later, Betsy reached down and picked up the man's blue shirt. She threaded the needle. Then she took hold of the fabric and, without another word, she started to sew.

Mary Ann, sullen as ever, was released from the man's grasp and she stomped off in the direction of their bunks without looking back.

'Who be the winner then?' asked another man.

'Them's the one what tells the truth,' answered a gentle woman in the sewing circle, and she continued her stitching as if nothing had happened.

****

Although the actual description of the fight between Betsy Wills and Mary Ann Proust is fiction, an altercation about the shoes was recorded in Flight's journal:

"1 Feb 1842. Mrs Proust found a pair of her shoes on Wills' daughter. A quarrel arose between Proust and Wills women. The two stood face to face yelling accusations at one another and denouncing each other's families. Mary Ann Proust was certain that her shoes had been stolen by, or on behalf of, the teenage daughter of James and Betsy Wills and she was determined to have them back. The verbal brawl soon turned into a physical one as the two commoners tussled and wrestled, pulling hair braids, and grabbing at shoes and stocking feet, tumbling to the floor in a flurry of skirts and petticoats amid the sound of tearing linen and brazen cursing. They fought until they were both spent and then the melee dissipated as fast as it erupted, unresolved, unpunished and with both parties unrepentant."

We will never know who the guilty party was or if, at a later date, the two women reached an amicable resolution. Whatever the outcome, a pair of shoes at that time would have been of value and worth fighting over.

A HERO AMONGST MEN

Albert Wills was halfway through giving thanks to God for the evening meal when he, his wife and children, all seated at the table with their heads bowed, heard an animal-like roar. Albert finished his prayer with a hasty 'Amen'. When the animal-like noises changed to sounds of anger, it appeared that the animal was quite definitely human.

Albert, well-known in the farming community for his calm and compassionate manner, was at first at a loss as to what to do. A perplexed Albert wondered whether it might be prudent to ignore the uproar outside and finish his meal but the noises became angrier and angrier until Albert stood up from the table, leaving the food on his plate uneaten, announced to his wife that he better go and see what all the commotion was about. The natives were restless and some of the houses belonging to the white settlers nearby had been burned down and for the sake of their family, he prayed that this must not happen to them.

He strode to the door of the wooden slab hut that he, his father and his brothers had built with their own hands in the early days when they had first come to New Zealand. It was a new land for the white man, but an old one for the people who had lived there for centuries. Albert was forever respectful to the original inhabitants, which was contrary to other opinions in the community, but Albert Wills was a God-fearing man and he had decided long ago that no good ever came from fighting or assuming superiority over those with different skin colour from your own. He had learned much from the Māori folk and studied their language. Knowing how to communicate with people was his mantra and it had certainly helped to keep the peace between his family and the Māori. Property belonging to the white settlers had been destroyed but nothing untoward had happened to any of the homes of the Wills' families. The assumption was that it was because of Albert Wills and his family's very attempt at understanding the Māori that no damage had been done to them.

So Albert was surprised to hear the commotion at the gate of his father's property, and not a little bit frightened as well, for the yelling grew louder and more threatening as he got closer to about a dozen angry men, all of whom seemed to be shaking clubs and fists. When the men saw Albert approaching they roared as one and made warlike gestures. Albert kept walking slowly towards the assembled group, his head held high. One man stood out from all the rest because he wore the chieftain's cloak, and it was to him that Albert addressed the group in the language of the Māori.

'Rangatira,' said Albert. 'I come in peace.'

The chief, dressed in a cloak made from long cords rolled from the fibre of the flax plants which indicated his status in the group, made no attempt to answer the white man. Instead, he swung his tomahawk towards Albert in a circular motion. A fire was in his eyes. He was a very angry man. The next swing of the tomahawk came even closer to Albert's head but Albert did not flinch. Instead, he repeated his words. The words did not affect the chief. They seemed to make him even more excited while the assembled group of men began to chant words of revenge. Some of the men held short clubs made from stone, others brandished longer ones made from wood, and these wooden ones were highly decorated. Two of the men on either side of the chief thrust their spears up and down into the dirt in a very threatening manner, and then both men pointed the spears in the direction of Albert's chest. It appeared a stand-off and Albert had no idea what had caused such animosity. He had been on good terms with the chief and had learned much from him. This was an altogether unusual situation and it seemed to Albert that things were getting serious.

The chief was a tall man. Taller than Albert, and it was this height that made him look even fiercer than his companions. His whole face was covered with tattoos, tā moko, and around his neck, he wore the famous hei tiki, a weighty greenstone pendant that gave him status and authority. He was every inch of his being, a chieftain. Albert had thought him to be a reasonable man. The two of them had had conversations over the years, and he had been made welcome at the chief's whare. To be able to converse in the chief's language had made life easier for them both, and Albert's stumbling over many of the Māori words had been a source of amusement. Both men respected each other so Albert was surprised at this anger from the Rangatira. None of the other settlers had bothered to try to reach out to the Māori in this way. Indeed, Albert's fellow farmers, by and large, held the belief that the native people were somehow lesser mortals, similar to children and should be treated as such. Albert did not agree with this line of thought for he had always held the belief that the greatest means of human communication is language which then leads to understanding, and he had felt honour bound to pursue this.

The chief suddenly, and without any warning, raised his tomahawk above his head and cried out:

'VENGEANCE FOR THE PIG!'

And it looked likely that Albert would soon be the victim of the raised tomahawk for the wooden gate that separated the two men never seemed more insecure.

Seeing their Chieftain raise his tomahawk as if to strike, a roar arose from the group and the two fierce-looking men beside the chief pummelled their spears even harder than before into the dirt. Albert did not flinch but kept his eyes fixed on the chief. He showed no outward fear but he trembled inside. Perhaps it was the calmness of the white man in the face of certain death that somehow unsettled the chief for he lowered his tomahawk. For a few moments, all was quiet.

'I know nothing of a pig', said Albert.

Hearing these words, the chief once again raised his tomahawk above his head but made no move this time towards Albert.

'Your man killed my pig'.

Albert was cautious. The tomahawk was still too close for comfort but he felt that the chief's anger had subsided and seeing this, his men appeared to have relaxed a little as well. It was enough for Albert to grasp the significance of the moment for he knew just who of his farm workers would have killed the chief's pig. He had admonished the man before as being too prone to using his gun.

The man was well known for taking a drink and it was then that he became belligerent and out of control. It would have been feasible that he had the drink in him and the gun loaded. If he had spied the pig, he would have revelled in shooting the unfortunate animal and bragged about it afterwards.

'I would like you to accept a pig of my own, Rangatira[1]. I knew nothing of this but be assured it will not happen again.'

The chief appeared to accept Albert's offer for he lowered his tomahawk, turned around and strode off in the direction of the Māori settlement. His men followed behind him. Albert could hear them talking but he did not understand their words. It was a somewhat relieved Albert who returned to the safety of his own home to finish his evening meal.

****

The altercation took place before the Wills's house was burned down, and before the family relocated from New Plymouth in the North Island to the Nelson area in the South Island in 1863.

The report in the Taranaki Herald reads: "But next day the Chief, with all his men armed, presented himself at the gate of the senior Mr Wills. He was very excited, brandished his tomahawk and vowed vengeance.

---

[1] Chieftain

Mr Albert Wills in the company of warriors at the gate, succeeded by tact and courage in inducing the natives to put down their weapons outside, and before they returned to the dairy the breach had been healed. This was the only difficulty the family had with their Māori neighbours."

As it is documented in the Taranaki papers that Albert Wills confronted the Māori chieftain and the newspaper is based in the New Plymouth area, I have assumed that the altercation between them took place there before the Wills's house was burned down, and before the family relocated from New Plymouth to the Nelson area in the South Island in 1863.

Sketch of Māori chieftain by the Author

A CORNISH FARMER

It has been said that farmers from Cornwall are farmers throughout, and it matters not a jot where in the world they find themselves. Wherever they are, they will grow their crops and tend their animals, look to the seasons, and love the land which runs like water deep within their veins. Albert Wills was such a farmer and when he undertook the long journey from Cornwall, he was that Cornish farmer. The only difference was that in New Zealand he owned his very own patch of earth. The Māori inhabitants thought otherwise.

'I can understand the Māori position,' said Albert to his wife, Ann one evening when rumblings of unrest in the district were growing louder. 'I doubt if any good ever comes from war and I have attempted to put an end to it before it starts, but I fear the worst.'

'I am fearful as well, Albert. I know how hard you try to keep the peace between us and them. After all, you have learned their language which so many others do not, and you're on good terms with the Rangitara. But I have heard rumours that there is a rebel native who is intent on revenge and plans to burn the homes of the settlers.'

'We should be on our guard, dearest, but we mustn't despair. I have heard the same rumours as well. You and the children might be well advised to take refuge in New Plymouth if that happens but I will stay and hold the fort, never fear.'

'Would that be wise? I would not want to leave you alone in the face of such danger. We have come so far since Cornwall, haven't we? This is our home now.'

'You are right. 'Tis a better life here than we could ever have hoped for in the Old Country but we must understand that to the Māori we are the interlopers and as such, they want us gone.'

‘I would not wish to leave.’

‘Nor I.’

That same evening, Albert and Ann were awakened by a red glow in the sky. Even though it appeared to be miles away, they both knew that another settler home had been put to the flames. Albert wondered if it was the time to be prudent and make provision for his wife and children to find safety elsewhere. He said nothing of this to Ann for he knew his wife objected to such an arrangement given their conversation of the night before. Her loyalty to him was paramount and he loved her for that but he was responsible for her safety, after all.

In the morning, they went about their business and neither spoke of the night before. At midday, Albert saw more smoke clouds rising in the east. His first thought was that the land might be burning from the forest fires. Trees had been felled and grassland burnt by both the Māori and the white settlers over the years but most of the land in the Taranaki region had now been cleared. The black smoke on the horizon could only mean one thing. Another house of one of the white settlers was on fire and if so, it could be that his home might be next on the list. It had to be a major fire, he surmised, because the smoke drifted higher and higher, darkening the cloudless blue sky and threatening to eclipse the midday sun. If it had been a minor burning none of this would have happened.

It was then that he heard the roar of human voices coming closer and in the opposite direction from the smoke. A moment before, everything around had been silent. Even the birds had ceased their constant twittering. Later, Albert would often relive those few minutes of silence and judge that that had been a premonition of what was to come. He saw no one; he just heard the rumble and the chanting getting ever closer and closer.

Ann was busy with the midday meal. She heard the sound and saw the smoke at the precise moment as her husband. It was indeed fortunate that the family were all together as their meal was about to be served for had it been later in the day, lives might have been lost. At that moment about twenty or so Māori men, dressed in warlike clothes, and with their voices roaring as if possessed by a demon, came into view. Some of the men carried spears and tomahawks but the danger came from those who held sticks burning with fire. They were angry, and they were determined, and every one of them was intent on revenge.

There was not a moment to lose. Albert, Ann and the children scrambled from the house just as the first fire stick was thrown onto the roof. There had been a dry spell for a few weeks and the flames burned quickly. Then another stick was flung through the window of the room where just a few moments before, the family had been seated waiting for their meal. Soon more sticks were thrown. The men were strong and they hurled the fire sticks with precision. Soon the house was engulfed in smoke as the fire crackled, sending shoots of red flames ever higher into the air until the building was a burning furnace, and the house that just a few moments before had been a place of sanctuary for the family, gradually filled with more and more smoke, leaving in its place, a charred ruin, already smouldering and burnt to the ground, and with it, the dreams of a generation.

The family fled, stumbling and fearful, to the top of the hill at the back of their home. The dogs followed them up the hill. Two of the dogs turned and barked at the scene below. It seemed they were as furious and as frightened as their owners were whilst the other two dogs ran ahead, panting, to finally collapse in a heap at their owners' feet. Below, the fire had now spread to the outbuilding where the farm machinery and saddles were kept. A hefty native threw his fire stick at the haystack and it, too, soon caught fire, burning the dray that had stood in front of it. Chickens scattered in every direction whilst the terrified horses, in a field at the back of the sheds, galloped in ever-increasing circles, and whinnied in fright. It was a nightmare scene. Albert and Ann stared motionless like statues, numbed by the sight in front of them until the youngest of their children, Betsy, started to sob. She clung onto her mother's dress, her tears running down her cheeks, still clutching her rag doll. There had been one thought in mind then, and that was to get away. All were fearful, and yet thankful they were alive for the vengeful men who had thrown the firesticks had no cause to harm the white settlers. Their mission had been to burn the settlers out, not to murder them.

****

New Plymouth proved to be a refuge for the family but Albert was restless. He wanted to return to his farm as soon as it was safe to do so. With a certain apprehension, the family returned to their burnt-out property and set about reconstruction.

'We will rebuild for we have the Cornish blood in our bodies,' announced Albert. 'We do not give up. This is our home now.'

Ann was a little less optimistic.

'Should the wars continue,' she said as if she had a glimpse into her future, 'we might need to move again. Your brother, James is thinking of relocating to the South Island... it's safer there. Your parents would come with us, of course. I believe the land around Nelson is fertile...?'

Albert did not answer. He was thinking of the farm and what he had to do next. But he had taken note of his wife's words for he, too, had spoken to James about moving.

'We'll see how things work out, Ann,' he replied after a few more minutes of thought. 'I fear you might be right though. I would not want to put our lives in danger ever again. I am a farmer through and through and nothing pleases me more than to see the crops grow and the animals well fed. For isn't it a fact that our ancestors tilled the soil in faraway Cornwall, and I am a Cornishman in this new land, don't you agree? We are forever farmers, no matter what happens or wherever the good Lord takes us. If it is to the South Island, so be it.'

****

The Wills family were always sympathetic to the Māori cause. However, as hostilities grew between the Māori and the white settlers, Albert Wills and his family found that they, too, were subject to intimidation which led to the burning of their home and the farm buildings. They were fortunate to escape unscathed. It was, therefore, inevitable that the decision was made to relocate to the South Island where the atmosphere between the two peoples was less volatile than at Taranaki.

A TRAGEDY

I remember that day well. The sun shone high in the sky and hurt your eyes when you looked upwards. Grandmother and Mother said the light was different in New Zealand from England. We must be careful not to stare at the sun. When Grandmother talked of England, she looked sad. Father was busy with the harvest and Mother was forever engaged with the younger children. My sister, Eliza and I were good friends and we played together.

Eliza and I liked to skip. Father had made ropes for us both from the flax. He had watched the Māori folk and learned how to take a sharp knife and scrape along the leaves, twisting the fibre into a rope. He had made another longer rope for us as well, and our big brothers, Albert and Thomas would swing that rope making it go faster and faster while Eliza and I jumped up and down, trying all the time not to fall. That day we set off along the track that led from our farm towards the river. Eliza could skip faster than I could but she was kind and she always slowed down a bit. Eliza's legs were longer than mine although she was my little sister.

'Race you, Mary,' she said although she knew I couldn't keep up with her. She could run and skip so fast that the rope threw up dust and stones. Eliza reminded me of a picture of an antelope in the picture book that Grandmother had given me. The antelope's four feet scattered dust too. That was in Africa and we lived in New Zealand. Antelopes don't live in New Zealand and we don't have lions here either. Lions eat you. Nothing eats you in New Zealand; leastways that's what Grandmother told me.

I started to pant like the antelope in the picture book. I tried to skip the way Eliza did but my left foot caught the bottom of the rope, and I fell, face down, onto the dusty track. I started to cry when I saw the blood on my hand. Eliza stopped skipping.

'There, there, Mary. Don't cry.'

But I couldn't stop crying and my hand hurt.

'Whatever will Mother say?' I sobbed. 'I've torn my dress, here.' And I pointed a finger, now with a tiny amount of my blood on it, towards a small hole in my pinafore.

'Mother won't notice. She's so, so busy. We'll ask Grandmother to mend it. Please don't cry, Mary.'

Eliza wiped both my eyes with her best lace handkerchief. Then she dabbed the wound on my right hand with the handkerchief. She took hold of my other hand and swung both our skipping ropes over her shoulder.

'Come on, Mary. Let's find something to eat,' she said. 'I'm hungry, aren't you?'

'There's nothing to eat here. Let's go home.'

'We'll find something, you wait.'

'Where?' I asked, and I sniffed because my nose had started to run and I was hungry too.

We walked slower now but I didn't want to skip anymore. I felt safe holding Eliza's hand but my other hand still hurt and I tried not to cry. All the time Eliza chattered away as if nothing had happened. We grew hotter and hotter under the summer sun, and I longed for something to drink.

I think we both noticed the berries at the same time. They grew on small shrubs along the side of our dusty track. Clusters of them hung, pendulum-like on horizontal stalks and some bunches of berries were hidden under the shiny heart-shaped green leaves while others were more accessible but all were round, purple and inviting, and just what we needed to gather on this hot day. I thought how sweet they would be and about how I wouldn't need to have that drink. We could eat the berries instead and I wouldn't be hungry either.

'They're the tutu berries, Mary,' announced Eliza in a voice full of importance. 'Father said we are not to eat them 'cos they make the cattle sick.'

'But we're not cattle, Liza... and I'm so, so hungry.'

Eliza frowned slightly and wrinkled her nose. I liked seeing her wrinkle her nose. It made her look funny.

'Well... the purple ones might be alright to eat but we mustn't touch the green ones, ever.'

It sounded like a command. I was hot, thirsty and hungry. Surely the purple berries couldn't do us any harm?

So it was Eliza who ate the first berry and then another one. She gave me a ripe, very purple one, to try. It tasted sweet and juicy. I picked another berry from the bunch and chewed it. The juices filled my mouth and down my throat and I didn't feel thirsty anymore. We both started to pick them, faster now, for the berries were delicious and we were very hungry. We counted as we ate them and Eliza said she had eaten more than me because she needed extra ones. I think I ate about ten but I couldn't count as well as Eliza. I felt hot again for it was midday and Mother would wonder where we were. Eliza liked the berries so much that she pulled about a dozen of them from another bush, and we walked, not skipped, all the way back to our farm. Eliza ate all the berries but I had eaten enough. I just wanted to go home.

****

That evening I felt very, very sick. I vomited all over my pinafore and Mother and Grandmother called for Father to come. I forgot all about my sore hand for my belly hurt so much. I heard Eliza crying all the time, and I knew that something was wrong. Grandmother tried to console me but the pain was so bad inside me that I pushed her aside with my hands. I vomited again. It was horrible. I heard the doctor talking to Mother and Father and then he was at my bedside. He carried a black bag and he had a grey beard and a bushy moustache. He had lots of hairs growing out of his ears. He gave me something to swallow and I vomited again, all over the bed. I felt very frightened.

Father sat beside Eliza's bed and held her hand. Then he cried out for the doctor. I had never heard his voice sound like that before. I was scared now. The pain in my belly wouldn't go away.

****

When the morning sun finally rose in the sky, I awoke to see Mother beside my bed, and her eyes were red from weeping. Then I knew that something dreadful had happened in the night while I tried to sleep. My belly was still sore but the terrible pain had gone. A deeper pain was to come. My mother started to cry. She held me tight in her arms, and then I, too, started to sob for I knew I would never again see my little sister, Eliza. And the two of us would not be able to skip along a dusty track beside bushes laden with sweet, deadly berries.

****

The ages of Eliza and Mary have thrown up a discrepancy. In the newspaper article from the Nelson Examiner and New Zealand Chronicle 13th February 1869 P.3, Eliza is seven years of age and therefore the older sibling. However, Mary's birth date is recorded as 1861 and Eliza born in 1863. Eliza died on 23rd January 1869 which is consistent with the newspaper article of 13th February 1869. I have decided to err on the side of caution and agree with the birth record rather than the newspaper report. An inquest was held on the body of Eliza and also reported in the Nelson Examiner and New Zealand Chronicle 13th February 1869 p3. The verdict concluded that she died from eating the poisonous tutu berries. And there were no suspicious circumstances.

Tutu berries (*Coriaria Arborea)*

A GENTLE ARTIST

People say I am such a talented watercolourist, that my paintings should hang in the most prestigious of galleries, and that my name should be known throughout New Zealand and beyond, but I doubt if any of that is true. I am an old woman now and what I have done with my life and the talent I have nurtured has been both my salvation and my curse. They say the artistic temperament cannot be understood by those less gifted but I disagree for I believe we all have something to give to others and that our life is a gift from God. An artist is just one of many talents given to us.

My life has been a fortunate one in lots of ways. My dear husband, John, was a God-fearing man who cared for his flock and he loved me. He encouraged me to paint and saw no harm in my spending hours outside at my easel. I was truly blessed with John as so many men see their wives as nothing but child-bearing slaves, existing only to serve their husbands. Without John, I doubt whether I would have had the courage or the endurance to pursue my art.

Oftentimes, I think that my best painting ever was the portrait I did of John because this came from my heart. He sat so still for me and he hardly moved a muscle whilst I worked. I think he used this time to meditate and perhaps that quiet time was for him, a respite from the demands of his congregation and his obligations. I know we both enjoyed the experience and I think he liked how I portrayed him. That's how I want to remember John for I have been a widow for almost forty years and the memories fade. Love endures and I will be with him soon, in death as in life.

I cannot remember how many paintings I have done now. Once I tried to count them up and the figure came to about three hundred or so, but there could have been more for I have been sketching all my life. Time changes everything. I can no longer hold a brush. My fingers are arthritic and my eyesight has dimmed. I recall how Charles Goldie told me that we artists never stop thinking of our art and how, even at the end of our lives, we would still yearn for the canvas and the brush. What a talent Charles had. I did admire his work so, and he was generous in his appreciation of my humble landscapes.

After John died, and so young he was, just forty-six years of age, leaving me with my three boys, I thought I could never paint again. We had known sadness during our life together. My firstborn son, Garfield did not survive infancy and when my second child, baby Elva Mary died in Opotiki, taken from us when she was just three months old, I blamed myself for both deaths. This was when I viewed my painting as a curse. In truth, had I not been so obsessed with my work; my only daughter might have lived. That is how it felt for me and I feared that we would not have any more children. Two infant deaths were a hard cross to bear. Although John tried to reassure me that it was God's will, the guilt lay in my heart for many years.

But it was when we moved to Ormandville that my painting became my salvation once again. It came from an unexpected source. One fine day I decided that I would take my sketchpad and pencils and try to capture a view of the hills beyond the vicarage. I hadn't sketched for so long. There was a gentle breeze blowing and I intended to capture the early morning light. The sun had not long risen in the sky. I drew a pencil line, and then another. The hill appeared on my sketchpad. Excitement grew, and I knew then that my talent was still there though it had lain dormant for many months. I was so absorbed in my work that I didn't notice that I had an audience. I turned around to see two children, a boy and a girl, aged about eight and ten.

'What are you doing?' asked the boy.

'Sketching the hill in front of us,' I answered.

'It's very good.'

I was a little taken aback at the compliment and I put down my pencil.

'Do you both like to draw?' I asked.

'Oh, yes,' the girl replied, 'but I could never draw like you.'

I laughed.

'It takes a lot of practice,' I said, 'but you're both young and you have a lot to learn. I couldn't draw like this when I was your age.'

'Father says it's a waste of time, drawing. Best to get a job.'

The boy looked sad as if he doubted his father's advice.

'It's not a waste of time, Harry,' scolded the girl. 'You can draw so well. Father can't draw,' she whispered.

'Would you like to draw me something, Harry?' I asked and I handed the boy a pencil and paper.

'I can draw too. And my name's Amelia.'

'Of course, you can, Amelia,' I smiled. 'Let's all draw that hill with the houses in front of it. And don't forget the trees too.'

A light breeze lifted Amelia's paper into the air as she scrambled to catch hold of it. I couldn't stop smiling at the antics of the girl but the boy didn't notice. He was already drawing lines across the paper and sketching two trees. I watched as he carefully outlined the house.

'That's very good,' I said. 'You need to keep the line of the house straight.'

I pointed to where I thought there could be an improvement.

He nodded. He was absorbed in his drawing. I remembered how I used to be at his age, and how my fingers had itched to hold a pencil. My parents encouraged me then. It looked like Harry's parents weren't quite so accommodating. I wondered where the children lived and what circumstances were like for them. I watched them work. There was childlike naivety in their drawings but my trained eye could see they both had talent.

I thought of my two dead children then, Garfield and Elva, and wondered why they had come into my head at that moment. I felt tears behind my eyes. I took hold of my pencil once again so the children wouldn't notice my distress. Art was my solace as it must be for these two.

'I've finished,' Amelia announced with pride in her voice.

'You can draw, Amelia.'

Amelia grinned.

'I've finished too,' said Harry. He showed me his drawing.

'Keep going, Harry,' I said. 'You and your sister are meant to be artists, don't you think?'

It was as if I had said something magic to the children. Amelia put her little arms around me whilst Harry grinned.

'You're a nice lady,' Amelia said.

Now it was my time to feel that something magic had happened to me as well.

'I'll keep drawing too,' I whispered, and it was then that the tear that had threatened me before, trickled down my cheek.

****

I never did see the children again although I asked people around me did they know of them. No one knew. I wonder sometimes whether they existed at all, or did I somehow dream the whole episode? But I believe whatever happened that morning saved me. I started to paint again.

****

Mary Wykes Wills was born in 1859 in Groby, Leicestershire, England. She married the Reverend Thomas John Wills in 1886. Her collection of 300 watercolours, 2 oil paintings and 13 albums, primarily of landscapes are held in the National Library of New Zealand. There is a portrait of her husband, the Reverend Thomas John Wills included in the collection. Mary died in 1942, aged 83. The meeting with the two children described in this story is fiction. However, Mary's eldest two children did die prematurely, a sad fact all too common at the time.

Studio photograph of Mary Wykes Wills
National Library of New Zealand

TEMPERANCE

The Reverend Thomas John Wills was a compassionate man. There was no doubt that he was a determined one. These two qualities were admired by many and mocked by a few.

He had been named after his Uncle Thomas John but he was always known as John. His determination to carve out his life his way was revealed at that early age. John was a clever man and learning came to him easily; he was also a man of conviction. This admirable trait extended to all people and in particular to the Māori with whom he had developed an understanding. He became fluent in the Māori language, and treated them with respect, for John saw all men and women as equal under God.

It was this belief that drew him to the Anglican ministry and he was ordained in 1887. At Opotiki, he first encountered the ravages too much alcohol caused. The isolated town was dominated by the brewery. John decided that limiting the sale of alcohol would not solve the problem. A total ban was necessary. With this in mind he became a leading anti-liquor campaigner and he was elected President of the New Zealand Alliance in 1900. To his dying day he maintained that it was the consumption of too much alcohol which caused untold misery and suffering to both the Māori and the Pākehā communities. This strong determination to address the social issues of the day brought him into conflict with the Bishop and others in the church hierarchy.

In his ministry, he had seen many examples of drunkenness and none more so than one morning when a poor woman appeared at the door of the vicarage with a baby in her arms and two scraggly children beside her. John guessed the poor creature in front of him was about thirty years of age but her appearance gave the impression that she was at least twenty years older than that, so emaciated and undernourished did she look. The baby cried and the children, two boys, were as thin and puny as their pitiable mother.

'Please, sir, can you help us?'

It was then that John noticed that there were black bruises on her face and arms.

'Of course, my dear,' he said kindly. 'Come out of the cold.'

It was winter and the woman had no coat. A well-worn and tattered white blouse covered her upper body. Her thin arms were exposed to the cold, and she shivered. Her boys, standing on either side of their mother, clasped her skirt and stared with black eyes at John. Neither boy uttered a sound. John saw that they, too, were as malnourished and frightened as their mother.

John ushered the little group into the front parlour and asked them to sit down.

'I don't want to impose upon your kindness, sir...'

The woman gazed longingly at the open fire. Its warmth seemed almost too much to bear.

'Come now. Sit by the fire, my dear. Boys, there's a stool for each of you.'

John pointed to the two stools on either side of the fire. Both were embroidered with fine needlepoint depicting mountain and lake scenes. The boys hesitated for a moment, and then sat down on the edge of the stools, unsure of what was happening and what was expected of them. The baby, perhaps feeling the warmth of the room, stopped crying. The woman sat down and it was then that John noticed something else. There was a scar across her left cheek.

'Now, how can I help?' he asked.

'I've nowhere to go. I'm not been much of a churchgoer, sir, please forgive me for that but I heard you were a good man and helped people.'

John smiled. 'Be that as it may,' he replied.

'It's the drink, sir. When it's in him, he's like a madman

then, and anythin' sets him off. I got this here scar when I didn't have his meal ready for him in time. Came at me with a knife then, he did, sir. I worry for me boys as he takes the whip to them for no reason whatsoever. Just seeing them there, them sittin' quiet an' all can annoy him. Why...?'

The woman paused for a moment and John noticed that she had tears in her eyes. It was as if she didn't know what else to say, that somehow she was being disloyal to her abusive husband, just talking about him in this way.

'You can speak freely, my dear.'

'Well, one time he accuses me of bein' with another man and me boys aren't his. As God is my witness, sir, I have never been unfaithful to him but that's just the way he is, that is when he's full of the drink. I tell you, sir, the drink's a curse.'

The Reverend John nodded. Of the social consequences of too much alcohol consumption, he was in complete agreement with this poor unfortunate woman and her children.

'Well, there's me thinkin' all the time he might change one day. But no. He's in and out of work 'cos of the drink, sir. Can't keep a job and what money he earns, he spends at the pub with his mates. All of them gettin' drunk together and causing misery at home. I tell you, I haven't a penny in the house sometimes an' I can't bear to see me boys go hungry and my darlin' baby girl, I've hardly any milk in me for the poor soul.'

She started to cry and John handed her a handkerchief. She blew her nose loudly. One of the boys got off his stool and put his thin arms around his mother's shoulders. He didn't say a word, just stared at the fire in front of him.

Outside a wind had started up and caused the windows in the parlour to rattle. John put another log on the fire. Rekindled, orange and yellow flames spread out along the log. The wind and the crackling of the fire was the only sound in the room.

'Have you any family you can call on?' John asked

somewhat tentatively.

'No, sir. My mother and father are dead, and my only brother was killed at the sawmill years ago. I've got a sister in Auckland but she doesn't want to know me. All hoity-toity is Maud. Said I've made my bed and I should lie in it. She never liked my husband an' thought right from the start that he was a wrong 'un. Now I know she was right but I didn't think that at the time. He was so handsome before the drink took hold of him. Anyway, Maud's done better than me. Married a baker and they own a bakery at Ponsonby. No, sir, I wouldn't call on Maud, never.'

The thought of her sister seemed to annoy the woman. The Reverend John thought it best to leave that particular avenue closed. Families, his own included, often had members that didn't quite fit into the mould. He tried again.

'Where is your husband now? Do you know?'

'Stormed out of the house, he did, after givin' me a black eye. See?'

She pointed a grubby finger in the direction of her right eye which did look as though it had been newly struck.

'Think that what made my mind up to go. 'Cos he's all apology when he's sober but that doesn't last for long. Says he'll never do it again but it's all talk. Soon as he has a few pints in him, off he goes again an' I know what comin' when he gets home. I just want to get away from him now. Had enough but as I said, I've nowhere to go.'

She looked miserable.

At that moment, the boy who had sat so quietly on the embroidered stool spoke.

'I'm so very, very hungry, Mother.'

The mother looked apologetic as if it was somehow an intrusion to be asking for food.

But the Reverend John's reaction was completely different. The pitiful voice of the boy asking for nourishment was to him another example of the social injustices which abounded in the world. It was his Christian duty to try to help as much as he could to alleviate the suffering of others. That people did not have enough to eat was to this good man as much an issue as excessive alcohol consumption. He had studied the story of Jesus feeding the multitudes with loaves and fishes and concluded that allowing people to starve was a sin. The Universe was an abundant one and there was enough for all.

'We will give you something to eat, my boy,' he said. 'There is soup already made and heating in the pot and enough bread for the eating. You will dine with us. Come.'

John led the woman and her children to the room next door where he and his wife, Mary, and their three boys always dined. The table was already set. He fetched more plates and cutlery and bade them sit down. The woman was unsure and the boys clung to her skirts once more.

'Oh, sir,' she said, 'I can't intrude upon your good self. The boy is always asking for food.'

'And so he should,' John smiled. 'He's a growing lad and there's enough for us all. Sit yourselves down and I'll summon my wife and boys to join us.'

The woman and the boys hardly muttered a sound during the meal and, although both John and Mary both tried to illicit some form of conversation, it seemed their unexpected guests were ill at ease in the company of such kindness. The soup and the bread were eaten with much enthusiasm, however, and John began to wonder when the little trio had last had a good meal. It was a very thoughtful priest who rose from the table.

This encounter between himself and the woman worried him for here were fellow human beings who, through no fault of their own, had become victims to the excesses of alcohol consumption. In a way, he felt powerless in the face of such human misery but in some strange way, this made his resolve stronger. He must do something. He must answer the call and become a beacon of hope. The woman and her children deserved a better life.

When the meal was finished he asked the woman to return with him to the warmth of the front parlour. Here all the kindness within the Reverend John was revealed to her, and in such a way that tears of gratitude filled her eyes for what was proposed was a way out of the unfortunate circumstances of her present life. She had been captive for so long in the hapless marriage, grieving, fearful, hating the sight and smell of a drunken husband.

John's suggested that he would write to the Anglican Trust in Auckland where women and their children found a safe refuge and that this letter would be written as a matter of urgency. In the meantime, he thought that the best course of action was to distance herself and the children from her drunken husband as soon as possible. He pressed some coins into the poor woman's hand. This was for the fare to Auckland and she was to stay at the Anglican Trust home until employment could be found for her and a safe dwelling for herself, the baby and the boys.

'Bless you, sir,' the woman said. 'I promise I will pay you back what you give me now. I'm a proud woman, sir, and beholden to none.'

After a few minutes of silence, she lifted her head and looked straight into the eyes of the Reverend John.

'I tell you, the demon drink is a curse indeed. I thought before I came here, that you would judge me, and you would tell me it was my duty to stay with my husband and suffer. You have given me hope today, sir, and I will not let you down. We will do as you say.'

She smiled.

'I might even visit my sister, Maud one day, us both being in Auckland then. The boys should meet their cousins, don't you think?'

Now it was John's turn to smile.

****

Although the meeting with the woman and her children is fiction, the Reverend Thomas John Wills, always known as John, was a prominent figure in the temperance movement in the nineteenth century, and it is possible that a situation similar to the one in this story could have taken place. He was a man of high intelligence, strong in his convictions and motivated by a sense of social justice as an integral part of his Christian faith.

Studio photograph of the Reverend Thomas John Wills
National Library of New Zealand

WINNER TAKES ALL

It was always about the cow. When Betsy decided that she would leave the dairy cow to one of her grandchildren in her Will, the cow became the topic of conversation amongst them all for hadn't Betsy brought seven children into the world, and those children now had produced an impressive number themselves, and it was probable there would be even more arriving after Betsy had departed this mortal coil? So the ownership of the aforementioned cow was the subject of much talk and just a bit of rivalry. Who, of that great number of grandchildren, deserved to have the cow?

It has to be said that the cow was a larger-than-life animal with a good-natured personality towards Betsy in particular, but even better than her sanguine character, she was a great milker. Betsy was very fond of the cow. She had been there at the birth, for hadn't she helped in the delivery of the little calf when the poor mother had been in such distress? The little calf was a fighter and Betsy had kept it warm with blankets and brought it into the house to lie before the fire as it struggled to live. Alas, the calf's mother did not survive the ordeal of the birth and she succumbed a few days later. To Betsy, the little calf was just another one to nurture, just as she had done with her babies. The calf paid for Betsy's devotions with loyalty and followed her around the farm in much the same way as a dog would. The calf grew up healthy and strong. She was soon a mother herself and her milk kept flowing, a full bucket every day. It was no wonder that Betsy loved her cow.

Betsy was a determined woman. She was also a character and whatever place she found herself, be it in Cornwall where she had been born, or Lower Moutere in the South Island of New Zealand where she lived most of her life, Betsy's tough personality kept her family in order, including husband, James.

She could see the funny side of life amongst all the adversity, however, and this perhaps was notable in her decision to leave the cow to her favourite grandchild, although she refused to divulge who this favoured one was. The grandchildren had their suspicions but not one of them was sure which one of them this was, which also led to both speculation and again, some rivalry. After all, having a good milker was an asset. The cow, oblivious to all this human conjecture, happily continued to follow Betsy around and she only allowed her surrogate mother to milk her. If anyone else tried to extract milk from her, she would swish her tail in their face and sometimes kick her heels in the air, upturning the bucket and on one memorable occasion she even caused the bucket, the milker and the stool to be upturned. The unfortunate milker fell backwards into the cow's carefully positioned, and newly deposited, dung. The furious milker stormed away to complain to Betsy that 'the cow was her problem from now on and she refused to have anything to do with it.' Both Betsy and her cow viewed the whole sorry episode with some amusement for the cow quite generously allowed Betsy to continue the milking, and she even gave a little more than normal on that occasion. But as Betsy aged and her hands became more arthritic, this presented a problem.

So Betsy devised a cunning plan. It is even possible that she discussed her plan with the cow but this, of course, is pure speculation. Betsy announced to all her brood of grandchildren that she had made a decision regarding the cow, and if any of them wished to take part in her experiment, they would have to spend time with the cow. This meant that they would be required to not only attempt to milk the intransigent beast but to brush her down, clean out her pen and, if that wasn't enough, put a rope around her neck and take her for walks about the yard. This challenge had to be done, announced the ever astute Betsy, 'before I die!' A couple of the lazier grandchildren decided then and there, that the prospect of having to do all that for a house cow was just not worth the effort and declined to take up the challenge as soon as their grandmother suggested it.

So in the end, there were just three of Betsy's grandchildren who took up the gauntlet. The great day arrived and the three contestants descended on the farm in time for the daily milking. The cow, however, seemed to sense that something was not quite the same for she refused point-blank to enter her pen. Instead, she bolted. The three contestants ran round and round trying to encircle the cow, all the time waving hands above their heads and shouting. But it was to no avail and the wily cow avoided them in much the same way as a bull sometimes can outsmart the bullfighter in faraway Spain. Betsy observed her grandchildren's efforts from behind the safety of the fence where the horses were kept. To say that she was amused would be an understatement. Her usual severe countenance broke into a smirk. Betsy was enjoying herself.

After about half an hour of this spectacle, the cow began to tire and reluctantly she allowed herself to be led into the pen by the first contestant. The cow, however, was not ready to have hands other than Betsy's anywhere near her. She bellowed. The first contestant tried and failed. The second of Betsy's grandchildren had a little more success. She was able to coax the cow to the milking position by enticing the beast with a bundle of hay but when she sat down on the milking stool, the cow swished her tail. This did the trick because the granddaughter received the whole force of the end of the tail on her face, drawing blood. Furious now, she stormed off leaving an empty bucket and an upturned stool.

Then it was Eliza's turn. She had watched the whole episode with much the same amusement as her grandmother and had devised a plan. She filled a bucket with water and took hold of a brush. She talked to the cow as she washed her down, making sure that she cleaned the cow's udder and that the cow was happy to allow her to do this. Then, she took some hay and hand-fed the cow, all the time whispering gently in the cow's ear. It seemed to do the trick because the cow calmed down and the tail swishing abated somewhat. Eliza was still wary of that end though. She kept out of the way.

Then, Eliza picked up the bucket and the upturned stool and laid her forehead on the cow's belly, the way she had seen her grandmother do. All the time she talked to the cow. Then she gently took hold of one nipple and squeezed.

Soon the bucket was full to the top with warm milk and the cow looked suitably relieved. Then Eliza gently placed a rope around the cow's neck and the two of them walked out into the yard to receive a cheer from Grandmother and laughter from the other two grandchildren. These two might have been thankful that they hadn't succeeded in milking the cow and that it would be Eliza who would have the responsibility of dealing with the crafty beast. We will never know the reason for their laughter but we do know that Betsy was delighted with the result.

After all, wasn't Eliza her favourite grandchild?

The actual description of the events concerning the family cow is fiction. However, Betsy did leave the cow to her granddaughter, Eliza, in her Will as this has been recorded.

SAVING SOULS IN INDIA

The girls sitting on chairs at the front of the hall giggled. They had spent the morning swimming and talking about boys. Now they had been told that they were to hear a talk about missionary work in India which didn't seem half as exciting as speculating about the male sex. In fact, they giggled so much that the Reverend Morris told them to be quiet. Miss Sowry would be along any minute to tell them all about her experiences at a Christian missionary school in India, something which might inspire them to follow her and do good work spreading the Gospel. Hearing this, the girls were silent. India was so far from New Zealand and none of the girls knew much about the country. One of the girls whispered to her friend next to her that the Indian boys might be more exciting than the local lads. This brought on another bout of giggles. The Reverend frowned. The girls lowered their heads and covered their mouths with their hands.

When Miss Sowry started to speak the girls stopped thinking about boys.

'Girls, I would like to begin with asking you to imagine a world where young women like yourselves are bound by a dissimilar set of rules to what you know. The young women I taught at the missionary school were no different from yourselves in so many ways but in other ways, you and they are poles apart. India is a country of such extremes. The girls at the missionary school were a product of all this for there is great poverty in India but side by side, great riches there as well. It is a fascinating country. I want to tell you something about my work there and what it was like to be a part of it and what joy it was to teach these girls about our Saviour, the Lord Jesus Christ.'

The girls at the front row were silent. Now they began to

imagine what Indian girls were like. The first thing that Miss Sowry told them was about the heat, how it sapped your strength and how she and the other missionaries would travel on overcrowded trains and then trek to the foothills of the Himalayas on horseback for the hottest six weeks of the year because it was cooler there. The girls were intrigued. How exciting it would be to ride horses that distance. None of them could imagine such a fierce heat. It had been such fun this morning to splash around in the cool water. If they lived in India they would want to be in water all day to escape such heat.

Then Miss Sowry explained that the religion of India was Hinduism. She showed them photographs taken in the streets of Ellore and some of the colourful processions where people and elephants jostled for space. One photograph showed a young Indian boy, adorned in all manner of fascinating attire sitting astride a huge elephant that was decorated with similar apparel. The girls wondered what it would be like to sit on top of an elephant. An elephant seemed a lot more exciting than a horse to ride.

By now, the girls in the front row were under the spell of these stories from India. Their chattering had stopped. They wanted to know more about this fascinating country. Miss Sowry showed them photographs of the crowded markets where rows upon rows of fruits, the like of which they had never imagined could exist in the world. When she held up another photograph of monkeys feeding themselves on these fruits while a white cow with a hump on its back stood in the middle of the street, the girls were so intrigued that one of them raised her hand and asked in all innocence whether the people or the monkeys were ever harmed by the presence of such a beast? Miss Sowry explained that the cow was sacred in India and allowed to roam freely around the streets. This explanation seemed to amuse the girls. Another question was directed to Miss Sowry and this time, a more serious one.

'Miss Sowry,' the girl asked, 'why did you go to India?'

This was a question that Zaidee had no difficulty in answering.

'I knew I had a vocation to serve God and spread His word,' she replied. 'I felt that God was calling me to missionary work and if I disobeyed, I would have failed Him. I never thought that I would be called to India but my experiences there have enriched my life. I have seen miracles take place in front of me and lost souls reborn through the acceptance of Christ as their Saviour.'

'Were the girls at your school Christians?'

'Some were. Others not. Some of the girls had parents who had become Christians and it was easier for those girls. They were the ones who could help girls who had not yet come to Christ.'

'Do monkeys come into the school?' asked one of the girls. Everyone laughed, even Miss Sowry.

'Yes,' she said. 'Often they would scurry over the walls and into the school. Once one of them was so cheeky that he snatched a banana out of my hand. When I chased him away he just ate the banana in front of me.'

A rather plump girl with pigtails at the back of the room put up her hand.

'Were you ever frightened?' she asked.

Zaidee was surprised at the question. None of the girls at her school in India would have dared to ask such a direct question to a teacher but this was New Zealand, and things were different.

'I was scared of the snakes at first,' she answered. 'They wrap them into small baskets and sometimes they bring them out and play to them. The snakes stand up and hiss. Yes, it frightened me seeing them but I knew God was with me.'

That seemed to satisfy the girl for she clapped her hands. Soon the room was filled with the noise of girls clapping.

Obviously, the idea of Miss Sowry confronting snakes went down well. None of the girls had ever seen a snake. After all, there were none in New Zealand.

The girls in the front row couldn't keep still. They fidgeted and they wanted to hear more about the adventures of Miss Sowry. How glamorous it would be to travel to such an exotic place as India and save souls there. There seemed so many souls to save and so many dangers lurking around every corner. How brave Miss Sowry must have been to venture into the unknown. They wondered what the girls were like at her school. Would they be interested in boys? Or would they pray all the time to save themselves from the snakes. It all seemed so exciting.

'Are the girls at your school like us, Miss Sowry?' asked one of the more studious girls in the front row.

'They are very dutiful,' the missionary teacher replied. 'They have respect for their parents and study hard.'

'What clothes do they wear?'

'They wear a uniform at school and on special occasions, a sari.'

Zaidee showed them a photograph of rows of brown skinned girls, all in neat uniforms and dutifully facing the camera. But when she showed them other photographs of those same girls wearing the free flowing robes they called saris, excitement grew.

'I should like to go to India,' one of the girls announced, 'and wear a sari.'

'Me too.'

'I would like to be a missionary, Miss Sowry, and do what you do. Then I could wear a sari and see the monkeys.'

Somewhat taken aback by the sudden enthusiasm of the girls, Zaidee smiled.

'Well, you have to study hard first. God will guide you to mission work if you have a vocation to do so but for the moment, you all need to concentrate on your studies.'

Everyone in the room seemed to be talking at once. Reverend Morris called for silence and the girls ceased their chattering and sat still, just like the Indian girls.

'I would like you all to show your appreciation to Miss Sowry for her very informative talk about the wonderful work done on the missions that she and all the other dedicated missionaries do, bringing the heathens to the Lord Jesus Christ.'

His request was answered with enthusiastic clapping.

'We will now say a prayer that the good work that is done in our missions around the world will continue. Praise be to God.'

The girls bowed their heads in prayer.

When the meeting ended the plump girl with the pigtails approached Miss Sowry. She was rather nervous.

'Miss Sowry,' she said in her timid voice, 'I feel God has been speaking to me today and that He wants me to be a missionary like you and go to India to save souls.'

Zaidee was busy gathering the photographs and her papers together and she was rather distracted.

'Well, dear,' she replied, 'if that is true and you have been called, there are many, many souls out there who are in the need of salvation but... perhaps you should concentrate on your studies first. After all, it is not easy saving souls, you know.'

The plump girl nodded her head. Miss Sowry was right. She had exams to pass and books to read. Then there was that other problem that had been worrying her of late. Boys!

****

Zaidee Sowry was the daughter of Albert Sowry and Laura Wills. She worked in the post office in the 1920's until she decided to be a missionary. She trained first as a midwife in Melbourne before going to India. This story is fiction and is based on her experiences in India where she was in charge of the Alexander Girls School at Ellore, Dornakal Diocese. She would return to New Zealand to do speaking tours on behalf of the C.M.S. (Christian Missionary Society). She worked at the school in India for twenty-one years until she was invalided out suffering from Dengue Fever and Malaria. She returned to work in the post office, first at New Plymouth and then Wellington. The house she built at Wainuiomata was donated to the C.M.S.

****

Zaidee on horseback on her way to Aru Kashmir, June 1931
From *Leeds to Woodville* by Betty and Athol Sowry

Miss Zaidee Sowry, 1926
From *Leeds to Woodville* by Betty and Athol Sowry

TWICE BITTEN
The Story of Eliza Amelia Wills

Eliza was a determined woman so when her husband, Joseph disappeared she decided to track him down and when she caught up with him, see him in court. The circumstances of their marriage were somewhat hazy. They managed to produce six children during their time together, three sons and three daughters.

Joseph was a "remittance man" and that should have been warning enough for Eliza but she was young, just twenty-two years of age. Marriage was the preferred option open to women and after all, her husband was a handsome sort of fellow with dark brown hair and brooding brown eyes. No wonder she was attracted to him then. Eliza soon found out after a few months of marriage that Joseph was lazy and somewhat adverse to work. He was forever changing jobs. Consequently, the lack of money in the household was the cause of many arguments; some of them decidedly heated for Eliza was no pushover. Their arguments usually ended with Joseph storming out of the house leaving Eliza angry and the children in tears.

Joseph's disappearances became so regular that on one occasion Eliza's eldest son, in all innocence, asked whether his father had got lost somewhere. He had been reading a story about a boy who had been washed up on a tropical island, never to be seen again. No doubt his father's absence had fuelled his imagination. Eliza could only reassure but her mind began to focus on how best to resolve this troubling situation. If Joseph didn't return soon, she decided there was only one course of action and that was to take the absent and indolent husband to court. A legal separation would be the best possible outcome, she reasoned. Then she would be free to go her own way. She had a plan as to how she would make ends meet without

Joseph.

Eliza had already brought six children into the world. She decided that she could help other women when their time came to give birth. This would be one way to earn extra money. In a short space of time women came to her for help and Eliza, ever resourceful, soon became known for her midwifery skills. This was one way but she was determined that Joseph should be forced to provide some sort of financial support. She had never been under any illusion that he was able to give her any emotional care. After all, the man had been missing for five years and before that, he would often disappear for months. The present problem was that no one knew where Joseph was.

In between delivering babies, the ever resourceful Eliza supplemented her income by teaching the piano. She was a talented pianist. Teaching came easily to her. With the midwifery and the teaching, money trickled in until one day her patience with the absent Joseph finally boiled over. She decided that something had to be done. He had got away with not meeting his responsibilities towards herself and her children for far too long.

When Eliza discussed the situation with Mr Tringham, the lawyer was sympathetic when he heard her story. Sympathetic, but business like.

'This is a most unusual case, Mrs Perkins,' he told her. 'We first of all have to locate your missing husband and, as he has not been seen for over five years, this could cause some difficulties before we are able to proceed with a legal separation.'

'Should the police be informed, then?'

The lawyer shook his head. There were too many missing husbands on the books these days, what with the men coming home from the war and finding things not as they were. War changed men and the women in their man's absence had often found solace in another man's arms. He doubted if this had been the case with Eliza, however. The woman in front of him was much too determined to fall into that trap.

Still, five years was a long time to be missing. Maybe the man was dead?

'I doubt whether the police will have much success in tracking him down. There are many absent husbands these days. Rest assured, you are not alone in this situation, my dear. Our best course of action is to publish an advertisement in the Auckland and Wellington papers to the effect that unless your husband comes forward, a Citation and Petition will be supplied to you and proceedings will begin towards a legal separation. Regrettably, if we do not hear from your husband before the thirty-first day of October 1918, I fear that the court may not be able to impose a demand for any financial support from the gentleman in question.'

He drummed his fingers onto the desk and then he leaned back in his chair. He was becoming somewhat weary of these cases. This was the third time this week he had heard stories from women in similar situations to Eliza.

'However,' he concluded, 'we won't give up hope. You certainly have a sound case for the dissolution of your marriage given your husband's somewhat aversion to work and his frequent absences. I see here that he lists his occupation as a driver and his place of residence, Wellington. Is this true?'

Eliza sniffed.

'Driver! That lasted a week. He's in and out of work. Can't hold a job. I've had to take in boarders to bring in money along with the midwifery and the piano lessons.'

'That is admirable, Mrs Perkins.'

'If you say so. And as for him being in Wellington? Doubt if he's still here. It's a small enough place. People get to know one another. No one has seen head nor hide of him for more than five years. He could be anywhere.'

The lawyer smiled.

'It certainly has been a difficult situation for you. As you are aware, your husband was sentenced to three months in Auckland Gaol in 1911 for not providing the £110 necessary to maintain yourself and his children. I have not been able to find anything about his whereabouts since his release from prison and, as you are only too aware, that was well over five years ago.'

Eliza stood up and said,

'Going to prison saved the bugger from paying me that time, now didn't it? I tell you, if I ever get hold of him, Mr Tringham, I will be the one who will end up in the gaol.'

'Quite so, Mrs Perkins. Rest assured we will do our best for you.'

Eliza was somewhat relieved to think the law was on her side this time and that in due course, she would be released from her unfortunate marriage. She thanked Mr Tringham by grasping the lawyer's hand and shaking it in a somewhat familiar way. The lawyer, unused to such display could only mutter some trite words of encouragement as he ushered Eliza to the door. Eliza, for her part was in a buoyant mood and treated herself to tea and cake at a tearoom on Lambton Quay.

None of the authorities were able to locate Joseph and in due course, Eliza was granted a divorce. Things did not end then, however. One of her male boarders was seventeen years younger than her but that did not deter the ever resourceful Eliza.

Whatever the reasons, she decided that marriage was a good option after all. One barmy summer's evening as the two of them sat side by side on the veranda, Eliza said,

'Warren, I think we should get married, don't you?'

Somewhat surprised, the object of Eliza's affection, coughed and spluttered, not sure of an answer. He looked around. The house was comfortable and given his landlady's ability to earn money by any means possible, marriage to her might not be such a bad thing. Warren, like the indolent Joseph, had difficulty keeping a job. Any money he earned ran like water through his fingers and the publican grew richer because of it.

A few minutes later he replied,

'Well, now, Eliza... I can call you "Eliza" now, can't I? That sounds like a good idea. Yeah, let's do it.'

And so it came to pass that Eliza married again but this time it was something like the proverbial jumping out of the frying pan into the fire because Warren Williams proved to be an even worse husband than Joseph. He was forever drunk and when he had the liquor in him, he was cruel to her. Eliza suffered. What with never knowing where he was and never seeing any of the money he earned when he was in work, it was like history repeating itself for poor Eliza.

It was no surprise to anyone that one day just three years after their wedding Eliza decided that enough was enough. She filed for a divorce. A legal separation was granted and maintenance was set at £1.10s per week. Eliza never saw a penny. Three years later an arrest warrant was issued to her second husband for failing to meet his obligations to her.

If you thought that Eliza would give up after two disastrous marriages, you would be wrong. Instead, she seemed to relish in her newfound freedom. One day, she announced that she had plans.

'I'm done with men,' she said. 'I'm not about to try again. As the saying goes, "once bitten, twice shy". Well, I've been twice bitten and thrice shy. And... '

She had a twinkle in her eyes as she told the family of her plans.

'From now on I'll do what I do best. I have decided to buy land out Pinehaven way and build a house on it. I intend to build the house myself with my own hands.'

And she did!

****

Eliza was the daughter of Albert Wills and Ann Joll. She married Joseph Perkins, a remittance man. A remittance man in nineteenth century Britain was usually the 'black sheep' of the family and was sent away from Britain to the rest of the British Empire and paid to stay away. He was generally of dissolute or drunken character and may have been sent away after disgraces at home. Whether this was true of Joseph is unknown. It is a fact, however, that Eliza divorced him, married and subsequently divorced Warren Williams and she did indeed build a house at Pinehaven, Upper Hutt, Wellington.

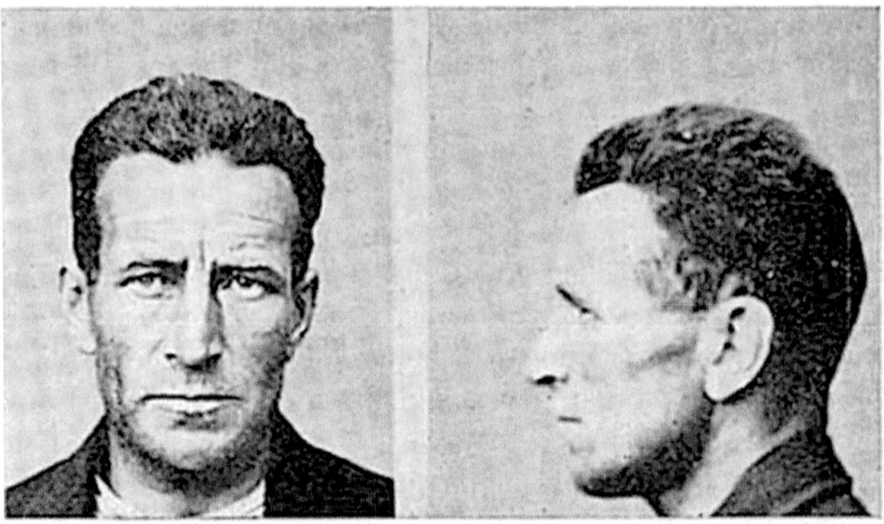

PERKINS, JOSEPH.

Eliza outside the house she built at Pinehaven, Upper Hutt, Wellington.

GOING HOME

It had been a difficult crossing. Choppy seas across the Tasman had meant an uncomfortable few days and the constant rolling of the vessel brought on bouts of sea sickness. The children cried. With just their mother to cling to now that their father was dead, not knowing why they were, all of a sudden taken away from their friends, every one of the seven of them bewildered and fearful at the same time. Their mother did little to reassure them except to say, "We are going home." It was no wonder that their young hearts were scared. When one of the girls vomited over the side of the ship and they were just an hour out from Brisbane, it seemed the whole world they had known had ended.

For the mother it was different. A widow now, her only thought in mind was to return to the place of her birth. Here she would find the familiar comfort of belonging for she had never felt at home in Brisbane. She had followed him over the Tasman because he wanted to be with his kith and kin. Without protest she had been at his side, right to the bitter end when he breathed his last; a young man taken from her too soon. All because of a terrible war that had left him broken although he never spoke of what he had seen on the fields of Flanders. She could never understand. Gassed there at the Front, she doubted if he had ever fully recovered but there had been so many other young men who hadn't come home. He had come home and she had borne him eight children. They had laid him to rest in a crowded graveyard beside the little girl they had lost many years before. It seemed the right thing to do. Grief is love with no place left to go but memory. All this would come later. There were seven mouths to feed and no time for either the grieving or the memory. These had been hard times and sometimes clinging to hope had been the only way to get through. That hope had been to return home.

****

The ship rolled as they entered the Cook Strait[2] for this was always a rough passage through to the calmer seas in the landlocked harbour. It was a cloudy day and the wind was up. Thick mist obscured the land on both sides so the mother could not make out the sights of home but when the ship entered the harbour, the mists cleared just a little and now she could see the sandy beaches. They passed by the familiar Soames Island[3]. How near to home she was now. Timber houses arranged like building blocks clung to the hills for this was a city hemmed in by mountains. Mount Victoria[4] came into view. There was a thin covering of snow on the top of the Remutakas and tears came into the mother's eyes. Seeing the snow brought the memory of her earlier life. Were these the tears coming without warning from a grieving wife and mother or were they perhaps the tears of relief that she was home at last? We will never know.

The present world was now. The children had to be gathered together for the ship was about to weigh anchor and soon they would all be ushered off to the shore to stand on dry land once more. Memories always come at the most unexpected times. A hundred years before her great grandmother and great grandfather had made a similar sea journey on the *Timandra.* These brave souls had sailed with their children from faraway Cornwall to New Zealand. There were sailing ships then and four long months at sea. The mother's journey was just a short three days. She knew the world she was going to. They had not.

The little fatherless family stood on Wellington's shoreline. A gust of wind lifted the mother's hat and blew it away like a feather to be caught by a stranger and returned to her. Everyone laughed.

---

[2] Te Moana-a-Raukawa

[3] Moutere o Somes

[4] Maunga Wikitoria

'Windy Wellington,' he said with a bow.

The children giggled as the mother reclaimed her hat. No tears of grief were behind her eyes now, only joyful ones.

'Yes,' she replied and then she smiled. 'For better or worse, it's a place to call home.'

****

Rheta Perkins was the granddaughter of Albert and Ann Wills. Her mother was Eliza Amelia Perkins (née Wills). She married John Payne and the couple had eight children. John died aged forty-one years leaving Rheta with seven children to rear on her own. One child had died in infancy. I wrote this particular story to give a picture of what life had been like in the 1930's and that her journey back to her place of birth had many similarities to her ancestors' sea journey a hundred years previously.

The Payne family in Brisbane before the death of John, probably in the 1930's

(From a family collection.)

HISTORY OF THE WILLS FAMILY IN NEW ZEALAND

It must have been a momentous decision for James and Betsy Wills to decide to leave the world they knew and undertake a journey to the other side of the earth. An unknown world was before them, and possibly it was for the other Cornish families as well, that the promise of a better life was the most compelling reason to leave. Cornwall, in the early part of the nineteenth century, was suffering from a recession brought about in part by imports of cheap alluvial tin from Malaya, now Malaysia. Consequently, wages were low. Life was hard and conditions were challenging. The hope of a new life and the possibility of owning land in the Colony of New Zealand would have meant for James and Betsy and their six children a gamble worth pursuing.

"James Wills is described at the time of the birth of his first son, Albert in 1823 as an 'innkeeper, Calstock'. If the economy in the area was depressed his trade was not likely to have been very flourishing."[5] By 1837, the Wills family had grown to six. Their youngest daughter, Betsy Rickard, was born in 1837 and in January 1840, the Plymouth Company of New Zealand was formed. The company merged with the New Zealand Company of London in 1842. Before the merger, the Plymouth Company sent six ships to New Zealand from Plymouth. The fourth ship to sail was the *Timandra*. The Wills family were on board that ship.

It appears that James and Betsy may have been less than truthful about their ages to secure the free passage out as the ages of assisted immigrants had to be below forty. As James was christened in 1800, and Betsy in 1802, it would have meant that James was forty-one and therefore not eligible. This discrepancy

---

1 Wills, Norman *A Good West Country Name*, Hamilton 1992 Ch 2 p 15

with ages was not an uncommon occurrence at the time and records were not as accurate as the present day. Suffice it to say, they, along with their children, Albert, Thirza, Maria, Thomas, James and Betsy, sailed from Plymouth on 2nd November 1841. Other Calstock families were also on board so there would have been the security of knowing friends on the ship but it must have been a traumatic moment in all their lives to see the last of Plymouth and the prospect of the long sea voyage ahead of them.

A notice appeared in the London and Plymouth Paper[6] regarding the sailing of the *Timandra:*

"New Plymouth, New Zealand. The Court of Directors of the New Zealand Company do hereby give notice that the new ship TIMANDRA, A1, 430 tons burden, is chartered for the conveyance of cabin passengers and free emigrants to the settlement of New Plymouth, to sail from London on the 10th, and from Plymouth on the 20th October. The settlement, to which about 500 persons have already emigrated from the West of England, has been located in the district of Taranaki, near the Sugar Loaf Islands. Further sales of land in England are now restricted to actual settlers, who will receive liberal passage allowance, and the TIMANDRA has been specially chartered on terms which will secure to families and others a passage to the settlement on liberal terms. By Order of the Court of Directors."

With this vision of finding a land of promise ahead of them, the Wills family said goodbye to their old life. The thought of a four-month sea journey to the other side of the earth must have been a daunting prospect for the family and not knowing what they would find at the journey's end would have made them apprehensive. However, the determined spirit is resolute in many a human heart. The decision that James and Betsy made to voyage to a new land and to a new beginning, and to face an

---

[6] Wills, Norman *A Good West Country Name*, Hamilton 1992 Ch 2 p 16

uncertain world there, is surely a testament that they, too, had that same indomitable spirit of determination.

And so the journey began. The assisted passengers were confined below decks in crowded conditions and with just two metres above the floors; it must have seemed that they had entered some sort of hell on earth. When the *Timandra* crossed the Equator the temperature rose to 82 degrees Fahrenheit and we can only imagine how stifling that must have been for the Wills family and their fellow passengers. There was also a good deal of sickness on board. Several children died and a young woman didn't survive childbirth. No record exists as to whether her baby lived.

Compounded with the crowded conditions on board, at different times food shortages caused problems as well. One memorable incident occurred when "They managed to capture and kill an albatross whose wing tip measured ten feet. The flesh was eaten by some of the emigrants and said to be good." [7] This surely would have relieved some of the hunger as well as provided some excitement for what must have been, at times, a tedious journey.

When they reached Cape Town on Christmas Day, Joseph Flight records in his diary:

'Went on shore, one shilling each way. Bought some oranges and lemon trees and one hundred vines. Many of the emigrants returned to the ship...? Wine cheap at Cape Town.'[8]

There appears to have been an altercation between Betsy Wills and Mary Ann Prout as the latter accused Betsy's daughter of stealing her shoes. This was also recorded in Flight's journal.

"1st Feb. 1842. Mrs Proust found a pair of her shoes on Wills' daughter. A quarrel between Proust and Wills women."[9] (Passenger list shows Prout).

---

[7] Wills, Norman *A Good West Country Name*, Hamilton 1992 Ch 2 p 17

[8] Wills, Norman *A Good West Country Name*, Hamilton 1992 Ch 2 p 18

[9] Wills, Norman *A Good West Country Name*, Hamilton 1992 Ch 2 p 18

A good deal of animosity also existed between the assisted passengers and the cabin crew but there is no record of this hostility resulting in fisticuffs. Given the proximity of everyone on board, it is no wonder that fights and disagreements would have broken out.

The Wills women appear to have excelled themselves in needlework however and stitched up several batches of clothes. The women were required to sew up garments as a means of "keeping the female steerage passengers gainfully employed."[10] Garments had been cut out before embarkation with the plan that the women would finish them during the journey. Thomas Woollcombe went on to say that "the ladies were entitled to keep for themselves one garment out of every five they made – men's blue shirts and white shirts and women's shifts." The garments were taken by the Plymouth Company and were to be sold in New Plymouth. The proceeds went to funding a school. Mr Woollcombe was also of the opinion that "the gratuitous education is never properly valued". The settlers were required to make some financial contribution towards the education of their children. James and Betsy would have approved of this arrangement as educating their children was viewed as essential to bettering oneself and would help their children to make a new start in a new land.

The *Timandra* anchored at New Plymouth on 23rd February 1842. All in all, the passengers and the crew on the *Timandra* fared better than others on similar emigrant ships.

"Here, then, had ended the Wills family voyage from England to their new homeland. Some families had recorded births and deaths on the way, but James and Betsy and their six children do not figure on any health reports, so we presume they all travelled fairly well."[11]

---

[10] Wills, Norman *A Good West Country Name*, Hamilton 1992 Ch 2 p 18
[11] Wills, Norman *A Good West Country Name*, Hamilton 1992 Ch 2 p 19

The land the settlers viewed was an abundant one. One of the passengers on board, Stephen Gillingham, wrote that "The town is situated between two rivers, both of which abound with mountain trout and eels, and their waters are as good as any I have ever tasted. It is a beautiful country, abundantly supplied with water and wood etc." The people on shore were "living in tents, huts formed of reeds or mud, and a few in one-storey houses."

Seeing all this before them, we can only imagine what thoughts and imaginings would have been going through the minds of the emigrants as they gathered their belongings together. They had come from towns where brick and stone buildings huddled together as a permanent fixture, and generations lived and died there, to dwellings that held no recorded past. Here, amongst the tents and mud huts, was their future and the old world they once knew, so very, very far away.

New Plymouth, 1863. From a collection in the Alexander Turnbull Library, Wellington

The Plymouth Company of New Zealand was the brainchild of Edward Gibbon Wakefield. He planned to colonise New Zealand and make money. He proposed to turn the colony into a model English settlement and for this to succeed; the colony would need white settlers. On 3rd October 1840, at a dinner where the Earl of Devon presided, a gift of a section in the Town of New Plymouth was promised to each emigrant upon their arrival. This was greeted with great enthusiasm. No doubt the news of this enterprise would have reached the ears of James and Betsy Wills and would have hastened their decision to emigrate. The possibility of acquiring land in the colony, something that would not have been possible for them in England, was beyond the dreams of the ordinary working folk of that time. Emigrating to New Zealand would have fulfilled their dreams.

"Under the Plymouth Company land scheme, a deposit of £10 paid in England entitled the emigrant to be allocated one town section of 1 acre and 50 acres of rural land (later reduced to a quarter acre and 25 acres). The total payment for 1 town payment and 1 rural section was to be £75, of which £50 was to be transferred to the Company's Emigration Fund. (Labouring immigrants were to be allowed an eighth acre). The Wills town section shows as No 92, on the inland side of Devon Road, between the Henui and Waiwakaiho streams.

The family took up a farm at Bell Block, in what was then shown as the eastern portion of Wills Road. One report in 1849 lists 'the Wills property at Mangaiti' as "one of the few areas that had been transformed from a wilderness to a farm."[12] There is no doubt that the Wills family intended to make a go of it in their new home. In fact, from letters written around the time of 1842 by other emigrants, no one seems in the least interested in returning to England and one even wrote that he would not return home even if he could be given a free passage. Others mention that the land is fertile and there are plenty of potatoes, fine crops and fine vegetables.

Conditions must have been hard during the first few years, however. New Plymouth was an isolated settlement and at times there was a shortage of food. The settlement was still reliant to

---

[12] Wills, Norman *A Good West Country Name*, Hamilton 1992 Ch 3 p 23

some extent on ships coming from England. In 1844 a dispute arose between the traders who sold flour and the New Plymouth merchants who sold drapery goods. The drapery goods were imported from England and the traders refused to sell flour when they could not dispose of the draperies. No doubt the matter was resolved as the colony became more self-sufficient. The emigrants earned more money than they could have done in England and work was plentiful. Tree felling was a matter of priority to clear the land. Sawmills sprung up in the area with sawyers being amongst the well-paid.

It has to be noted that the Wills family were sympathetic to the Māori cause and defended their rights. They appeared to be on reasonably good terms with the indigenous people and when strife erupted between the white settlers and the Māori in 1848, a message was sent to the Governor by the Māori chief that Mr Wills and his family were to remain in undisputed possession of their land. This was the time when houses and buildings were being set on fire as a protest at the white settlers' claims on the Māori land. Albert Wills, the eldest son of James and Betsy had learned the Māori language and was able to communicate with them. Perhaps this understanding on the part of Albert's family saved them at that time from being burned out.

However, a notable incident occurred which was duly reported in the *Taranaki Herald* when the Chief and his warriors arrived at the gate of the property of James Wills after a farm worker had killed a pig belonging to the local Chief.

"But next day the Chief, with all his men armed, presented himself at the gate of the senior Mr Wills. He was very excited and brandished his tomahawk and vowed vengeance.

"Mr Albert Wills in the company of warriors at the gate, succeeded by tact and courage in inducing the natives to put down their weapons outside, and before they returned to the dairy the breach had been healed. This was the only difficulty the family had with their Māori neighbours."

This amiable state of affairs between the two communities was not to last.

"In 1859 trouble flared up when a minor chief offered to sell land in the Waitara Valley. His right to sell was opposed by a more senior chief who occupied part of the disputed block of land with his followers."[13] "The problem was exacerbated when the governor, Colonel Thomas Gore Browne, prepared to survey the land despite the conflicting claims, and then proclaimed martial law. Māori took the proclamation on 25th January 1860 as a declaration of war and it was the government forces that carried out the first hostile act on 6th March when troops destroyed a deserted pā. As the Maori put it to John Gorst, a civil commissioner,

"Land was bought at Taranaki; we heard it was bought improperly, and presently disturbance arose about it. We had not heard that the *Pākehā* was at Taranaki until the soldiers had gone on board the ships, then we heard. Now this offence was from the *Pākehā;* hence we said, we are strangers to one another. We are divided, you on one side, we on the other."[14]

The Wills family did not escape the strife this time. A rebel Māori group burned down the houses of both James and Albert Wills. Hostilities increased. The area was now at war and a decision had to be made for the safety of them all. Several families had already left the district including most of the Wills family who had moved to Nelson on the South Island where clashes between the two communities were infrequent. Albert's sister, Thirza, her husband and their family had already done so. So in 1863 Albert, his brother, James and their families along with their parents, James and Betsy, made the move from

[13] Bohan, Edmund *Climates of War: New Zealand in Conflict 1859 – 69.* Hazard Press, 2005 Prologue p 25

[14] Gorst,J.E. *New Zealand Revisited* ch X p 178

Chessell, Gwen *Separate Lives: The Story of Sir George and Lady Grey* Hopping Mouse Press 2014 ch 15 p 272

Taranaki and took up a Crown Grant of land in Lower Moutere, in what became known as Wills Road.

It was on Wills Road that a school was built in the isolated area. The school was aptly named the Wills Road School. Albert and his wife, Ann Joll were to remain at Lower Moutere for the rest of their lives.

Albert's brother, Thomas and his family were the only ones of James and Betsy's children to remain in Taranaki. Fluent in the Māori language, on occasion he was able to sort out tensions between the two communities. However, he narrowly escaped with his life when his good friend Reverend Whitely was murdered.

Always sympathetic to the Māori cause and anti-war, Albert, his father and his brothers were true pioneers. They were farmers throughout and cleared the land, grew their crops and tended their animals. The women were equally hardworking surviving numerous pregnancies, tragedies and deaths of their children. In both men and women, their Cornish roots were strong, strengthened by their early life and by the endurance of the long sea journey to the new land. They had a strong sense of social justice and the hope of a better world in the land that they and their descendants would forever call home.

Social justice and speaking out about it were at the heart of many of the Wills's family members. One of the most prominent was the Reverend John Wills, the son of James, who was an outspoken advocate for the temperance movement in New Zealand. He became President of the New Zealand Alliance and devoted his life to raising awareness of the social deprivations arising from the abuses of alcohol and it was recorded that "he brought a different style to the Church"[15]

The Reverend John's sons were equally prominent in public affairs and the eldest son, Webster Harold was a teacher of the

---

[15] Centennial Booklet of the Church of the Epiphany, Ormandville (1985)

Māori language. He wrote a textbook for students, *Lessons in the Māori Language,* continuing the family belief in social justice for all.

The Christian faith was strong in some members of the Wills clan. A granddaughter of Thomas John Wills, Zaidee Sowry was an advocate of the temperance movement as well as being a missionary at Ellore, Darnakal Diocese, India for thirty years.[16]

Although the Wills family were by and large anti-war, the grandsons and great-grandsons of James and Betsy served in both World Wars of the twentieth century, many of them losing their lives in these conflicts.

With the passing of James in 1896 and Betsy in 1898 any ties that would have bound the family members to Cornwall were loosened and by the turn of the century, their descendants had greatly increased in number. All these descendants would consider themselves to be New Zealanders. James and Betsy would have been proud of them. They had, indeed, made a better life for themselves.

---

[16] Sowry, Betty. Edited by Betty Sowry, Clive V. Sowry, Athol Sowry. *Leeds to Woodville, The Family of Joseph Sowry in New Zealand 1862 - 2005*

Present day shoreline of New Plymouth (2023)
From a photograph by Jeanette Clarkin-Phillips

THE JOLL FAMILY
ORIGIN OF THE FAMILY NAME

The name is linked with the Old Norse *jol.* It has also been suggested that the name derives from Jolfr (Norse), Jolles (German), Jolle (Dutch), Joly (French). The Old English word *jolif,* means jolly, merry or happy.

It also has to be mentioned that the ancient Celtic word for the devil is *Joll.*

THE SOUL OF AN EMIGRANT WOMAN

Elizabeth Treliving, aged eleven would often glance at young Samuel Joll as he sat beside his parents at chapel on Sundays. Of course, not one of her siblings noticed, and her mother and father would have been amused at a young girl's infatuation. Elizabeth thought Samuel was handsome and not at all like his elder brother, Joshiah. Rumour had it that Joshiah was a brute and bullied his younger brother. The Jolls and the Trelivings were farmer neighbours and it was natural that the two families would gossip about each other.

Samuel was a strong lad and already his path in life was chosen, or so it seemed. Farmers needed blacksmiths and Samuel had the strength to wield the hammer over the anvil. Elizabeth sometimes made an excuse to walk past the smithy and hope that she could watch Samuel at work. It was all rather exciting.

One day Samuel noticed Elizabeth. He had finished shoeing a large grey stallion and was in the process of walking the horse to the fence to be tethered there when he caught sight of Elizabeth. She was carrying a wicker basket and when she saw Samuel, she blushed and dropped the basket with its load of turnips onto the ground.

'Why, Miss Treliving,' said a concerned young Samuel. 'Let me help you.'

And he proceeded to scoop up the turnips in his strong hands and load them into the basket while Elizabeth, flustered now, tried her best to help. She was aware of the proximity of Samuel, and as they loaded the turnips back into the basket, Samuel's huge blacksmith's hand brushed, ever so slightly, the tiny hand of Elizabeth. Their eyes met and Elizabeth's face reddened even more. Samuel, awkward now, coughed to hide his nervousness and the moment passed. But neither Samuel nor Elizabeth ever forgot that one precious moment.

****

The banns were read out in the Wesleyan Chapel, Calstock, Cornwall. Samuel Joll and Elizabeth Vanderband Treliving were to be married on the Sixteenth Day of May in the Year of our Lord, 1829, and this marriage had the approval of the two families, both families being members of the same parish. It was welcome news and cause for celebration that the young couple would remain on the land of their birth and be blessed with many children. On hearing those words, Sarah, sitting quietly next to Elizabeth, squeezed her sister's hand.

'Lizzie', she whispered, 'You're lucky. Samuel's a good 'un, ain't that so?'

Elizabeth didn't answer for her eyes were full of tears. Whether the tears were from the emotion of the occasion or joy we will never know but Elizabeth agreed with her sister. Samuel would be a good husband, and wherever and whatever happened in their lives together, she believed he would be faithful to her, as she would be to him. They would be happy to stay in Calstock, farmers forever, and raise many children to carry on. Elizabeth was just twenty-two years of age.

****

Elizabeth and Samuel were indeed blessed with many children. Five came in quick succession and the steady routine of their lives seemed to Elizabeth to be a settled one. She was contented enough and the children took up most of her attention. True to her sister's prediction, Samuel turned out to be a responsible husband. He didn't take fools lightly and sometimes Elizabeth despaired of his stubbornness but she kept her thoughts to herself. She knew better than to antagonise him when the mood was upon him. It had to be said that it was a happy enough marriage and in most things, they seemed to be content until one day when all that changed.

Samuel came home in a rage.

‘Enough is enough,’ he shouted. ‘I’ll have no more to do with him.’

Elizabeth knew just who he was referring to because the animosity between Samuel’s elder brother and Samuel had been simmering for as long as she had known them. She murmured some words of reconciliation but Samuel was having none of it.

‘He clouted me with a bridle for the last time, I tell ye. I told him that I’d had enough of his authority, lordin’ it over everyone. I be goin’ to Plymouth to buy a farm in the New Zealand Land Company.’

Elizabeth heard the words but her mind could not believe them. Surely Samuel would calm down? But her husband’s mind was made up.

‘It’s not just Joshiah,’ he said after a few tense moments. ‘The Land Taxes are cripplin’ us. There’s no future here. Leastways we can make a new start in New Zealand an’ be all the better for it.’

‘But, it’s so far away… the other side of the earth. Calstock is our home and has been for generations, how can we leave it?’

‘We are going. My mind’s made up. Tomorrow I be off to Plymouth to get a passage booked for us all and find out about the land grant.’

Elizabeth knew that once Samuel’s mind was made up there would be little she could do to change it, but she despaired. She had thought that this was her life, safe with her children around her in the only place she had ever known. To leave her mother, knowing that she would never see her again was a cross too hard to bear; to leave the familiar and set off on a journey into the unknown, to a country so far distant that it didn’t bear thinking about, to try to make a life there amongst strangers, knowing that she would never return to Cornwall and that she would live and die in a faraway land was the most painful thing she could imagine that could have ever happened to her. At that moment, she inwardly cursed Samuel for she knew that there was no other option for her. She would have to be the dutiful wife and follow him but she did not want to. She had hoped for something more out of life and in her wildest imaginings that did not include moving away from her family and friends to the other side of the earth. The thought of the four-month sea journey terrified her and what she might find there at the end of this was even worse. She began to think that God was punishing her for some misdemeanour or other, and if she prayed hard enough, all would be forgiven and Samuel would come to his senses. It was a faint hope indeed.

Whatever Elizabeth's fears were as the impending departure drew ever closer, she kept them hidden. Samuel had been able to purchase a section of good land at Omata, near New Plymouth and he was so full of enthusiasm for the new venture that he spoke of little else. His enthusiasm didn't transfer to his wife. Elizabeth went about the business of packing and reassuring the children as best she could, and the tears she shed when she said goodbye to her mother were silent ones and made more poignant because of this.

The first sight of the *Timandra* did little to allay her fears. It was a cold November morning when the Joll family gathered along with the other emigrants on the wharf at Plymouth. The *Timandra* was a fine clipper but Elizabeth could not admire the vessel. To her, it looked like a prison to which she would be confined, crowded together with about two hundred others, plus sheep destined for the new colony, and no way to escape for at least four long months while the world she knew gradually faded into a bittersweet memory.

But Elizabeth was stoical and kept her sadness hidden, busying herself sewing the garments that the steerage women were required to do to keep them occupied, and trying as best she could to keep her children happy and pacify a sometimes explosive husband. At times, she despaired of it all, especially when the sea sickness caused her untold misery and the stench of humanity confined below decks upset her fastidious nature. Then New Zealand felt like an impossible and foolish dream.

When she glimpsed the towering peak of the mountain the white men had named Mount Egmont and the journey was at an end, her relief was palpable.

'This be our home now. An' 'tis a land of opportunity, ye mark my words', Samuel announced as the family clambered onto the whaleboat, all thankful for the safe passage. Tired, bewildered and relieved that the long sea journey was over at last, Samuel and Elizabeth and their five children, along with the rest of the emigrants, collected their baggage and gathered together on the sandy shore. They could never have imagined how very different this new land was from the world they had left behind. What was ahead of them would be hard, backbreaking work and the challenges would sometimes seem insurmountable but it was a new beginning and that had to be something. At least, that is what Elizabeth hoped for.

Perhaps her newfound optimism was shattered somewhat when they first saw the new settlement. It was nothing like she had been led to believe. The township, if it could be called that, consisted of tents and rough houses built from rushes and sedges. There was an overwhelming sense of pessimism Elizabeth discovered. And she, too, wondered why on earth had she allowed herself to come halfway around the world to this. But Samuel was undeterred. He set about clearing the land that he had purchased at Omata, building a shelter for his family while Elizabeth was left with the younger children in New Plymouth. Here, she struggled. Food was in short supply and an infestation of rats added to her misery.

In due course, she and the children joined Samuel and her life in New Zealand began. Here, pregnancy followed pregnancy and she was to have another five children. As the years went by, and the family prospered, memories of her earlier life in faraway Calstock diminished. Her father died in 1856 and when news reached her of her mother's death in 1867, she shed the tears she had kept inside herself for all those years. She had realised that life presents many challenges and amongst all the struggles, there was much joy mixed with sorrow.

One summer evening, she and Samuel sat side by side in the garden of the home that Samuel and her sons had built in New Plymouth. The Joll family were now so much part of the community that she could no longer imagine a world away from here. She put down the book she was reading and looked at Samuel. Everyone called him Growler now because he grumbled a lot about everything but Elizabeth loved him, despite his shortcomings.

'All our children are New Zealanders now, Samuel, aren't they?' she murmured.

'What's that, woman?' Growler grumbled for he was hard of hearing and especially so when his wife requested something or other.

'I said, our children are New Zealanders now. Are we, do you think? Or will we forever be Cornish folk.'

'We be New Zealanders now. All of us. The Cornish blood be runnin' in our veins but this is our country an' we are blessed to call it so.'

Elizabeth nodded.

'Aye, that we are. A place to call home.'

And she turned the page of her book and started to read once more.

****

Although the description of Elizabeth's character is fiction, certain events described in my story did happen in her life and they have been recorded. Elizabeth would have been like so many emigrant women of the time who had no other choice but to follow their husbands, to endure numerous pregnancies and see the premature deaths of some of their children whilst all the time they struggled in an unfamiliar and sometimes harsh environment so different from what they had left behind.

Elizabeth Treliving Joll

Captain Frank Skinner was a troubled man. It was all because of a regulation from the New Zealand Company about the hygiene on board the emigrant ships which decreed that chloride of lime had to be sprinkled liberally on the bunks and sleeping quarters to prevent the spread of disease. As an antiseptic and disinfectant chloride of lime was the preferred method. Captain Skinner was duty-bound to obey and enforce this directive. However, the practice was viewed with suspicion, and at times hostility by the emigrants. Right from the start when the application was first implemented there had been complaints that clothes and bedding were burnt and that the sailors were somewhat lax in their application. It was something that appeared to be universally disliked and Captain Skinner was ever mindful that this hostility could spread to rebellion, even mutiny if left unchecked. His only course of action to prevent this occurring was to order that it must be done, without hindrance, or there would be consequences if not obeyed.

This directive was soon to be tested and it was Samuel Joll, the blacksmith from Calstock, who caused the biggest problem, and it was Samuel who provided some amount of excitement on board the *Timandra*. Given that the long sea journey was tedious most of the time anything out of the ordinary had to be cause for much talk and speculation. Samuel Joll, as strong an ox, was not a man to be messed with.

Samuel was a stubborn character and once provoked, there was no stopping him. Like the other emigrants, he was wary of the chloride of lime treatment and things came to a head one morning when his wife, Elizabeth was confined to her bunk bed. Poor Elizabeth had suffered from sea sickness for most of the voyage, and it just happened that this was the day that the Captain had issued the command to his men to sprinkle the dreaded chloride of lime treatment over the emigrants' sleeping quarters in the steerage area.

The chief mate, Mr Thompson had a full bucket and began to spread it over Elizabeth's bed. The sight of the woman lying there, helpless and sick, must have excited him for he grabbed her blanket and started to pull it off the bed exposing her thin body.

'Ye'll 'ave to get yesel up, Missus,' he said in a rough voice, 'or ye'll be covered in the stuff.'

He then started to sprinkle the chloride of lime about the berth. Elizabeth didn't answer. She was so worn out and weakened from the constant vomiting that the thought of moving from her bed was the last thing that she could contemplate doing. Instead, she groaned and told Thompson to be gone. This annoyed him. He happened to be in a bad mood as he had been disciplined by one of the senior officers a few days previously for not applying the chloride of lime properly over the steerage passengers' bunks.

Thompson tried to pull the covers from Elizabeth, whilst still holding the full bucket in one hand, and that was when Samuel lunged towards him, spilt the contents over the floor in the tussle, and wrestled the bucket from a very angry chief mate. Another bucket was called for but this time Thompson threw some of its contents over Samuel, and then he turned his attention to Elizabeth. He gripped her thin shoulders. Then he proceeded to pull her by force from the bed. This was too much for Samuel. He seized the second bucket and in the ensuing struggle between the two men, this bucket landed on the floor. Half the contents spilt onto another bed.

'Take yer hands off of me wife, ye lecherous bugger,' roared Samuel. He took hold of Thompson by the collar. Then he landed an almighty punch on the man's chin causing Thompson to topple on top of Elizabeth. Elizabeth, by this time, had forgotten how ill she was and tried in vain to push the half-unconscious chief mate off her bed. Samuel, seeing his wife in such distress and very angry, heaved the unfortunate man to his feet and punched him once again, this time in the stomach. Thompson groaned and toppled to the floor.

The whole episode took only a few minutes but it just so happened that it was witnessed by the ship's doctor.

'Get hold of the Chief Officer,' the doctor yelled to another sailor who all this time had stood, looking somewhat gormless, not knowing quite what to do.

In due course, the Chief Officer arrived.

'Put this man in irons', ordered the Chief Officer.

'Ye'll do no such thing,' roared Samuel and he hit the officer with such force that he, too, fell to the floor.

By now the ship was lurching and everyone was finding it harder to stay upright. Samuel took this opportunity to make himself scarce leaving Elizabeth groaning on the bed, half covered in chloride of lime whilst the fellow emigrants cheered. The sailors were no friends of the steerage passengers and the sight of one of them getting their comeuppance from Samuel was cause for celebration. The Chief Officer struggled to his feet and holding his hand over his bleeding nose, called for the hand bolts to restrain Samuel. This brought forth more jeers and shouting from the emigrants as word got out that Samuel Joll was taking on the sailors.

By now Thompson had struggled to his feet and barked an order to the sailor whose duty it was to deal with the Joll's sleeping area. This sailor had managed somehow to coax Elizabeth from her bed. He then proceeded to disinfect the bed and the floor. Elizabeth, groaning in pain from the sea sickness and worried as to what was happening to Samuel, balanced herself as best she could whilst her children looked on, frightened. There was still no sign of the pugnacious Samuel.

Captain Skinner was informed of the altercation and he decided that an example must be made of Samuel. He could ill afford to have this sort of insubordination on his ship. It was for the passengers' health and safety that the chloride of lime had to be applied, and if the emigrants thought that this procedure could be prevented by the use of force on the sailors who were doing the work, this would cause no end of trouble. Discipline had to be maintained for both the emigrants and the crew and the Captain was ever mindful that it was his duty to maintain order.

Shortly after noon the crew and the emigrants were summoned. By now, Samuel had been located and Captain Skinner ordered his men to bring Samuel to the poop deck to hear his punishment and have the hand-bolts put on him. This directive was greeted with some resistance from the emigrants. Samuel was quite popular with his fellow passengers and somewhat of a hero. He had never been one to bow to authority and for this reason, given that the English class structure was maintained in such a rigid fashion on board the ship, his defiance was legendry. When he stood in front of the Captain, restrained by the irons, and his punishment read out to him, a cheer of defiance rang out from the passengers. Captain Skinner was having none of it. Samuel was told to apologise forthwith but the obstinate Cornishman refused to do so.

Poor Elizabeth was witness to all this. She was torn between loyalty to her husband and admiration for his zeal in protecting her, to the embarrassment that this had happened so late in the voyage as the ship would soon be anchoring off the coast of New Zealand within the next few days, and she would not need to have anything more to do with Captain Skinner, the sailors or most of her fellow passengers. So she stood silently as the Regulations were read out and Samuel was taken away. She wondered if he would apologise but she feared his intransigent nature would prevent this and she would be left with gathering her children and their possessions together when the ship finally reached New Plymouth. She feared that Samuel would be a marked man and they would not receive any of the promises that had been made to them from the New Zealand Company.

Samuel stood motionless with his legs apart to balance himself against the swell of the clipper as the prevailing southerly winds pushed the *Timandra* through the heavy seas. They were making good speed and all hands were on deck. All afternoon he stood there and not a word of apology did he murmur. The iron bolts hurt his wrists but he didn't flinch nor did he retaliate when the passing sailors jeered at him, confident that the powerful Cornishman was sufficiently restrained, they taunted him without mercy, but he didn't budge one inch. Elizabeth and the older children distraught at the thought of Samuel a prisoner, and fearing the shame of it all, remained below decks so as not to provoke any lewd comments. The sun disappeared below the horizon but Samuel remained defiant.

Captain Skinner summoned the Chief Officer to his quarters.

'Is Joll offering an apology for his behaviour?' he asked.

'No, Sir. The man's cross-grained and not budging. A good flogging would be for the good of him.'

'Agree, but he's an emigrant and paid his way, such as it is. Be glad to see the back of him. How long has he been restrained?'

'Eight hours, Sir.'

'And his wife?'

'She and the children have remained in their quarters, Sir. Keeping out of sight. The chloride of lime has been applied throughout,' he added with a smirk.

'Good. We'll have no end of rebellion if Joll gets his way. The steerage passengers have been a difficult lot this time, I must say. We are too lenient with them. Joll will remain where he is until he apologises. Have you had any problems with the punch that the wretched man gave you?' he added, somewhat condescendingly. Captain Skinner was not a man who showed much emotion as to the well-being of others and his unexpected question took the Chief Officer by surprise.

'No, Sir. Thank you for inquiring. Aye, he inflicted quite a blow to my chin. He's a strong 'un but apart from a bruise or two, not much pain.'

'Good. I will see Joll now. An apology is called for. Summon the chief mate. I require an apology to you both.'

The Chief Officer saluted. He would relish hearing an apology from his adversary although he doubted, given the man's obstinate nature, whether that apology, if it did come, would have much sincerity. The Captain had the authority though and an apology would be forthcoming however it came. They were just a few days out of New Plymouth. Neither he nor the Captain wanted Joll in irons when they embarked. Be good to see the back of him.

When Samuel was brought before the Captain, the Chief Officer and the chief mate and made to stand in front of the assembled group of sailors, he still had the hand bolts on. Once again the Regulations were read out to him and he was told to apologise. Samuel looked the Captain right in the eye and said nothing. The Captain wasn't used to this sort of insubordination and he could feel the anger rising within him. He agreed with the Chief Officer. This man deserved to have a flogging.

'Apologise!' He barked.

Still, Samuel didn't flinch. He continued to stare at the Captain. No sound was heard about them bar the flapping of the sails and the gentle swishing of the waves. It looked as though there could be no resolution until Samuel apologised. They were just days from New Plymouth and the Captain had no wish to see the man still in irons when the clipper anchored. He repeated his request. Then Samuel spoke in his broad Cornish accent, and when the Captain heard the words, his face reddened and he clenched his fists.

'I be tellin' ye this, Captain Skinner. If an apology ye are after, so be it. That's all I have to say on the matter.'

'Release this man and be gone. I'll not see the likes of you again, Joll, nor would I wish to.'

The chief mate obeyed the command and as he unlocked the hand bolts, he whispered in Samuel's ear,

'You're a dead man, Joll if I ever set eyes on you again. Mark my words.'

Then Samuel smiled.

'Who be dead first then, Thompson?'

****

When the *Timandra* anchored off New Plymouth, the steerage passengers, along with their possessions, were bundled into the whaleboat in much the same manner as the Southland Down sheep that had also survived the journey.

Relief was felt by all and none more so than Elizabeth Joll who now had her husband back, freed from his chains. But it wasn't for long before the Cornishman had other ideas.

'I have unfinished business to attend to,' he said to his wife, 'an' I be doin' it now.'

Elizabeth, who by now was vexed with the whole episode, saw her husband approach a man who was observing the emigrants' arrival with some interest. Samuel spoke to the man and the next thing Samuel was paddling towards the *Timandra* in the man's canoe.

Captain Skinner was on the upper deck overseeing the disembarkation when Samuel Joll approached him. Samuel was a good bit taller than the Captain and this height difference in itself, made for some unease on the part of the Captain. His posture stiffened when he saw who it was. *Was there no end to this cursed man*? He thought.

'I bid ye farewell, Captain Skinner. I have to tell ye this an' I do so with complete sincerity. I would advise ye not to come ashore while I and my family be there. Good day to ye.'

And with that, Samuel turned on his heel and left the ship. There is no record of the Captain's reply.

****

The incident described in this story was officially recorded in the ship's Journal. It must have caused some amount of excitement on board the Timandra. I have attempted to describe Samuel 'Growler' Joll's character and his obstinate nature which would have led to the events which took place. As there are two versions, one from the Journal and one from family lore, I decided to combine the two accounts to add to the drama and to make for a good story.

GROWLER AND THE BULLOCK CART

Samuel 'Growler' Joll, hereafter known as Growler, was a hefty man, broad in the shoulders with strong muscular arms to match. His occupation as a blacksmith and a farmer and a liking for hard work were legendary. Growler could be stubborn on many an occasion and this Cornishman did not take fools lightly but from the moment he arrived on New Zealand's shore, his one object was to succeed in the new colony by any means possible.

In the early days of the settlement, New Plymouth's streets were made of clay. In wet weather, the clay turned to mud and made it hard to move about. It has to be noted that Growler was something of an improviser and he first became known in the district for his strange conveyance which he made himself. In the early days of the settlement, there were no horses or bullocks so Growler decided to construct a cart-like contraption in the shape of a donkey cart which was pulled by Growler and one of his sons, two goats coming next and two dogs with one of the sons being the leader dog. In wet weather, the cart was pulled with some difficulty and a fair amount of cursing over the muddy streets. It became quite a sight. Flour from the mill was loaded into this strange contraption and Growler and his sons pulled hundreds of tons of it, some to be exported to Wellington.

Life became easier for everyone when the bullocks and the horses arrived in the town and with their arrival; Growler's strange contraption became redundant. But Growler was undeterred. By this time, he had acquired more land for farming and bought several sections in the town of New Plymouth. Growler was making his mark.

One particular wet day there was an incident which turned Growler's life around forever. New Plymouth's streets were still made of clay, and as it had been raining for weeks, the muddy streets were just about impassable, especially for the bullock wagons. On the day that changed Growler's life, a bullock cart had managed to get stuck in the middle of one of the main streets. No amount of cursing and whipping the bullocks could budge them. The beasts were straining their utmost but they were stuck fast, unable to move no matter how hard they tried. The weight of the full cart made things even more difficult for them.

A small crowd had gathered in the rain to watch the spectacle, including Growler. Now, Growler was not known for his patience but when he saw the bullocky inflicting such pain on the poor beasts, this was just too much for our Cornishman. He let out a yell:

'You be gettin' nowhere, them poor beasts can't move an' inch and there's no amount of whippin' and cursin' will move them.'

The bullocky was none too pleased with this intervention.

'You keep yer nose out of it. Or I'll do for you too,' he yelled at Growler and flicked his whip in a threatening manner.

'No man on the earth has any right to treat an animal like this. Them poor beasts are in pain an' tired out an' the whip ain't helpin', just makin' it worse for them. Can't you see they are tryin' hard but no way can they get out.'

The commotion had brought even more spectators to the scene. Someone who knew Growler cried out,

'You be tellin' him, Samuel Joll.'

There was a cheer from a few of the other men who knew Growler and mutterings that the Cornishman was right. This was too much for the bullock driver. His pride was being threatened and, instead of listening to Growler, he raised his whip once more and lashed one of the bullocks with such force that the poor beast bellowed in pain.

'That be it, then.'

And Growler pushed his way through the crowd, ploughed through the mud to confront the bullocky who by that time was cursing even more, heedless to the ladies present. When he saw Growler approaching in a threatening manner, he raised his whip again.

'Keep away', he shouted. 'This here's none of your business.'

This brought boos from the crowd.

'Too right it is. I'll show ye how it's done.'

Growler, who by this time was almost knee-deep in the soft mud, was not deterred. With a mighty heave of his broad shoulders, he lifted the cart, just a few inches at a time, and then he tried again and again until it could be seen by all that the dray and the bullocks were moving at ever a slow pace out of the quagmire, but moving nevertheless.

The crowd, who by now numbered about twenty cheered as the bullocks struggled through the mud, pulling the heavy load behind them. A few minutes later the beasts were on the drier ground and the four stood, heads down and panting.

The bullock driver was none too pleased with the way the whole episode had gone. Rather than thanking Growler, he swore at him. His rudeness was rewarded with more boos from the crowd but there was no reaction from a very weary Growler who turned his back on the man. Instead, he plodded through the thick mud and crossed the road. He was last seen heading towards the general store. Behind him, he heard cheers and his name but he didn't turn around.

****

Whether it was from Growler's obstinacy not to be seen weakened in front of the crowd or because he did not want to give the bullock driver more verbal ammunition to throw at him, he had been determined to pull himself across the road to the general store. It was there that he collapsed. That evening what had happened became apparent to everyone. Growler was in extreme pain. The exertion of lifting the heavy dray out of the muck had injured his spine. He would be crippled for life.

In later life, he would sit outside his house in New Plymouth and grumble at the world, the people in it and life in general. Someone named him 'Growler' and the name stuck.

****

A reference by Fred B. Butler in his book, The Early Days of Taranaki, states that one bullock cart was stuck in the main street for many months so it must have been a fairly common sight during the rainy season in New Plymouth. The events described in this story were included in The History of the Joll Family compiled by Esmene Chatteron (née Joll) and Phyllis Lomas (née Joll). Growler was such a memorable character in the family folklore that I felt he deserved to have some stories written about him, albeit fictionalised.

Samuel 'Growler' Joll

GOLD FEVER

I suppose you could call me an adventurer. Although that's not what my father called me when I first heard the rumours that gold had been found in Ballarat and Bendigo. He called me a 'fool' and 'no good will come from prospecting' and, he added that I was a young man and strong. He needed me to help around the farm, me being the eldest and this is what was expected of me.

We had quite a row about it, I remember. I reminded him that I had been useful to him from an early age for hadn't I helped with his stevedoring and clearing the bush? I was an expert bullock driver and carted the timber as we cleared the land to make way for our dairy herds. I didn't dwell on the fact that I had joined the Taranaki Bushrangers when the Māori Wars broke out and I got a medal for my service. I think that my father had been proud of me for doing my bit and just a little envious too. It was a subject that we didn't talk about much, my father, Samuel, being anti-war and all that. I had my thoughts about the wars as well. My father insisted that we make 'a go of it' in New Zealand and even though he agreed that the natives had a reason for us not being there, we had to make the most of it and not be chased out from our homes. We had made the long journey from Cornwall to better ourselves. There was no way we were going back to England, and if we had to fight the Māori to be here, so be it.

But the wars were over now and we had begun to prosper on our farm. The Jolls had settled into this new land and we had no intention of moving. After all, there were enough of us to keep the whole thing going and I wouldn't be missed. So the lure of gold and adventure in Australia took hold of my imagination and I thought if I don't go now, I'll never do it. Of course, my mother wasn't too keen on my idea either. She agreed with my father that the chances of finding gold and becoming rich were just a dream, and it was her opinion that it was far better to stay on the land and make our fortune here. I, however, had other ideas for the gold fever had got into my brain. Every waking hour, I made plans to get myself over to Ballarat and Bendigo and dig up the biggest gold nugget I could find and prove to them both, how wrong they were. I would return to New Zealand a rich man.

So I began to collect what monies I had and booked a sea passage to Victoria.

My mother shed a tear as I announced my intention and my father grumbled a lot. My siblings were envious though and my brother, John desperately wanted to come with me. But it was I who was the adventurer.

I stayed in a hostel in Melbourne for my first night on Australian soil. It was full of rough men; most of them seemed intent on getting to the gold fields as quickly as they could. The talk was there was plenty of gold in the country for the digging but the problem was to stake a claim before the gold ran out. Most of them had decided to walk the seventy-mile track as everything was so expensive in Melbourne. The shopkeepers in Melbourne were making a fortune from the eager prospectors but I needed to buy a canvas tent, a mattress, a shovel and gold pan, and a wheelbarrow to carry all this. Pushing this over rough ground did not appeal but it was a necessary purchase if I was to have any hope of finding gold. I had heard a rumour that all the equipment I would need could be bought from the stores at the goldfields but prices were extortionate there by all accounts so I decided my best option was to buy everything in Melbourne and then head for Ballarat as this place, according to the men, was where most gold was to be found. I thought if I could travel by stagecoach it might be easier for me but when I finally managed to locate a stagecoach which was heading for the goldfields it was so expensive that it wasn't an option. The talk had been that the journey in the coaches was so rough that a lot of people decided to get off and walk anyway.

Two of the men from the hostel were also enquiring about the costs of the coach journey. Both of them eyed me with suspicion and I must confess, I was a little nervous about sharing a coach with them. I thought if I were to strike gold and they were anywhere near me, my life might be in danger. Gold changes men. I decided that I would walk. It was a three or four-day walk but I would get to know the country this way. I began to think that perhaps my father might have been right after all. I was glad to get out of Melbourne and into the country.

So I pushed my wheelbarrow and slept under the stars along with dozens of other men. The country was so different from the green fertile land of New Zealand. Dry and dusty and I was fearful of the snakes. But there was a wonder there for me too. The eucalyptus forest we pushed our way through was a magical place for me. At times, I glimpsed the black bodies of the natives behind these trees. They appeared and disappeared as if they were ghosts and I wondered what they thought of all these people trudging through their land, all of them intent on pursuing a dream of riches.

The gold, like the natives, had been there for millennia undisturbed. I trudged on.

I must confess my first sight of Ballarat did nothing to quench my earlier fears. The talk was that about four to six thousand people, mostly men, were flooding into this area every week. All of them pursued the elusive gold, and all were filled with enthusiasm and anticipation, and a fair amount of optimism. Despite my fears, I felt the same.

As far as the eye could see the whole area in front of me was covered with hundreds of canvas tents and I wondered how it was possible to even find a place to stake a claim, let alone erect a tent. Bark huts and more substantial buildings were also in evidence. I surmised these belonged to more prosperous miners and their families. Everywhere, men were panning for gold along the riverside whilst others were busy digging so that mounds of dirt lay everywhere. Wooden shafts, their frames like so many scarecrows, completed the surreal picture. Smoke drifted upwards from the dozens of fires. I heard voices calling and cursing in so many languages that I wondered how it was possible to hear anything over the din. I had never seen such a gathering of humanity in all my life. I pushed my way through the crowd and asked a rather surly Englishman where the Claims Office was located because this was the first thing I had to do. His directions led me to a wooden building where there were already a few dozen men waiting in a queue. I paid for my claim with what little money I had and was directed to an area about two miles from the main part of the town. Here, on this patch of earth beside the river, I would make my fortune. Or so I thought.

The next day I set to work. I knew very little about the process of extracting gold and very soon I realised that it was no easy task. It was backbreaking toil from dawn till dusk. The dust, mud and the constant flies almost drove me to madness at times but the lure of gold was stronger than any of this. I laboured on. I dug a shaft, bought another pick, an axe and a crowbar from the store at over-inflated prices and learned how to use the pan to find the gold particles. One day my labours paid off and I saw for the first time, specks of gold which were heavier than the sand and the gravel. I picked the precious metal from my gold pan and carefully placed them in a bag for safekeeping. The next day I took them to the assayer and received some welcome cash for my endeavours. I began to think my fortunes had turned for the better.

I was fortunate that the miner beside me was a friendly sort of fellow. He told me he was from Basel in Switzerland and had been at the goldfield for six months. He planned to find enough gold so that he could pay for a passage to bring his wife and three children out to the goldfields and from there the family could eventually settle in this new land of opportunity, as he saw it. He had been a teacher in Basel and he spoke perfect English. The knowledge he freely gave me about the workings of the mining world proved helpful and we assisted each other whenever it was needed. With so many opportunistic and unsavoury characters on the goldfield, I was indeed grateful that Jűrgen was next to me.

'It is a sick fever, this searching for gold,' Jűrgen said to me one evening as we shared a meal in front of the fire. 'It gets into a man's soul and takes hold there. Every day we hope that this will be the day we find the biggest nugget and our troubles will be over. I fear there is a lot of disappointment though.'

'I think that you are right, my friend. I have been digging for three months and barely covered my costs of living here. At this rate, I doubt I could pay the passage back to New Zealand.'

And I told him my father's reservations about my plans to find a fortune.

'Ah, my family likewise, Samuel. My father was angry when I told him I intended to travel to the goldfields in Australia. He said I was deserting my wife and children to follow a dream that alas, would come to nothing. I would like to prove him wrong, but sometimes I fear he may have been right. But then, we hope that the next day, all will change.' He shrugged his shoulders.

'Will you give up?'

'It is possible. I miss my wife and the children. But what day will that be? That nugget might be hiding there tomorrow, just waiting for me.' He smiled.

'Yes, it is indeed something like an addiction, or perhaps an obsession? You are right, Jűrgen. Tomorrow we might make our fortune.'

I spoke these words but I was already beginning to have my doubts.

The days turned to weeks and I found just small particles of gold, hardly enough to cover my costs. These small particles captured my imagination, however, and I began to think there had to be a seam of gold, lying further from the surface, taunting me. Although my body ached with the heavy work, my mind would not give up.

It was about five months of hard work before I discovered a small seam of gold. I now had enough money to think of other ways I could make my fortune. Two things happened which hastened my decision. The first thing was that Jűrgen told me he was leaving the goldfield.

'Now, Samuel, 'he said, 'I have to tell you, my friend, that I have found enough gold here to bring my wife and children to me.' He stated one evening after a particularly hot day when we both had struggled with the work and the heat.

'I intend to stay in Ballarat. The town begins to grow and there are more and more children here. I am staying in this country because I work once more as a teacher. I have a job at a new school and I have a house for my wife. The school board has told me that I can move there after the holidays. It will be difficult for my wife at first. She does not speak any English but she is a strong woman. The children will grow up Australians and I am proud of this.'

Jűrgen took a sip of tea.

'Maybe my father was right after all. This gold fever is a blessing and a curse. I have found enough gold but the work is hard and I am tired now. I want to teach once more and to see my wife.'

I had been thinking along the same lines but it would not be the same for me without the companionship of this Swiss man. Living under canvas through all weathers had begun to weary me and to survive in these conditions had become a constant battle. The lure of the gold was no longer there for me.

'I will miss you, Jűrgen,' I said after a slight pause. 'You are right. It is possible to keep going, full of hope that we will find the biggest gold nugget one day, but I fear that will not happen for us. We have exhausted this claim and I have no desire to keep pursuing the dream. For every man who finds the golden nugget, hundreds don't, and those who don't, die like old men long before their time.' I concluded sadly.

'Ah, true words. Samuel. True words indeed. What will you do? Go home to your family in New Zealand?'

I shook my head.

'No, I will stay for a while. I have a plan,' I said.

I did indeed have a plan.

I had observed that the men on the goldfields who made the most money were not, by and large, the miners. Although some men did strike it rich, and when that happened news travelled like wildfire around the camp, most of them toiled with little reward except having to contend with fighting the elements, sickness and loneliness. Money was not made from what came out of the ground but by those who provided the services. The Chinese had arrived on the goldfields in their droves, some of them were miners but the ones who sold their vegetables from their gardens were the real winners and, although I had little to do with any of them, I couldn't help observing that they were better clothed and well fed in comparison to the rest of us. The shopkeepers, too, were doing a roaring trade selling their goods at often extortionate prices. I decided to look around and see if there was anything I could do which would bring in more income than the miserable amount of gold particles I was toiling to find. It seemed, in this instance, fortune was on my side.

It all happened by chance. Or was it Fate that I met a bullock driver named Paddy O'Brian? Back on the farm, I had become an expert in handling the beasts and, I must say, I enjoyed the work. Paddy had a wagon and a team of six bullocks and he provided a service to the miners for he would transport supplies to them at a price. Paddy told me he had tried prospecting when he first arrived on the goldfields.

‘Sure,’ he said to me, ‘I be tellin’ ye this, young man. ‘Tis a mug’s game, this diggin’ for gold. Was laid up with dysentery an’ that’s what did it for me. Up in Queensland I was a drover and I thinks to meself, why don’t I get meself a team of bullocks and a wagon and bring the goods to thems what’s lookin’ for their gold?’

He chuckled.

‘An’ sure thing, by all that’s holy, it worked. In a matter of weeks, I was bringin’ in more than I had done after six months of pannin’, an’ I was enjoyin’ meself.’

‘I drive the bullocks too,’ I said. ‘Back in New Zealand, on my father’s farm.’

‘Well now, ain’t that somethin’, me lad, a fellow bullock driver.’

And Paddy spat onto the dry ground and shook my hand with such a firm grip that I thought my hand would break.

‘I’m lookin’ to go back home to Queensland. Been away from the wife and kids too long by my reckonin’ an’ I don’t want to take the beasts and the wagon back there. Me beasts are young an’ strong an’ this is the work for them here.’

It seemed like the gods had answered my call.

‘Would you be interested in selling them then, wagon and all?’ I asked. I could hardly believe my luck.

‘Sure thing,’ Paddy the Irishman replied, ‘Give me a fair price an’ they’re yours.’

I thought for a moment and gave him an offer.

‘I like the look of ye, young fella,’ Paddy said. ‘Let’s shake on it.’

And so, with that mighty handshake and a lot of luck, I became a bullock driver again, and like Paddy, I never looked back.

****

Samuel Joll of Waitara was the eldest son of Samuel ‘Growler’ Joll and Elizabeth Treliving Joll. He did find his fortune on the gold fields of Ballarat and Bendigo. The description of his time there is fiction. He returned to Waitara a rich man and this has been recorded. His farm, Riverdale was one of the finest in the Taranaki district. He married Elizabeth Langdon Jonas and the couple had thirteen children. Samuel died at Waitara in 1899.

JOHN AND CHIEF TE HĀPUKA

When I was old enough to make a life for myself, I looked around to see where I could best purchase land to continue the family tradition of farming. My father, Samuel and my mother, Elizabeth were born to the land. Both their families had been yeoman farmers in Cornwall. It was in our blood. There were problems for them in Cornwall, however, and the promise of land in the new Colony of New Zealand was a tempting one for them. I was just a child when they and my siblings emigrated on the *Timandra* to New Plymouth and it was here that I spent my early years.

I followed my brothers and gained the knowledge needed to drive the bullock wagons and work the land, and I also learned to respect the Māori people, their language and their customs. The kinship I felt with the Māori was to be of great benefit to me when I purchased land at Hawke's Bay for it was there that I chose to settle, on the other side of the country from my childhood home in New Plymouth.

Certainly, I was no stranger to hard physical labour. With determination and a vision, I cleared the land. I used my bullocks to help with the road construction. Hawke's Bay was a rough and lawless place and I had to keep my wits about me especially when the Māori chiefs began to wonder whether they had been right to dispose of their lands to the pākeha. There were many Māori chieftains in Hawke's Bay but it was Te Hāpuku who was by far the most influential and he had established himself in the area where I took up my land. Te Hāpuku was more vocal and belligerent than the other chieftains. When I first met him, I was wary of him I must say for I had heard many reports about him. I had been given the nickname of 'Taranaki Jack' by my fellow settlers because that was where I hailed from and it was with that name that Te

Hāpuku addressed me. He had no doubt heard the white men calling me by that name. He spoke a little English and me a little Māori, so we were able to communicate in a somewhat clumsy way.

My first contract upon arrival at Hawke's Bay was to use my bullocks for road construction and so replace the rough tracks already in evidence. The bush was being cleared at a rapid rate and I presume the Māori chieftains viewed this activity with some suspicion, and none more so than Te Hāpuka. At first, the chief had been active in selling land to the pākeha but now as more and more white settlers arrived, he began to have second thoughts and he was convinced that he had been cheated. A block of land where I worked had already been granted to Te Hāpuka for the establishment of a Māori college. The wily chief began to think that he would not have the influence that he had enjoyed for so long with his fellow Māori chieftains or with the ever-increasing number of pākeha. He decided that he would obstruct any more progress as a way of reclaiming his authority. I had been warned about Te Hāpuka but I had no idea what he was planning.

I worked hard and I already had my sights set on acquiring more land to farm successfully. I intended to grow wheat and other crops once the land was cleared and the roads built. I also planned to raise cattle and sheep to supply two butchers' shops that had recently opened in the town, and I was thinking all these thoughts when I encountered Te Hāpuka and his men standing in the middle of the road. My bullock wagon was full of crushed lime and I had not expected to see the very angry Māori chief blocking the road. Te Hāpuka was known for his arrogance and he held up his hand to me.

'Stop! What have you in that dray?' he asked in his broken English.

I was perplexed by his attitude as I reasoned this was none of his business. I decided that some form of humour might be appropriate in the circumstances. His men did not appear to be threatening me in any way but I thought that Te Hāpuka might want to make a big display in front of them to assert his authority over the pākeha.

A light-hearted approach might be the answer to the problem and Te Hāpuka and his followers would then move aside to allow me to pass with the minimum of fuss. I glanced at my load of crushed lime and decided there and then on an answer.

'Huka,' I said. I knew enough of the Māori language to know this was their word for 'sugar'.

All Te Hāpuka's followers laughed out loud. One of them decided that my answer was so funny that he rocked back and forth holding his sides whilst another man hopped up and down in the manner of a jack in the box. The latter's antics brought forth even more laughter. Te Hāpuka, however, was not amused at this display of levity by his men. He drew himself up to his full height and came right up to me in a threatening manner.

'Taranaki Jack,' he said in his arrogant voice, 'does not laugh at me. I am not to be made a fool.'

'Huka,' I repeated because, by this time, I too was laughing.

This remark was greeted with even more laughter. Everyone but Te Hāpuka was in stitches. This did not meet with the approval of the now annoyed chief. He shook his fist at me.

'Taranaki Jack has made big mistake.'

I did not take his threat seriously given that his men appeared to have been as amused as I was by the whole episode. I commanded my bullocks to move and flicked the whip over their backs and the dray with its load of 'sugar' moved at a slow pace along the newly constructed road leaving Te Hāpuka with a face like thunder and standing, legs apart, in front of his men.

****

I woke in the morning to find that Te Hāpuka had the last laugh on me after all. Sometime in the night whilst I slept he and his men had sawn through the spokes of the wheels of my dray. It would be many days before the wheels could be replaced and the dray was out of action for a few weeks. I decided that I would need to be more careful in future about describing its contents should I encounter the vengeful Te Hāpuka again.

****

John was a son of Growler and Elizabeth. He farmed at Hawke's Bay. The events with the Māori chief were recorded in The History of the Joll Family compiled by Esmene Chatterton (née Joll) and Phyllis Lomas (née Joll). I have attempted to describe a young man's humour in this story. Te Hāpuka was something of a character and had become famous enough that, on his death bed, he was visited by Governor George Grey.

John married Fanny Jane Harrison and the couple had six boys. Tragically, John was gored by one of his bullocks and was seriously injured. He was confined to his bed for two years and he died in 1879, leaving his widow to raise the boys on her own.

FROM SMALL BEGINNINGS

Had I been able to look into the future I must confess I would have been amazed. Who would have thought that my humble dairy would one day be visited by the Queen of England and that I would have a memorial to my memory elected in a park that bears my name?

****

Farming runs through the veins of the Joll family for a long time back. My ancestors were yeoman farmers in Cornwall and when my father, Samuel decided that he could make a better life for himself and his family in New Zealand, it was without any hesitation that working the land would be where we would make our livelihood. I must say my interest had been in the dairy industry. To gaze upon a contented herd of cows munching away on fields of green grass, knowing that I have seen most of these cows being born and nurtured the calves until they would repay me with yields of rich milk was to me a magical thing. I suppose I always had the dream of owning a dairy factory. Once the land was cleared and we made peace with the Māori, I decided to put my vision into practice.

The herds were productive I must say. The rich volcanic soil of South Taranaki allowed nourishing grass to grow in profusion and my cows grew fat on it. In no time I was supplying the local population with milk but therein lay my conundrum. My cows produced more milk than I could sell and the surplus presented a problem. It was then that I decided to use the excess milk to make butter and cheese. I suppose my father, Samuel was sceptical at first.

'Ye be layin' out too much of ye capital, my boy,' he told me. 'Best to limit your herd and concentrate on milk production. There's where the market is.'

But I wasn't deterred. I did, indeed, run into debt the first few years and times were hard establishing the factory but I refused to allow the pitfalls and the challenges I faced in those early years to get the better of me. When I opened my first factory with my name above the door, *T. J. Joll Dairy Co,* it was to me the most exciting thing that I had ever done. At last, all the hard work in getting to this point was visible to all.

Butter and cheese would soon be made there and as production grew, so did my ambitions. I decided to invest in more land, more cows and build another factory. This one was to be a bigger one than my original building had been with more equipment. I knew that to increase production I needed labour.

'Ye be mindful of who ye employ, my boy,' admonished my ever-perceptive father, 'ye be best to keep your costs down and be wary of who works for ye. Ye want loyalty in your staff, not shirkers.'

In this, I couldn't have agreed more. I decided that I would never turn a willing worker down and that I would repay them accordingly. After all, I owed my whole business to my herd of cows and the hard work of my employees. It was only right that my workers benefitted from my successes.

Another problem presented itself with my search for willing workers. Quite a few farmers in the district would have nothing to do with the local Māori. Memories of the wars between our two peoples and prejudice against them prevented the farmers from even considering employing the natives. However, I spoke fluent Māori and had gained their confidence. Some of my earliest suppliers were the Māori and very soon I was employing quite many fit young Māori men in my factories. I must say they proved to be as equally hard-working as their white compatriots. I was seldom disappointed with either worker. Perhaps my father's advice stood me in good stead in this regard.

I was twenty-nine years of age when I married, and I must say that I was fortunate in my choice of wife as Louisa proved to be an ideal companion with a keen acumen for business. We were the perfect partnership and our dairy factories increased in number as did our fortune. Soon the name T. J. Joll, and butter and cheese would be forever linked.

To be a dairy farmer and factory owner has been my greatest joy. Fortune did indeed shine on me. I am forever grateful to have been able to pursue a career path that I chose myself. Despite my father's initial scepticism, I remained true to my roots and farmed land as generations of our family had done before me. And I do so love my dairy herds.

****

My privately owned dairy factories are not only the largest enterprise in the whole of New Zealand but perhaps in the whole world. Had I lived to know this and not fallen from that tram car, who would ever have guessed that from such humble beginnings, all this could have happened?

****

Thomas Langdon Joll was the son of Growler and Elizabeth. He founded the Joll Dairy Company. Queen Elizabeth and Prince Philip visited the dairy years later so it was an enterprise of note in the district by then. There's a statue of Thomas in New Plymouth. He fell from a tram car in Wellington and died from injuries sustained there.

Memorial to Thomas Langdon Joll, New Plymouth

Dairy entrepreneur Thomas Joll is commemorated with this marble bust at Ōkaiawa's Joll domain. Joll established a chain of privately owned dairy factories around Ōkaiawa in the 1880's. After his death, the company became the T.L.Joll Co-

operative. Over the next half-century, it expanded to become one of the major dairy companies in South Taranaki. In 1963 the company amalgamated with its main competitor, the Kaūpokonui Dairy Co-operative, to form Kiwi Co-operative Diaries. In 1992 Kiwi Dairies merged with their north Taranaki equivalent, the Inglewood-based- Moa-Nui Co-operative. This merger consolidated Taranaki's dairy industry until the formation of the national dairy giant Fonterra in 2001. Photograph by Ron Lambert.

Ron Lambert, "Taranaki places – Waimate plain', Te Ara – the encyclopaedia of New Zealand.'

http://www.TeAra.govt.nz/en/photograph/26012/thomas-joll-memorial-okaiawa Story by Ron Lambert Christensen, Edward Percival, 1907-1982. Royal Tour party at Bell Block Co-operative Dairy Factory, New Plymouth. Photograph taken by Edward Percival Christensen. Tourist and Publicity. Ref: 1/2-042081-F. Alexander Turnbull Library, Wellington, New Zealand./records/22763283

Royal visit to the Joll Dairy

There can be no doubt that Samuel 'Growler' Joll was one of the most enthusiastic emigrants to board the *Timandra* on 2nd November 1841 at Plymouth Harbour bound for the Colony of New Zealand. Life in Cornwall for the blacksmith and farmer had become difficult due to the economic recession after the Napoleonic Wars, and perhaps even more challenging for the young Samuel was the frustration of having to submit to his elder brother, Joshiah's authority. When the news of the formation of the Plymouth Company of New Zealand [17] reached Samuel with the promise of acquiring substantial land there, he must have viewed this as his way out and a means of bettering himself. Samuel had married Elizabeth Vanderband Treliving, the daughter of a neighbouring farmer in 1829. Both Elizabeth's family, the Trelivings and her mother's family, Parnell Blight were yeoman farmers.

The Jolls were to become part of what has been called 'the Cornish Diaspora'. Over a quarter of a million Cornishmen and women and their children left Cornwall between 1815 and 1920. Samuel and Elizabeth accompanied by their five children, Ann, Samuel, Sarah, John and Eliza left Cornwall bound for New Plymouth in New Zealand, never to return.

Life on board the *Timandra* had its fair share of challenges and at times the four-month voyage must have seemed that it would never end. When the obstinate and determined Samuel was put in irons for assaulting crew members and only released after an apology, the long sea journey must have been even more fraught, particularly so for Elizabeth and their children.[18] The *Timandra* finally arrived in New Plymouth on 23rd

[17] Wills, Norman A Good West Country Name Ch2 p.15

[18] Chatterton, Esmene and Lomas, Phylllis The History of the Joll Family ch 3 p 7
Flight, Josiah Journal of the Voyage of the Timandra 1841 - 1842

February 1842 and Samuel and Elizabeth set about establishing themselves in the new colony. They were to produce another five children and so it could be said that their offspring were first-generation New Zealanders.

Samuel set to work to clear the sections of the land that had been allotted to him. In the early years, the settlement struggled due to food shortages and disputes with the Māori over land rights. At that time, the Māori were divided into two groups and inter-tribal warfare between the anti-land selling parties and those who were agreeable to selling the land to the white settlers, they called them pākeha, was frequent. Samuel's family had settled at Bell Block and Waitara and both these areas were part of the contested land which would have made for an anxious time for the family. These disputes led to the Taranaki Wars between the Māori and the pākeha. Samuel's sons served in the war.

By the end of the war, the Joll family were established farmers in the area and beyond. Samuel acquired land in New Plymouth and built a substantial house in the town. He died there in 1879 and Elizabeth in 1882. They are buried together in New Plymouth.[19]

The eldest daughter of Samuel and Elizabeth was Ann, She married Albert Wills whose family were also on board the *Timandra*. They were to have thirteen children. One daughter Eliza died through eating the poisonous tutu berries and the other two in infancy.

The eldest son, Samuel, worked with his father from an early age. However, the discovery of gold in Ballarat and Bendigo took the imagination of the young man and he travelled to Australia to try his hand at gold mining. Very soon, he decided that prospecting was more a matter of luck than anything else and he procured a team of bullocks and

---

[19] Chatterton, Esmene and Lomas, Phyllis The History of the Joll Family ch 3 p 9

transported goods to the miners on the goldfields. His decision paid off and he returned to New Zealand a rich man.

Probably the most well-known Joll was Thomas Langdon whose enterprising genius paid off handsomely when he established a small dairy factory. As his suppliers increased so did his factories until the Joll Dairy Company became the biggest privately owned factory in New Zealand, and possibly the world. He is honoured by a memorial which stands in the T.J. Joll Memorial Park in Okaiawa.

Sarah, Samuel and Elizabeth's second daughter married and had twelve children. Her husband was the founder and senior partner in a large coach-building business. Sarah died aged fifty-three.

John accompanied his parents on the *Timandra.* He followed his father's footsteps and became a farmer. He moved from New Plymouth to Hawke's Bay where he had many dealings with the Māori chief, Te Hāpuku.

Eliza, the third daughter would have celebrated her first birthday on board the *Timandra.* When she turned twenty-one she married a blacksmith who was originally from Cornwall. The couple had five children. Their first child, Mary Elizabeth, died in infancy.

Thomas was the fourth son. At the age of fifteen, he worked bringing supplies to the troops during the Māori Wars. He married and had a large family. A widower, he married again.

Mary and Elizabeth Joll both married. Mary to a Scot who was a Headmaster who turned to farming in Taranaki and Elizabeth married a blacksmith. It is interesting that Eliza and Mary both married blacksmiths. This surely would have made old 'Growler' happy!

David Joll, the youngest son met an untimely death by accident aged only thirteen years. He died on 13th March 1865, the very day of his thirteenth birthday. He was working for his father loading timber, carting it and unloading. When the load was discharged he jumped onto the cart, having one foot in the cart and one on the pole. He gave the bullocks a poke to make them go faster. He did not look where he was going and the wheel caught against the gatepost, slid up it and the cart was upset and fell on David, the rail striking him on the head.[20]

After Samuel and Elizabeth died their children and their descendants made a life in New Zealand, were proud to call themselves New Zealanders and proud, too, of their Cornish roots. It is to the courage and determination of Samuel 'Growler' Joll, whose compelling desire was to make a new life and to start afresh in a land so far away, that those generations who came after him give thanks.

---

[20] Chatterton, Esmene and Lomas, Phyllis The History of the Joll Family p 24

Samuel 'Growler' Joll

Joll Street, New Plymouth

ORIGINS OF THE FAMILY NAME BAKER

The origin of the Baker surname is thought to be Anglo-Saxon and have come from the English-Scottish border region, though it is common enough to have spread across Britain and the English-speaking world. Baker is an occupational name, coming from the Old English word 'baecere', which means to dry with heat. Baker in Irish is Báicéir. The meaning of Báicéir is someone who baked as an occupation.

BAKER FAMILY: The Circus Stories

HOW IT ALL BEGAN

It's the Irish in me, I guess. Haven't we always been wanderers, leaving our native land for a better world and us having the longing to return back home someday? It was Australia that beckoned me, and me being the eldest in the family, I had the yearning to seek my fortune and make a name for myself far from my poor broken country for the famine had been upon us and the English were after making us slaves. Was it no wonder the ships were full of poor Irish souls hoping for a better life?

I wanted something different for my life. I don't know when I first became fascinated with the circus but I do remember my amazement at the skills of equestrians and the death-defying aerial tricks of the trapeze artists. When the circus toured Ireland something stirred in me, call it restlessness or a hankering for adventure. Who knows? All I know was that the thrill of the circus had got into me and wouldn't leave me. When I was ten years of age I announced to my parents that I had no intention of staying in Ireland and that I would run away and join the circus. I suppose this was greeted with some amusement as there were no circus connections in the family but I was determined. I had found my path in life.

When the circus came to town I played truant and spent the time hanging around the circus tent, getting in the way no doubt, but all the time loving it. From an early age, I had an affinity with horses and I became an accomplished rider. The skill and agility of the equestrians was something that I would aspire to, I decided this after watching the bareback riders doing all manner of acrobatic stunts. So I practised some of the manoeuvres on my pony whenever I could. I had many a fall. Once, whilst standing on my head and trying to balance on the pony without a saddle, I was thrown and badly injured my shoulder. Nothing would stop me. My dream did not die despite the bruises and the grazes and the despair of my parents.

I got to know the circus performers and I suppose the Irish luck was with me. I showed off some of my acrobatic skills on my pony and I caught the eye of the proprietor. The next thing I was part of the circus and off to perform at the Dublin Hippodrome. My dream was taking shape but the restlessness was upon me. My countrymen were departing Ireland for America and Canada and Australia. At twenty-two years of age, I decided that I would join them. There was an opportunity for circus artists in Australia I was told, and so as soon as I had the money ready, I booked my passage to that faraway land. There was nothing to fear I reassured my parents. Mary and Joseph and all the saints would watch over me.

Sure, I was certain the saints were there on the journey for wasn't it the most miserable of voyages? Rough seas and sickness prevailed. I saw people die and then be flung overboard with hardly a prayer to save their poor souls. Us steerage passengers were herded together like cattle and in some cases, treated the same. The stench below decks was like nothing on earth and I was relieved beyond words when we finally glimpsed the Australian coast. The ship took days to sail along the eastern side of the country and I was amazed at the distances. Surely, this vast country had to be the land of opportunity for me.

My dream was to own a circus and tour the country but first I had to find people who would help me. I needed to become part of a circus again and learn more about that fascinating world before I could realise my dream. It was in North Queensland that I first made the acquaintance of the circus folk that would help me on my way. I must say those first few years were hard. The intense heat of the tropics and all the wild thunderstorms were wearing on me, and at times, I confess, I longed to be back in Ireland with the soft rains and cool climate but I knew my life was no longer there. When my parents and siblings arrived on the *Jumna* I knew for certainty that Australia was to be my home.

I must say that my fortunes changed for the better after I met my Alice.

What a woman she was. We were able to buy horses and a large tent. My dream was taking shape. We performed well and soon the Baker Circus was becoming well-known in North Queensland. *Fun in the Stockyard* was our great act and Dick Turpin's ride always brought cheers from the audience.

Our first child was Henrietta, named after my dear Mammy, but the poor wee colleen did not survive and she died two days after she was born. Then another Henrietta arrived and we were blessed. I must say we have been blessed with our children for they all followed a circus career and every one of them became as accomplished and as fearless as myself on the horses. Our lovely Barbara Henrietta became Babs and then we called her Babarina for that name sounded so much more artistic on the billboards. When Lorenz, Frank, Willie, Kathleen, Dorizzio and Cissy arrived the Baker Circus was complete. Our family was an act in itself, well, that's what the newspapers said.

Often as we toured Queensland some of my brothers and sisters joined the circus to help out as best they could. It was a right old Irish gathering then. We were all saddened, especially my poor dear mother, when The First World War took my brother, John Francis from us. As an Irishman, I questioned the futility of a war which brought nothing but suffering. John was a saddler and his skills were much in demand by the Army. Like myself, John had the love of horses in his blood. He would have hated to witness their suffering in the mud and despair of Flanders fields. I went to Mass and lit a candle for him when I heard the news of his death.

We prospered during the War for people needed distraction from the misery taking place in faraway Europe and our circus acts and the animals always brought in the crowds. At Wonderland in Sydney, four thousand people turned up. That probably was one of our greatest achievements.

We took the circus to New Zealand and did circling tours around the two islands. One of our most popular acts there and in Australia as well was *Dick Turpin's Ride to York.* Being on horses was great fun for all of us. Our wee Willie was a superb horseman and contortionist and he had quite an engaging manner. The crowds loved him. I got six wagons built for me in Auckland for the show as the old ones we had in Australia were long past their prime. It was the Elder Brothers who built the wagons for us and they were nephews of the old horizontal-bar performer who was well-known in Australia. We are circus folk and it's a small world.

Things began to be difficult for us when the Great Depression of the twenties hit us. The crowds thinned a bit and the takings were down but we carried on for we knew no other way of life. We had established the circus in New Zealand by then and I had bought some forty acres of land there so we could rest up over the winter. This was a good move as being on the road can take its toll on all of us sometimes. I was ever looking for different acts and new circus artists of repute. I must say a few of them stayed with us for years. Happy Jackles, the clown with his dogs and monkeys and La Belle Cora, the Dental Queen along with Thomas Kadama became our friends for life.

I have few regrets in my life. I'm a wanderer so the circus world suited me just fine. My family are dear to me. My Alice is the love of my life. The circus has been forever, my world. Who could ask for more?

****

Although the facts surrounding William John 'Jerry' Baker's establishing the circus in North Queensland, are shrouded in mystery, I have endeavoured to draw upon the many newspaper articles to write this story. It is fairly certain that

Jerry arrived on the Jumna before his parents and siblings and that it is likely that he had been exposed to circus life in Ireland before he emigrated. I have been unable to access his marriage record or birth certificates of any of his children, except Barbara (Babs). Babs, 'Babarina' as she was known by in the circus, was born in Brisbane. Jerry was fairly diligent in providing his name and other members of his family for the Census Records at the time, the address given being 'the circus tent'. There is no doubt that the Baker circus was a success both in Australia and New Zealand. Jerry's untimely death, however, seemed to put an end to the business.

AN UNEXPECTED ENCOUNTER

Everyone was tired. Chefulo and Senorita Chefalo after their daredevil act had retired early along with Happy Jackles who grumbled as usual and declared he was so weary after the night's performance that he too, needed sleep, and a lot of it. Happy Jackles moaned to anyone who would listen that he was fed up with running around the ring, squirting water and making everyone laugh. Kathleen, Babs, Dorrizzio and Frank after practising a few more tumbles and somersaults took themselves off to their beds. Although Frank and Kathleen kept their siblings awake whispering about a new routine they planned for the next performance which involved both of them performing a death-defying somersault act on two of the ponies. They were yet to inform their father of their new routine. Both decided it would be best if their father saw their act but only after some practice. He would then be more in favour. Or they could approach their mother first as she was more likely to agree as she had been a great acrobat in her day. If Mother was on their side, Father would follow.

Most of the monkeys had ceased their chattering and were huddled in small groups in their cage. The Chinese piebald donkey, the only one of its kind in the whole of Australia was such an obstinate creature that everyone who had anything to do with him was usually in despair, closed his eyes and seemed to all intents and purposes to fall asleep. The leopards and the Bengali tigers housed in their separate cages had stopped their endless pacing up and down and resigned themselves to sleep. The horses and the trick ponies too, had all performed well and after a good feed of some oats and hay appeared quite happy to rest. All the animals were fed and watered. The sun slid below the horizon on a peaceful scene.

It was around midnight when Jerry Baker made his final

check of the menagerie before he, too, would go to his bed. Jerry always made his rounds at the end of the day. As the proprietor, it was his responsibility to make sure that all was well. He enjoyed this time of the day as it was usually a peaceful time to say good night to his animals. They had all performed well except perhaps for the donkey that refused to do anything for his trainer and stood looking defiant. At least the obstinate creature brought laughs from the audience because of his stubbornness. Happy Jackles had been summoned to the rescue and attempted to coax the donkey to do something. The audience erupted into laughter at the clown's antics. It had been a good night and Jerry was pleased that his dummy, August had made people laugh. He had put August to bed next to his wife, Alice. Jerry was rather fond of his dummy and the two of them were a class act. They always made the audience clap and cheer whenever they appeared. Sometimes August seemed to know more than anyone else in the circus but that's how it was with a ventriloquist act.

When the Baker Circus rolled up to entertain people in the country towns crowds could be expected to pack into the big tent. The circus with its nail biting acts and menagerie of wild animals, with trick ponies and mules and clowns to entertain, was always an unforgettable evening for the folk who lived in towns where not much happened. Tonight was no exception. It had been a very profitable night with about five hundred folk turning up and some had to be turned away at the entrance. A promise of a seat at the next performance seemed to pacify most folk apart from the few awkward ones who demanded to be allowed in, then and now. That required tact and Jerry with the gift of the Irish banter was a master of tact. He thought there was something about a circus that brought out the best in most people, and he could handle the worst. When the tent was full and the money rolled in everyone was happy.

Tonight the lions had roared their loudest, snarling and

thrusting their giant paws at the Count who cracked his whip and showed no fear when he turned his back on the magnificent creatures. It was such a spectacle to see one man showing such control over these fierce animals that the people clapped so loud their clapping seemed like a deluge of rain falling onto the canvas roof but Jerry knew that a few folk in the audience would be nervous. A worried mother had once admonished him for causing her young son to cry with fear. Jerry's beloved lions performed well most nights, balancing on stools and jumping through the hoops of fire.

Jerry's nightly ritual started with the monkeys and ended with the lions. He had a special affection and respect for the lions for they brought in the crowds. The lions were up there, top billing, alongside the acrobatic feats of his children with their superb horsemanship. His son, Frankie was probably the youngest equestrian act in the whole world and his daughter, Kathleen on the trapeze had to be the star act. He was proud of his children for they were as supple as the monkeys and as fearless as the lions.

The circus had three cages that housed the lions in a rather confined space but it had been thought prudent to give the creatures a little bit of room to move about. Some circus owners were not so generous preferring to keep as many wild animals penned in one cage to save costs. Jerry was not like that. He respected all his circus animals and tried to give them the best life possible, given that they were such an important part of the show.

He often looked into the eyes of the wild creatures and wondered what they thought of being captured, destined to spend their lives in cages and balancing on stools to delight a crowd of humans. But then he decided that they probably didn't think, just accepted their lot in life. At least they were fed well and looked after, and knew nothing of what it would be like to be free.

Jerry always checked that the padlocks on all the cages were secure. If one of the wild creatures escaped there would be no end of trouble from the authorities and a heavy fine would be issued for him to pay. He couldn't risk that. Once six Bengali tigers had escaped out Goondiwindi way and all hell broke loose until three of the creatures were recaptured. The other three suffered a worse fate as they were shot. Their French trainer had decided that these three were too dangerous and it wasn't worth the risk of having them roaming free. Escaped circus animals didn't do much for the reputation of the circus although it gave good publicity. People from miles around had queued to see the runaway tigers and paid their money to go to the circus.

Perhaps with all these thoughts going around in his head, Jerry wasn't thinking too clearly when he inspected the lock on the second cage. The two larger lions were awake and pacing back and forth. And it was there when the unexpected occurred. He had his back to the cage and he was close to the bars, too close, as it transpired. He felt nothing for a few seconds. Then he heard the lion growl, followed by a deafening roar, and the sound of his shirt being ripped. Claws from a huge paw struck him on his back, again and again. He felt the pain and then the wetness of blood seeping from the wound. As he fell to the ground he heard both beasts roar as one.

****

'Your husband's a lucky man, Mrs Baker,' the doctor said. Alice was a resourceful woman. When she had seen her husband bleeding and in pain, she had feared the worst. She would rouse the whole town if necessary to find the doctor. The doctor wasn't too pleased, however, to be awakened so early and had to stitch up the injured circus owner. He was a rather cantankerous old doctor and always grumbled when the circus came to town. There were always more injuries to contend with what with people falling off the seats and tripping over wires. So Mr Baker with his back half torn away from a lion attack was just the last straw.

'And you, Mr Baker', he declared in a rather condescending manner, 'I would suggest you shoot the beast.'

Jerry's back throbbed. He was probably in some sort of shock and he was so weary, as weary as his whole circus had been just a few hours before. All of them would be now fast asleep he figured, even his lions.

'Well, now, doctor,' he replied after a few painful moments. 'I hear what ye are tellin' me, that I do, but I want ye to know, by all that is holy, those lions are my friends, wild creatures that they are, an' I would be doin' them an injustice if I was to do as ye say. An' I have a question to put to ye, sir, how do ye know if the lion meant me harm or was he not just sayin' "good night" to me?'

****

This story is based on fact as reported in the newspaper, The Daily Mercury 11th August 1908, page 3.

Jerry Baker did sustain injuries and recovered fully. Whether he did his rounds of the circus at the end of the day is pure conjecture but it is indeed possible as he was the owner of the Baker Circus and would have had full responsibility for both the performers and the captive animals.

STUCK IN THE MUD

To the people who gathered to see the procession of dozens of horses pulling cages on drays and carts filled to overflowing with all the paraphernalia, the arrival of the massive Baker Circus was quite definitely the event of the year. This was a tantalising peep into another world. When the circus arrived in the country towns, the locals were convinced that the circus people had to be a breed apart. The performers did not conform to the accepted norm. They were talented and fearless, no one could deny that, but circus folk preferred to wander from place to place and not put down roots like the rest of the population, so the idea of constantly wandering, with no fixed abode except the circus tent, was an inconceivable one to the majority of people who came to see the shows.

Of course, wandering was the very reason for being in the minds of the Baker circus performers, as it is for all circus folk, for that matter. Wandering and packing up after a few nights did present problems, however. One of the major challenges was the weather. Sometimes under the canvas tent the heat was so intense that the performers argued and the animals were so bad tempered that coaxing them to do their tricks was a challenge. The stifling heat and the pressure of performing well, keeping the circus animals cool and making sure that everyone, both people and animals, had enough water to drink was always a problem during the droughts. All this added to the pressure that the people, who sat enjoying the show, never could have imagined happening.

The heat was one thing, but there was even more of a problem when that heat turned to rain. And in tropical North Queensland, where the Bakers started their circus career, the rain often turned to floods. The long cavalcade of horses pulling those drays over flooded creeks and dirt tracks, sometimes through a downpour, must surely have tried the most patient of wanderers.

Such an occurrence happened one week in early April when it had rained without mercy for days. The dirt tracks, which were the only means of travel for the circus, had turned very quickly into a quagmire. The horses struggled to pull their heavy loads through the thick mud whilst they battled against the continual downpour. The captive animals panicked. Locked in their cages and feeling the full force of the rain, the poor creatures paced back and forth. The lions were particularly unsettled, and their continual roar upset everyone.

'Doubt if we'll be puttin' the big tent up tonight at this rate,' Jerry Baker announced to his troupe of bedraggled performers. 'Sure, it's not about to let up by the look of it. No soft rain o' Ireland in this place. By all that's holy, makes ye wonder what it's all about.'

Jerry was knee-deep in the mud. There was mumbling from the group. All of them were fed up, and tempers could erupt at any moment. Of all the circus performers, the clowns were the most likely to cause trouble, but even they realised there wasn't much anyone could do against the full force of the wet weather. The acrobats felt it the hardest for they needed to exercise daily, and this had become impossible to do. No way could they somersault in the heavy rain over the thick mud. Everyone, it seemed, was on edge as the circus cavalcade ploughed along through the deep tracks at a snail's pace. Often a dray would become bogged, and it was all hands to the wheel to move it along. All this caused even more deep furrows and made it even more difficult for the carts behind.

The circus troupe and their menagerie had battled through the rain and the mud since dawn, and most of the performers were in agreement with the boss. They had no chance of getting to the next town in this weather. As the dishevelled group pushed and pulled their way up a slight hill, they were surprised to find a cart blocking their way. Now there was no way of getting through.

'What have we here then?' asked Happy Jackles, the clown. He was dressed in an old Army overcoat and a broad-brimmed hat. He didn't look at all like a clown.

'Problems ahead, Jack,' answered Kathleen Baker, the world-famous trapeze artist. If she could, she would have leapt over the cart, somersaulted through the mud and curtseyed to the applause of her fellow performers.

'I'm gettin' fed up with all this, Kath,' grumbled Jackles. But then, Happy Jackles wasn't all that happy most of the time.

'Ah, come on, Jack, you wouldn't want any other life, now would ye?' Babarina Baker, the contortionist, had overheard the conversation. She was trudging behind her sister and wasn't all that bothered about the mud and the torrential rain. But then, Babs was always an optimist.

'Looks like there's some folk stuck in the mud,' said Dorrizzio Baker, the fearless bareback rider.

'How in hell are we going to get by then?' grumbled Happy Jackles.

'Oh, come on, Jack, show a little Christian charity. Can't you see there's a mother holding a baby, and the other kids look like drowned rats?' It was the turn of La Belle Cora, the Dental Queen, to add to the conversation. Cora, who defied death every performance, hanging by her teeth and attached to the tightrope, was perhaps the most charitable of the entire troupe. She was liked by all for her gentle nature and rarely had a cross word to say about anyone.

As they got closer to the stranded cart, they could see that the mother and baby were in some distress. The baby cried as if it was about to be abandoned and left alone in the rain while the poor mother, wet to the skin, tried her best to comfort the child. The other four children wallowed in the mud and seemed not to notice the distress of the baby or their mother. The father was nowhere to be seen.

The entire circus procession halted. The rain continued to fall. By this time, Jerry Baker had arrived on the scene. He ploughed through the mud towards the woman and her children.

'Ye are in a spot of bother, so ye are,' he said in his soft Irish voice.

The woman nodded. The baby, seeing the stranger, stopped crying to resume a moment later. The mother had to shout to be heard over the rain and the baby's wailing.

'Our poor horse is fair spent,' she said. 'We've been stuck here for two days with only a fly sheet for cover. Not seen a soul 'till youse turned up. My husband's exhausted, what with trying to push the cart through this muck.'

Just then, a thin man of about forty, clad in a tattered overcoat and a tartan cap, appeared as if from nowhere. He did look exhausted, and he was soaked. Jerry held out his hand to the man.

'We'll soon get ye out of here,' he announced. 'We're the Baker Circus, and there's a lot of us about to lend a hand.' Jerry never missed an opportunity to publicise his circus.

One of the children, a freckly-faced boy of about ten, interrupted.

'Have you got an elephant?' he asked. 'An elephant could pull us out.'

'Can I see the lions?' enquired his brother. He, too, had a face full of freckles.

'I'm scared of the lions,' his sister said. She didn't have any freckles, but the hair under her rain-soaked hat was gathered into a long plait which reached to her waist. 'I love to see the people on the tightrope. Last year we...'

'That's enough, Gaby,' her mother admonished her. 'Let the nice man speak.'

Jerry took the opportunity to study the bedraggled family.

He decided that the best thing he could do for them was to get them out of the mud and offer them a lift. Their horse did look exhausted and in need of a rest. He could hitch up one of his stronger ponies, and this would give the poor creature some respite.

'Where are ye headin' for?' he asked.

'We've come from Mackay,' the man answered, 'and we're on our way to Clermont. That was the plan before all this rain stopped us.' He concluded with a shake of his head. The shaking caused droplets of rain to fall from his cap.

'Well now,' said Jerry. 'That's the direction we're goin', so I propose that we get ye out of here and give ye a lift with the circus.'

Hearing this, the four children jumped as one, sploshing the water and mud in every direction.

'Can we ride with the tigers?'

'I'd rather see the monkeys. I think they're funny.'

'You're funny,' laughed the smaller freckled face boy, and he flicked some mud in his sister's direction. She let out a wail.

By this time, a small group of circus performers had gathered around the stranded family. Even Happy Jackles had ceased his moaning and agreed to help push the cart. Frank Baker took hold of the horse's reins and gently coaxed the exhausted creature to keep moving. Frank was a great equestrian, and his love of horses seemed to do the trick for the horse responded, lifting first one front leg and then another, and the cart began to move forward ever so slightly. But it was the lion tamer, the strongest man in the whole circus, who managed to free the cart out of the muck and, for his efforts, received cheers of appreciation from all.

The men unhitched the horse, fed it some hay and allowed it to rest. Throughout all the drama, the rain did not let up, and everyone, including the horses, was soaked.

'Well now,' said Jerry, 'we'll rest here a while and then keep going. We've still to get through Logan Downs an' that's always a challenge even in the best of weather.'

'Yeah, you're right enough, Mr Baker. We didn't think the hundred and seventy miles or so to Clermont would have been such a trial for us. Fair grateful to you all. We was about at our wit's end when you turned up. Never expected to meet a circus out here in the back of beyond.' He added, 'Be glad when the rain stops and things dry up a bit.'

****

On the other side of Logan Downs, the unthinkable happened. The Baker Circus, with all the menagerie and loaded carts, became stuck in the mud. No amount of pushing and shoving could move the heavy loads. The circus was stranded.

'Think it's our turn to come to the rescue, Mr Baker,' said the man and his wife smiled. She looked worn out, but she had a lovely smile, and the smile changed her whole face.

'We're ever so thankful to you all,' she declared. 'Aren't we, Bill?'

Bill nodded.

'We'll go on to Clermont and send some rations out for you all. The horse has recovered now, and he's a strong one. We should make good time. Looks like the rain's clearing up a bit at last.'

'Well now,' Jerry said after a few seconds, 'that sounds like a mighty good idea. Ye can tell them in Clermont not to expect the big tent to go up tonight, but never fear; the show will go on.'

This optimism seemed to impress Bill. He laughed and shook Jerry Baker's hand.

'I have to tell you, Mr Baker,' he said, 'before all this happened, I always thought you circus folk were a queer bunch, not sayin' anything against youse, that is, but all this wanderin' around, never settlin' down, couldn't quite fathom it out, you know.'

Then he added, 'Looks like circus folk are like us after all.

Just takin' a different path, I reckon. That's all.'

Everyone in the Baker Circus would have agreed with that philosophy, even Happy Jackles, the clown.

****

The Baker Circus did get weather bound somewhere between Mackay and Clermont in North Queensland. The Daily Mercury reported this incident on 1 April 1910 p.6. I have taken some liberty naming a few of the performers, particularly the clown, Happy Jackles and the Dental Queen, La Belle Cora. Both were employed by Jerry Baker at different times. Whether they were present during this incident will never be known. I am almost certain that the Baker children would have been there, however. I have called the man stranded in the mud, Bill, but this is fiction. Again, we will never know his name.

A CLASS ACT

'If I work without the net, it'll bring in the punters.'

Kathleen Baker stretched, and in the blink of an eye, she somersaulted twice, and then she proceeded to walk on her hands. A moment later, her small body flipped like a tossed coin so that she landed on her feet. She somersaulted again. This time she managed to propel her body even higher into the air. Kathleen found it difficult to sit still. She had been somersaulting with her brothers and sisters all her young life. This was all she knew. The idea of being on the high wire without a safety net below had captured her imagination. She just had to convince her father.

Her father didn't share her enthusiasm. He supervised Kathleen's every act and was proud of his acrobatic children. Of course, the entire family had been balancing bare-back on horses and performing all manner of acrobatic tricks ever since they could walk. One child followed the other, but Kathleen was the one who was forever dreaming up new tricks. This latest idea of hers was even more daring.

'No, Kath,' her father said, 'no way without a net. We'll bring in the crowds without putting ourselves in danger. And ye know, they come to see you on the high wire, safe. They don't want to look at ye spread out on the floor with all your bones broken or worse.'

'I practise sometimes without the net. What's the difference?'

'I know ye do. But the crowds can sometimes put ye off your game. Just takes some idiot to start shoutin' an' next thing, ye have fallen to your death. I won't have it an' your mother would skin me alive if she thought I'd let ye do it without the net.'

Kathleen pouted. She knew that her father was right, but sometimes she just liked to tease him. When she balanced on the wire, all fear left her, but then Kathleen was perhaps one of the most accomplished female trapeze artists in the whole of Australia, if not the world.

They were due to pitch the tent in Cairns at Christmas time. It would be hot in the tropical North Queensland's summer, and the high wire was so close to the top of the big tent that it was always a few degrees hotter there. Hands would sweat, and the slightest misjudgement could end in tragedy. Kathleen knew this, for she had become known as the Queen of the Wireworkers, and she was used to performing in all weathers.

She also knew there was no more use in arguing with her father. Once his mind was made up, that was it. A few minutes later, and after another somersault, Kathleen propelled herself to the side of the big tent. Here, she opened a bag and took out her euphonium. She sat cross-legged on the grass and blew into the brass instrument. Her small fingers worked the magic, and very soon, the sounds from the euphonium could be heard all around the circus tent. Madame Leoni, the trapeze artist from 'Frisco, called out to Happy Jackles, the clown, and the two of them performed a lively dance in front of the seated Kathleen. They waved their arms in the air in tune with the music, and soon a small crowd of performers gathered around the energetic couple. Hearing the music, Kathleen's brother and sister, Frank and Dorrizzio, arrived and very quickly joined in the dance. Frank tossed his sister into the air as if she was as light as a feather. Dorrizzio, as supple as all the acrobats, somersaulted backwards onto the grass, and in one quick movement, she leapt from there onto her brother's shoulders and raised her arms in the air to the cheers from the small group. Kathleen stood up and playing her euphonium, marched the small group around the circumference of the tent. She had a plan.

If her father had known her plan, he would have quite probably disapproved, but then, Kathleen had a way of getting around him, and it usually was after she had performed her tricks to the audience. Then he would shake his head, and her mother would scold them both. But both parents would agree that their Kathleen was a star act.

Cairns was predictably hot and humid. Dark, ominous clouds gathered in the eastern sky. At three o'clock in the afternoon, those black clouds emptied just as everyone was putting the big tent up for the next day's show. Drenched to the skin and out of sorts, the circus folk grumbled, but to Kathleen Baker, the rain was a welcome relief from the stifling heat, and when the wire was in position, she climbed the ladder and stepped along the wire with ease. Sure-footed as a mountain goat, Kathleen was as much at home on the wire as she was walking on the ground eighty feet below.

The next day the same heavy downpour arrived as the day before, but this time the tent was up, the animals were ready, and the performers were primed to go. At eight o'clock in the evening, a large and enthusiastic audience greeted the performers. So great was the crowd, and so popular was the Baker Circus that people had to be turned away. Five hundred additional seats were required, and the ever-resourceful Jerry Baker assured the disappointed folk that this would be done for the next evening's performance.

The horses came into the ring first and were greeted by clapping and laughter from the audience. *Fun in the Stockyard* was always a sure winner. One horse, in particular, dashed around the ring with young Frank Baker clinging onto the animal's back. This brought forth cheers of admiration for the length of time that Frank had been able to maintain his balance. Little Miss Babs, soon to be called Babarina, came in next. She astonished the audience with her contortionist and tumbling acts. The horses were followed by two mules and a frisky donkey which set the mood for the rest of the evening.

The most exciting acts had to be from the trapeze artists, and they always performed at the end of the three-hour show.

The net was positioned below, and to rapturous applause, the fearless acrobats climbed the ladder to the high wire. Kathleen took a deep breath, clenched and unclenched her hands and watched as Madame Leoni, suspended in mid-air, held two of the Baker children by her teeth. This fearless performance amazed the crowd, but when a thick-set local man was invited to climb the ladder and also be held by her teeth, the crowd went wild. This was followed by a thin, scrawny-looking sailor who, when held in the same way by the indomitable Madame Leoni, was spun around at the same furious rate. When the sailor reached the safety of the ground, he was so giddy that he tumbled to the floor and had to be carried back to his seat to cheers from the audience.

By now, the crowd was in great humour, but what came next delighted them even more. It was Kathleen's turn. Dressed in a blue leotard festooned with sequins and white leggings, she stepped onto the wire. Her balance was perfect. She performed acrobatic turns and was caught in mid-air, not once but three times. The crowd clapped, but it was her final act that brought the audience to their feet, and her fellow acrobats applauded with as much enthusiasm.

Kathleen had somehow managed to carry her euphonium up the ladder and had left it on the platform. She stepped onto the wire with the brass instrument in one hand. There wasn't a sound from the crowd far below. The whole audience held their collective breath. Kathleen strode along the wire as if she was walking on air, and at the centre, she stopped. Then she stood on that wire with one leg and, with the hand that held the euphonium, brought the instrument to her lips. For a moment, she hesitated, and it looked as if she was about to fall.

High above the audience, Kathleen did something that no one had attempted before. Balancing on one leg, she started to play her euphonium. The whole performance lasted for less than a minute in time. The crowd below were silent. Then

Kathleen tossed her euphonium to her companion acrobat who was standing on the platform. He caught it in his left hand and raised his right arm to the audience. Then Kathleen executed a perfect turn on the wire. This was greeted with applause, but when she left the safety of the wire and performed a somersault on the way down to the net, people got up from their seats, clapped and cheered. Ever the performer, Kathleen somersaulted when she reached the net. In one beautifully executed movement, she leapt over the net, raised both arms in the air and ran to the opening in the tent, disappearing from view.

Later, after the circus had closed for the night, Kathleen met her father. He had seen the whole performance. He had been just that little bit afraid as his daughter performed her daredevil act, which could quite easily have ended in tragedy.

'Kathleen, my girl,' he said, 'that was some performance ye did there. Whatever made ye think that ye could do that stunt without a net below ye?'

It was then that Kathleen exhibited more than a daredevil smile.

'Why, Da,' she replied, 'I had no thought to work that act without a net... just wanted to see the look on your face. It sure brought the crowd in, though, didn't it?'

And Jerry Baker, father to all these amazing acrobats, had to agree.

****

This memorable act by Kathleen Baker was reported in the Cairns Post on 23rd December 1910, page.5. By that time, Kathleen was becoming well known in the circus world, and she received a flattering reception on her entry to the ring. I have fictionalised the story as there is no way of ascertaining just how old Kathleen was when she performed this clever feat.

A TALE OF TWO STARS

Two of the favourite animals in the Baker Circus were the donkey and the monkey. The donkey arrived on the scene to replace a few of the horses, and in no time at all, he became a special attraction. Children, in particular, loved him and he would stand quite patiently and let them stroke his long head with a 'hee haw' now and then. If they tugged his ears, however, he would 'hee haw' louder, and raise his head up and down, so that the children ran away. But if one of them gently stroked his long ears, he would immediately try to nuzzle them for this was a donkey that had rather sensitive ears. He was also a very friendly donkey.

It was no wonder that the donkey became very popular and his fame spread from town to town. He was also a greedy donkey and munched his way through so much hay that Jerry Baker wondered at times if this particular donkey had been a good investment. The horses didn't eat quite so much. He had a particular liking for cucumbers. His name was Sloper and he was the only performing Chinese piebald donkey in the world. Perhaps this status gave him some of his more unusual characteristics. He was a particular favourite with the clowns but everyone in the circus had a soft spot for him. Extra hay was always given to Sloper, and the occasional apple or cucumber was munched by him with enthusiasm, despite the misgivings of Jerry. Sloper was just that sort of donkey.

Sloper seemed to like circus life and the constant moving about. It was the clowns who trained him to do tricks but to say that they had succeeded would be something of an understatement. This donkey had determination and obstinate nature. No one ever knew if he would respond in the way he had been trained to do when he entered the ring. It was anyone's guess. When the strongest of the clowns picked him up, nine times out of ten there wasn't a movement of the eyelid and Sloper showed no interest in what was going on. This disinterest, however, encouraged the crowd to cheer.

When Sloper heard the clapping and the shouting of encouragement, he would respond but not always in the way he had been trained to do. One of his tricks was to leap through a hoop in the manner of a performing dog. This is when Sloper's stubborn nature was seen by all. Much to the frustration of the clowns this act nearly always failed. The unresponsive donkey just wouldn't jump through that hoop and no manner of encouragement, including sometimes the sight of a cucumber, would make him budge. Often the crowd would start to chant loudly, *C'mon, Sloper, you can do it,* for Sloper's antics had become well known. His trick, then, was to lie down in front of the hoop while the clowns jumped around him and tried to persuade him to move. One of the clowns would leap through the hoop himself to try to encourage the obstinate creature. This act always had the crowd in stitches of laughter. Sometimes Sloper would stand up while this was going on but his disinterest was obvious to all. Most times he just ignored the whole thing. For all these reasons, no one could guess what the donkey would do next. In one memorable performance, he just walked out of the ring in the direction of the opening in the tent as if he was bored. No amount of cajoling by the clowns could persuade him back into the ring.

It wasn't too long before the clowns and everyone in the circus began to realise that Sloper, despite all his obstinate ways, was a rather clever donkey. He had learned his tricks with ease but it was he that decided whether he would perform them or not. Despite this being a cause of frustration for the clowns, it was also a challenge for them and they, too, decided that the donkey's behaviour was a crowd pleaser and not an altogether disappointment. Sloper, it appeared, ran the show.

As so often happens in the animal kingdom, friendships can

spring up between different species and the most unlikely of animals. Sloper had made friends with one of the monkeys named Micky. This particular monkey was loved by all the circus folk. He was allowed to roam freely during the day and was only locked in at night with the other monkeys. Micky was more than a match for the donkey for he was clever as well. He was an inquisitive sort of monkey and had become very popular. He also was a great hit with the children and performed all manner of mischievous antics when they were around. When he entered the ring to do his tricks he wore a little red jacket and a yellow bandana around his neck.

When it was discovered that Micky and Sloper had become friends, the clowns thought it would be a good idea to arrange that the two animals were in the ring together. This proved a great success and in no time at all, Micky was on Sloper's back, performing as many somersaults as the human acrobats. He had no difficulty speeding through the hoop at a great rate. One of his antics, which always brought applause, was to run right around the circle of the hoop and then leap forwards and backwards through the hoop. All the time, Sloper lay on his side; his eyes shut, and showed no interest in watching the capers of his monkey friend. But the greatest trick that Micky did was to climb a ladder which was held in the air by two of the clowns, swing on the top rung by his tail and then leap to the ground so fast that it left the audience gasping at the agility and the speed of the animal.

Sloper and Micky became such a popular act that when the donkey and the monkey came into the ring they were greeted with clapping and shouts of encouragement. The acrobats and the lions always got top billing but Sloper and his friend were certainly up there with the star attractions.

Given the fact that Micky was allowed to roam around the circus, it has to be said that he did get into a fair amount of mischief. One day he was observed teasing the performing bear by climbing over the top of its cage. The bear growled and appeared to be very annoyed at the antics of the monkey. It was only when Paul Rougal, who trained the bear and also the six Bengali tigers, arrived on the scene that Micky scuppered. Undeterred, Micky had to be chased away from the bear's cage the very next day. After a few more similar incidents Micky finally seemed to become bored with the bear and didn't venture near that particular cage again. When Sloper settled down for the night, Micky did likewise. At least everyone knew where Micky was then, safe in his cage with the other monkeys.

It was when the circus arrived in Herberton that the unthinkable happened.

The big tent was packed out on Thursday and Friday and Sloper and Micky were greeted by the usual enthusiasm and applause. Both animals performed well. Sloper even managed to climb on top of a line of boxes and 'he hawed' loudly while Micky perched on his back and held onto his friend's long ears. Sloper never seemed to mind if Micky touched his ears. It had been a good night all around.

For his reward, Sloper was given a cucumber but Micky did not fare as well. He had given up teasing the bear and instead, he leapt on top of the leopard's cage and was busy amusing himself, annoying the leopard by poking his hand through the bars. Then for his next trick, he scampered along the sides of the cage. All the while he chattered away and this seemed to irritate the leopard even more. The leopard paced back and forth. He growled. Once he tried to grab Micky's long tail but the monkey was more agile. Micky babbled away, shot to the top of the leopard's cage and sat there, looking down on his adversary. Then he proceeded to scratch himself as if the whole game was a complete bore. Unfortunately for Micky his tail now swung close to the leopard's outstretched paw. The leopard was angry. He was no bear. It all happened in a blink of an eye. The leopard roared, lashed out and seized Micky's tail. The now terrified

Micky screamed but it was too late. The strong jaws of the leopard pulled Micky through the bars, chewed up the little red jacket and yellow bandana and spat them out. Before anyone could stop him Micky became the leopard's meal.

The circus troupe were devastated by the event for they all had a soft spot for the mischievous Micky but perhaps the saddest of them all was Sloper. For days he refused to perform his tricks and would come into the ring and just stand there, head down. He couldn't even manage a 'hee haw'.

One day Happy Jackles, the clown, had a brainwave. He dressed a little girl monkey called Daisy in a red jacket and yellow bandana similar to the ones that had been chewed up by the leopard. He brought Daisy into the ring. Here, he proceeded to teach her tricks when Sloper was busy munching grass and away from the tent.

The big day arrived and Sloper and Daisy were introduced. Sloper, who had been gradually losing all interest in performing since the demise of his friend, spied Daisy all dressed up and sitting on the other side of the hoop. He let out an enormous and joyful 'hee haw'. Then, to everyone's surprise, he jumped through the hoop and stood next to Daisy. She immediately climbed up his tail and perched on his back the way his old monkey friend, Micky had done so many times.

From then on, they performed their tricks like the stars they were. Sloper lived to a grand old age and had many monkey friends over the years. Every one of them wore a little red jacket and a yellow bandana.

****

This story is based on two facts. There was a piebald Chinese donkey named Sloper that was part of the Baker Circus and the monkey did meet his untimely death. Whether the two animals performed together is unknown. However, the report about the monkey's demise was recorded in the Cairns Post on 26th October 1910, page 4. Sloper, too, was mentioned in the

Ohinemuri Gazette, Volume XXVIII, Issue 3741, page 9.

A NEAR MISS

Babs Baker stretched and yawned. It was early morning and she had just awakened from a deep sleep. She had been dreaming and her dream rather unsettled her for she had dreamt that she had fallen from the high wire and landed, face down on top of Peko, one of the clowns. Then, as that image faded, she was transported back in time and she saw her mother, balancing on the same wire and calling out for her. It was all rather unsettling.

Her mother always believed that dreams could be warnings and Babs felt that way about her dreams as well. The trapeze artists were a superstitious bunch. Maybe this was because with every act they defied death, swinging through the air, balancing on bars, catching people in mid-flight but for all the danger, not one of them could imagine a life doing anything else. Every performance was different even if the routine remained the same. The audience dictated that. If the audience clapped and cheered and showed enthusiasm, it somehow transferred to the acrobats and the trapeze artists but if the audience was non-responsive, as it happened on rare occasions, the performers just had to do their best and not think too much about the crowd. After all, high above and close to the top of the tent, was another world for them and one in which none of the people below would ever get to experience.

Babs was known for her contortionist acts. Her small body could twist itself into so many near impossible positions that people watching her, could hardly believe a human could do such things but then, Babs and the other Baker children had been performing and practising all these tricks from when they could walk. With her grey blue eyes and dark brown hair, Babs, who had been renamed Babarina for the benefit of the circus publicity, had become well-known as a graceful and talented star performer.

She had perfected her art so much that Tybel the Great, as he called himself, had insisted that she accompany him when he performed his acrobatic tricks. He was the catcher for Babs. She swung, holding onto the bar, and then somersaulted in mid-air to be caught by Tybel. Sometimes she performed a double somersault. Always Tybel's strong hands caught her. The death-defying dental act, the iron jaw trick, was always their last turn. Gripping a piece of leather, the aptly named Iron Jaw, between his teeth Tybel caught Babs with his hands and with perfect timing, and a lot of practice, she secured the other end of the iron jaw between her teeth. Then she swung below him, turning round and round in graceful circles, all the while the two of them, locked together by the iron jaw, swayed back and forth thirty feet from the safety of the net. The act ended when Babs and Tybel locked hands again, and Babs caught hold of the other swing from her fellow artist who all this time had stood on the platform. Once safely back on the platform, Babs raised her right arm to the applause of the crowd. True to say, Babarina and Tybel the Great were a class act.

Babs and Tybel always practised their acts before any performance. Both were perfectionists and sometimes, this led to some rivalry between them for Tybel was insistent that he had the top billing and Babs would always be his assistant. Babs did not view this in quite the same way but she kept her peace. Tybel could get rather volatile if things didn't go his way.

When Babs arrived at the big tent, Tybel was already there. He was limbering up. His arm and leg muscles were as taut as any champion athlete and this strong physique and fearless disposition had been the reason he was a much sought-after artistic performer.

'You're late,' he barked at Babs when he saw her.

Babs did not reply. She was used to his outbursts. Instead, she began to stretch her small, thin frame and performed the warm-up exercises that she had been doing all her young life. Then, as if to annoy Tybel even more, she somersaulted right around the circle of the ring. Tybel was strong but he was no match for the acrobatic prowess of Babs when she somersaulted. Not half as subtle as Babs, Tybel could only look on in envy sometimes. However, he made a point of reminding her that he was in charge just about every day.

After about ten minutes of exercising, Tybel announced that it was time to practice their routine with the swings. His supple body climbed the ladder to the platform with an agility that always brought gasps from the crowd. He could ascend to the top of the tent in five seconds which was something of a feat. Babs followed him but instead of climbing the ladder, she shimmered up the pole on the other side of the tent. The trapeze artists always practised early in the day before the rest of the circus got going and two of their fellow acrobats were already in position on the platforms. A command from Tybel had brought the circus hands into the ring and the three men dragged the safety net into position. This was the rehearsal for the evening performance. Everything had to be worked on. Every little detail had to be perfect for any slight hiccup could spell disaster.

The evening show started on time and to a packed house. It was a responsive crowd and there was much interaction between the audience and the performers. The trick ponies with their acrobatic human companions had particularly delighted the audience and everyone, both people and artists, were in great humour by the time the twenty-first act on the programme was to take place.

This was the final trick before the close of the show. Tybel, defying gravity and Babs in mid-air performing somersaults had already brought the crowd to their feet. Then it was the Iron Jaw trick which was the twenty-first item and the most challenging. The ringmaster announced the last trick and asked for complete silence.

In the large tent, there wasn't a murmur. Babs, standing on the platform and ready to launch onto the swing felt a tremor of apprehension. She heard her mother's voice, just for a moment, and then she caught hold of the swing. Tybel was already on the other swing getting ready to perform the catch.

Babs took a grip of the bar and swung. The performance brought forth appreciative clapping from the crowd for she appeared as if she was flying. Tybel on the opposite swing was doing the same. They were partners in motion. Then the ringmaster asked for silence as Babs hooked both her feet around the bar to ready herself for the catch. She swung once and then twice, and the third time she managed to grip Tybel's hand while her other hand fumbled for the iron jaw. Tybel had his iron jaw already in his mouth waiting for the connection. They had practised this act so many times and with such precision. Timing was everything. A moment's hesitation could spell disaster.

For a split second, it looked like the two were connecting and Babs would delight the crowd by swinging in graceful circles below Tybel but something happened. Just as she tried to fit the iron jaw piece into her mouth, as she had done so many times, her other hand slipped from Tybel's clasp.

It was thirty feet to the safety net. She fell like a bird, twisting her body as she plunged downwards. Tybel, seeing this happening, swung to the pole and endeavoured to lower himself to the ground but in his haste, he slid so fast down the pole that he collapsed in a heap beside Babs. Four attendants rushed to the scene to try to help both performers. Tybel collapsed into the arms of one of them. Both Babs and Tybel were semi-unconscious.

A doctor was called for and Doctor Crawford, who had been enjoying the show as much as the rest of the audience until this happened, arrived on the scene, fearing the worst. Tybel had several injuries to his palate and several of his top teeth had been pulled away. These teeth had probably been loosened whilst he and Babs were struggling to connect the two parts of the iron jaw. Falling from such a height did the rest. Babs was in severe shock. Both artists were carried away on stretchers in front of the now-silent crowd. The ringmaster announced the end of the show and the crowd left the big tent in an orderly if sombre procession.

Later, both Tybel and Babs talked about their near-death experience for both of them recovered in a matter of days although Tybel was unable to perform the iron jaw act for a long time after.

'We were lucky,' he told Babs and then he growled. 'Next time get your timing right.'

Babs was silent. It was just like Tybel to blame everyone and not himself for she wasn't sure what had happened up there either. All she could think of at that moment was her dream of the night before, and her mother's words.

'I'll remember,' she said quietly.

****

This painful accident occurred on 16th November 1912 and was reported in the Wanganui Chronicle.

The actual cause of the accident was not recorded and I have created a story based on the newspaper article. It is possible that no one knew the reasons for the fall. Whether Babs Baker and Tybel got on or not is pure conjecture. Whatever happened, Babs lived to tell the tale and had many adventures afterwards.

THE HEART OF A LION

It was looking into the eyes of the old lion that Alice Baker found hard, but knowing what she had to do was even harder. The old lion had been born into a captive world and had lived his whole life in a cage. When he was released it was only to sit on a stool to roar. The crowd of humans made such a noise when the old lion roared and the keeper cracked his whip to make the old lion and the other lions, sitting on stools beside him, growl even louder. Then he and the other lions would thrust their paws with claws outstretched towards the keeper to pretend to strike, growling all the time, and the humans cheered and clapped. When the old lion and two of the other lions jumped through hoops of fire, the humans cheered even louder. Then it was back to the cage and a hefty bit of meat for all that trouble.

Alice Baker and the Baker Circus had had a difficult year but the old lion did not know that. His world was a cage and a circus ring. In the human world, a light had gone out of the lives of the Baker Circus. On the train between Ohakume and Waimarino Jerry Baker had died, all alone, to leave his grieving widow, Alice and his family to try to pick up the pieces and come to terms with their loss for it is fair to say that with Jerry gone, the circus could never be the same again. It had been Jerry whose vision had been to be a circus owner and in this endeavour, he had succeeded beyond all his wildest imaginings. William John Baker, always known as Jerry, was the Baker Circus.

Alice and the family along with their circus workers mourned. Their grief was even more poignant for the event had been unexpected, but then Life throws challenges at all of us, and sometimes, we weep. At first, Alice found it hard to come to terms with what had happened. When she had said goodbye to her husband, he had been full of his usual enthusiasm and optimism for he had been planning an addition to the circus and had managed to recruit a team of four performing jugglers whom he had been negotiating with for over a year. He had been off on the train to meet the two men and two women and to sign the contract. He was delighted that they had agreed to join his circus and his last words to Alice had been to assure her that these four jugglers would bring in the crowds. They were very talented and made people cheer whenever they performed. He also had in mind to purchase two more lions as the old lion was showing signs of age and something would have to be done about him. The old lion had been born in Australia and had been with the circus all his life. It would be sad to see him go but the circus was a business and Jerry was a businessman. His other lions were younger and had been born in New Zealand while on tour and it made good business sense to bring in some even younger animals to train when the old lion was gone. Jerry was always planning new things for the circus and Alice agreed with most of his plans however far-fetched some of them were. She was a strong woman and she had her family about her but for her, Jerry was irreplaceable.

Jerry had had a special affinity for his lions and this was even harder for Alice. Every night Jerry would say 'goodnight' to his lions. When one really old lion, aged thirty-five, had died in the South Island while the circus was on tour, Jerry had put a brave face on it but she knew he had shed a tear for his old friend. Except for the old lion, most of the ones they had now were between two to five years of age and they had many years left in them. They were all black-maned African lions and in good health.

It was a costly business keeping all these animals. The lions along with all the other circus animals were fed every day at four o'clock in the afternoon and the straw bedding in their cages had to be changed then. The lions were fussy and wouldn't eat anything that had been cooked or salted so to keep them in good condition they fed on good fresh beef. Jerry had calculated that the lions ate about one hundred and eighty pounds of beef each day.

The costs began to increase everywhere. The circus hands and the performers had to be paid. When the circus rested for the winter, the animals still had to be fed. When they toured, the crowds didn't come as much as they used to and the whole enterprise was beginning to run at a loss. Alice and her son, Frank who had taken over his father's role, knew that it couldn't go on.

At Palmerston North, the lions were housed in their cages at the Showgrounds. Their roars unsettled the local folk and it was then that Alice decided that it was time to call it a day. The lions, along with all the animals would have to be sold. The performers and the workers would have to find other circuses. Her talented acrobatic children would have to do the same. Jerry Baker's circus had ended.

'I'll try Wellington Zoo first to see if they will house the lions until we can find another circus for them,' she told Frank.

'How about the old one, Father's favourite?'

'Doubt if any circus would want him,' was his mother's reply.

'Poor old Malik,' Frank said.

All their seven lions had names although they didn't respond to their names with quite the enthusiasm of a dog. The old lion had been named Malik for that meant a King in Africa and Jerry had thought that particular lion exhibited all the characteristics of a leader.

'If we can't get any satisfaction at Wellington Zoo, we'll just have to try some Australian purchasers,' Alice was thoughtful. 'Maybe old Malik will find a home back there where he was born.'

'I hope so,' answered Frank but he doubted his words even as he spoke to them.

****

Alice took the train to Wellington and pleaded with the officials at the zoo to take her beloved lions. Her pleading fell on deaf ears. They would be too costly to house, she was told, and there were not the proper facilities to keep seven lions in captivity. That would require major building work to be done which would add to the costs. It was not a feasible proposition. When one of the officials was told the age of the old lion, he laughed and said that one would not be worth the £600 she was asking. It would be best to try other circuses. The zoo didn't want any of them.

The plan to sell the seven to other circuses was even more disappointing. Alice had reduced the price per lion from £600 to £300 but even this met with disinterest. It cost £3 per week for feed and bedding. No way could she keep the lions.

'We will have to do the unthinkable, Frank,' she told her son. 'There is no other way.'

'I know. It's Malik I will miss the most of all of them. If a lion can be a friend, that one is.'

They were both silent for a few moments, thinking of their lions, especially old Malik.

'It will be a mercy,' he added but there was sorrow in his words.

****

The sad day arrived and the vet administered poison in the milk to the first two lions. Much to everyone's surprise this procedure was unsuccessful. The lions were used to raw meat, not milk. The two lions refused to drink the milk. Another procedure would have to be done. Malik, as if sensing the end, crouched on the floor of his cage, swished his tail and put his old head between his paws. The vet and the Society of the Prevention of Cruelty to Animals officer discussed the situation between themselves and then they both approached Alice and Frank with their mutual decision.

'Mrs Kelly,' the vet said. He was a kind man and a professional but he found his task a difficult one to perform. These magnificent creatures, living their lives as captive beasts through no fault of their own, deserved a humane ending. The young ones, full of pent-up energy paced back and forth in their cages as if they, too, sensed something was amiss.

'Mrs Kelly,' the vet continued, 'we will need to try another approach. Tomorrow I will administer the poison into the meat and that should put an end to all this.'

'Thank you,' Alice replied, saddened by the news. She had hoped it would all be over in one day.

Alice did not sleep that night. She tried not to dwell too much on the next day but she knew in her heart it had to be done. With the death of the lions, the circus would die as well.

****

It was a bright sunny morning and the young lions were eager for their food but not old Malik. Because of his age, he was weakened and a lot of the fight had gone out of him. Alice despaired that he would not eat the meat but just leave it. Then poor Malik would have to be shot because there was no other way. To see her old friend end his life like this would be hard to bear.

The poison was administered and after a few growls of pain, the lions appeared to go to sleep but not old Malik. He refused to eat the meat. He sniffed it with not much enthusiasm, and then he sank back onto the floor of the cage. Alice was distraught.

'My old Malik,' she whispered to the supine creature, 'eat your meat for it is all we can do.'

She looked into the old lion's eyes as she had done so many times before and something stirred within her for old Malik seemed to understand. He rose to his feet. His legs shook slightly, and for one heartfelt moment Alice thought the old lion would sink to the floor again, but as everyone held their collective breaths, he approached the offering of the deadly meat and took a huge bite, and then another.

****

The incidents are based on fact. Whether the old lion was called Malik is fiction. Writing this story in the twenty-first century when attitudes have changed towards the keeping of wild animals in circuses the story could be viewed as sentimental. However, from all accounts the Bakers held great affection for their lions and this must have been a very painful day for them. The Horowhenua Chronicle of 28th July 1926, page 2, headlined the article as 'Seven Lions Poisoned: Ignoble End at Palmerston' so it is possible that the reporter viewed the sad ending of the lions with much the same feelings as we do in our time.

BABARINA IN AMERICA

I have known no other life but entertaining people. My beginnings were in the circus and that world has held me in its magical embrace for as long as I can remember. I'm old now and my joints no longer function as in my youth. I can sometimes move my body in ways I used to, much to the amazement of my contemporary old ladies. We laugh often about the days of our youth but if I were to tell them my story, it would make them blush. You see, I will be an entertainer till I die.

I've moved around all my life. No grass ever grew under my feet. I want to tell you a little story about my life in America and what adventures I had there on the vaudeville circuit. It all began after our circus folded in New Zealand. My dear father died suddenly of a heart attack on a train travelling between Ohakune and Waimarino. It was the way he would have wanted to go but his death hit us all hard, especially my mother, Alice. We found it almost impossible to keep the circus afloat after that. My father was the brains of the outfit. He was a showman through and through. It was he who made the decisions. The circus world was changing anyhow and people were finding other means of entertainment. When our big cats had to be put down, I guess that was the end of the Baker Circus.

They say in an ending there is a beginning and I had to find work. My feet were itchy. I needed to leave New Zealand. There was a world out there and the world was America. I was twenty-four years of age when I set sail for California and the vaudeville circuit awaited me. I visited my Uncle Michael and his lovely wife in San Mateo before I started work. We Irish can travel the world with a relative in just about every country. Uncle Micky was a lorry driver. He could never get his head around his brother owning a circus and us kids being acrobats.

Touring from place to place gets tiring sometimes but it's an addiction too. Always the next town awaits you and then the next and the next. As I said, I have known no other life nor have my brothers and sisters. We are circus people. My sisters joined me at times. Lorenz is an amazing trapeze artist and I love to sing. We received some good reviews from the American theatrical magazine, *The Billboard*.

I kept all the good reviews in a little box my mother gave me when I was ten years of age and sometimes I take them out and read them. It's then I wonder at what I did and all the places I have seen.

When I crossed over to Mexico I had a great time there. You get to understand the crowd and the Mexicans were fun, clapping, cheering us on and all this got the adrenalin going. Performing my acrobatic act at the Capital Theatre in Portland, Oregon was quite calm after the Mexicans. I travelled all over America and Canada from Vancouver to Boston and all places in between. I would try my hand at anything that was asked of me; working the high wire, somersaulting on the ground and sometimes I was asked to sing. I love to sing but these days my voice hasn't the power it used to have.

Then there was Clarence Oswald. I married him but that's another story. We settled down for a while in Los Angeles. I suppose I've spent a lot of my life in California but always on the move, even there. When I got too old to do the acts on the stage, I decided to train dogs to perform. I've always loved animals. The Baker Circus was a menagerie. Why, we had Bengali tigers, lions, monkeys, dogs, donkeys, leopards, even an elephant once, and always our horses. My father started the circus with horses. My brother, Frank could balance himself on a horse at four years of age and perform somersaults on their backs at six. I like horses, too, but it was dogs I had a liking for and this is where my story gets interesting.

I had five Pomeranians and I taught them to do all manner

of tricks. I dressed them up with little conical hats and frilly dresses. This is what the punters like to see. My dogs could do all manner of stunts. Spinning, leaping through hoops, balancing themselves on see-saws, jumping onto my shoulders and I loved every one of them. I had a particular favourite called Roxy. She was a black dog with bright little eyes and she was the star act. The other dogs were all brown so Roxy stood out in the group.

We were on the stage in Boston when the unexpected happened. For the finale, the dogs, to a few bars of Offenbach's *Can Can*, balanced on their hind legs and stood in a line similar to the girls who danced the infamous music. This always brought claps and cheers of approval. This evening, however, Roxy refused to join the line of other dogs. Instead, she leapt onto the small table that I used as a prop for my act and spun in a fast circle. First clockwise and then anti-clockwise. Then, as if she knew she was the star act, she jumped down and, with the music still playing; she proceeded to walk on her hind legs in front of the other dogs. By this time, sensing that something wasn't quite right the other Pomeranians ended their act. Instead, the four of them started to wag their tails furiously and bark. I was at a loss as to what to do next but the audience, not knowing that this performance was completely unrehearsed started to cheer. Roxy, ever the star, seemed to sense that she had performed a memorable trick and to the delight of the crowd and to my surprise, she leapt into my arms, tail wagging and proceeded to lick my face. It brought the house down, as they say.

After the show finished I was accosted by the reporter from the *Boston American*.

'Miss Baker,' he said, and I always remember he had his notebook out and was already scribbling, 'Miss Baker,' he continued, 'that was a very impressive act. Your dogs are amazing. But I thought fox terriers performed better. Why do you use Pomeranians?'

'All dogs can be trained,' I replied.

He wanted a story so he kept the questions coming.

'It must take an enormous lot of time and effort. Why, that black one was superb. When did it learn to do all those tricks?'

I thought of Roxy. After the show, it almost seemed that she expected to have top billing. I must confess she received an extra treat from me for her unrehearsed act. I decided, then and there, that I would train her to keep that particular performance for the next shows. Like my father, I always knew how to play to an enthusiastic audience.

'Well, I think sometimes the dogs tell you what they want to do. I like the Pomeranians. They are clever and always want to please.'

'And the black one?'

'Well, that's another story,' I said.

My reply seemed to satisfy him for he went away mumbling to himself. I must say I have lived in America for many years and I have lots of memories of my time here but somehow when I look back that act with my Pomeranians in Boston has to be one of the highlights of my life. Roxy lived to a grand old age and the other four dogs passed away before her. If I had been younger and Roxy had been alive then, we would have performed many an acrobatic stunt together. I'm certain of that. The little dog taught me a lot. Maybe, it was she that trained me?

****

Babs (Babarina) Baker was the most recorded of all the Baker children who performed with the circus. Born in Brisbane in 1903 she did travel the world. She lived in America for most of her life. I have attempted to write a little about the life of a theatrical performer in the early twentieth century. Babarina did train Pomeranians in later life. The report about this particular act appeared in The Boston American on June 22nd,

1943, Suffolk County Massachusetts. Babarina was referred to as a "Vaudevillian" in the article. The story about the Pomeranians is fiction as there is no way of knowing the names or even the number of dogs that Babarina trained.

Miss Babarina Baker
From a flyer for Sole Brothers Australian Circus Date Unknown

TRIALS AND TRIBULATIONS

The magistrate was a puzzled man. He had listened to many cases between a man and a woman but this had to be one of the most intriguing he had ever witnessed.

One glance at the man in question was curiosity itself for the defendant was dressed in Army uniform although he told the court that he had been discharged in 1919 and there was no reason that he should continue to wear the uniform. He had served at the Front and been discharged as being unfit for service having suffered an injury there. He hadn't another coat to his name. The old Army jacket, now torn at the sleeves, was his only garment. Hearing this, the magistrate decided not to pursue the matter further. Instead, he sank back into his rather ornate magisterial chair, drummed his fingers on the bench, and called Mr Tringham who was appearing for the plaintiff.

The magistrate and Mr Tringham enjoyed many a whisky at the barrister's bar and often or not, lively discussions about the various cases and the characters involved had engaged them to the early hours. The magistrate was certain that whoever won this particular case would be discussed at length with his friend afterwards. It was not every day a wife, married for just one week, took her husband to court for maintenance. The reporter from the *New Zealand Times* was already in the court busy taking notes.

'Do you admit that you have not provided your wife with adequate maintenance for her support?' asked Mr Tringham when the young man appeared in the dock.

John shuffled his feet. He was short in stature and the heavy Army overcoat enveloping his skinny frame made him appear even gaunter. Here was a man who had witnessed untold suffering, the results of which showed on his face. He mumbled that he did admit he hadn't paid anything towards his wife's maintenance. Mr Tringham asked him to repeat his answer.

'That is so,' intoned Mr Tringham. 'I have a question for you. My client alleges that you and she, having been married March last, remaining together for just one week, and you have been involved with another woman during that time and that you left your wife for this other woman. I believe that your wife agreed to take you back on two occasions but she would not live with you again. How do you plead?'

John appeared not to hear the words. He coughed and did not reply.

'The defendant will answer the question put to you,' the magistrate said from his lofty perch.

Mr Tringham repeated his question and this time John admitted that there had been another woman but they were no longer together. This seemed to satisfy Mr Tringham and he decided to pursue the matter of maintenance. His client was living with her mother at present as she had no other means of support. There seemed to be some discussion as to how John was supporting himself as he was no longer able to work due to his injuries. He was a broken man, haunted by events that he had witnessed in the war but Mr Tringham had a duty to his client. Somehow John must be made responsible for his laxity. His story as told by his wife was that her husband relied for his livelihood on his Army pension of £4 6s 8d a month.

'Can you please tell the court how you are managing to live given that you are not working and it appears that you only have your Army pension to support yourself?'

'The circus,' mumbled John.

'What do you mean... the circus?'

'I help out.'

'And are you paid any wages for this "helping out"?' Mr Tringham asked in a somewhat sarcastic tone.

'No.'

'Am I led to believe that you work in the circus and are not paid for your labour? I must confess I find that a most preposterous notion.'

John did not reply and the magistrate told him to answer the question put to him.

By now, the interest of the court was aroused and the reporter for the *New Zealand Times* even more so. He had already filled two pages of his notebook with scribbles. Surely he would receive a pat on the back from his editor for this intriguing case.

John mumbled that he received no money from the circus but he was given his bed and board in exchange for the work he did.

'This sounds most irregular,' said Mr Tringham.

'Well, that's how it is,' John snapped. He appeared somewhat angry at the line of questioning.

The magistrate cautioned John again and instructed Mr Tringham to refrain from any judgment. To which the barrister nodded in agreement.

'Very well, Your Worship,' he said. 'There is another matter, perhaps a more serious one that has been levelled at the defendant. My client alleges that her husband has been selling whisky to the Māori and as the court is aware, this is a serious offence, punishable by imprisonment or a hefty fine. What do you say to this?'

'It's not true.'

'Very well.'

'It has also been alleged that you are travelling in the company of a female member of the circus troupe. What is your answer to this?'

'Not true.'

'Speak up, man,' the magistrate was becoming irritated with the whole procedure. He was a little deaf in the left ear and as intriguing as the case was he was also becoming hungry. The defendant wasn't helping his cause by his constant shuffling of feet and mumbling.

'I have many friends in the circus.'

'And is this particular female, a special friend?'

'No.'

'Is she not the woman that you have been conducting an affair with?'

'No.'

'I put it to you if this is the case that you are not in an adulterous relationship with the particular female from the circus, and consequently, this would give your wife grounds for a divorce, how is it that these rumours have been allowed to be circulated?'

The magistrate interjected and cautioned Mr Tringham to not speculate. However, he ordered the defendant to answer the question put to him.

'I can't be responsible for what people say about me,' said John.

'That is not answering the question. Are you, or are you not conducting a sexual relationship with the aforementioned female?'

'No.'

'So this is not the same woman that you admitted to having an affair with?'

'No.'

'I see.' Mr Tringham shuffled some papers and decided to go back to the question of maintenance. Not providing for his wife would be enough grounds for a separation and the alleged adultery could be put to rest, at least for a time.

When he heard the possibility of sexual misconduct the reporter licked the tip of his pencil and scribbled harder. This was a story that his readers would revel in. When Mr Tringham's line of questioning returned to the question of how John could support himself, the reporter stopped writing.

'I will return to the subject of your employment, or lack of, with the circus. Can you please tell the court how it is that you do not receive any wages from the circus proprietor?'

Mr Tringham was puzzled about this peculiar situation. He

thought that circus folk were a different breed to the rest of the population but even they should pay some form of remuneration to their employees. John was still adamant that he received no wages.

'I get by,' he muttered.

'Very well,' And Mr Tringham sat down.

The courtroom was silent as the magistrate decided the fate of John. It had been a most curious case but a man was duty bound to provide for his wife. In truth, the magistrate was sympathetic towards John. The magistrate could only imagine what horrors the young man had witnessed at the Front. No doubt the torn Army coat indicated that the ex-soldier was penniless and lacking any direction in his life. The law was the law, however, and a decision had to be made.

'I have listened to this case carefully,' he said at last. 'Given the somewhat unusual circumstances, I have no hesitation in granting a separation order and maintenance to be set at £1 per week.'

The courtroom buzzed but the magistrate wasn't finished yet.

'However,' he continued, 'I do not believe that the defendant went with a circus for nothing.'

He brought down the gavel and said, 'Case dismissed.'

****

Later that evening the magistrate joined Mr Tringham for a drink at the barrister's bar and the subject returned to the case of John. Over a whisky and cigar smoke, Mr Tringham was able to enlighten his friend and colleague.

'I admit I was somewhat puzzled about the circus as well,' he said. 'However, John's wife filled me in with a few details. It appears that John's uncle is Jerry Baker. You must have heard of him... owner of the Baker Circus... it's quite an attraction around New Zealand... well, all the Baker family are involved with the circus. They're a strong Irish Catholic family. John would have been taken in with them, no questions asked.'

'Well, well, well. Glad we've cleared that one up.' The magistrate leaned back in his chair, blew a waft of cigar smoke upwards and said, 'Least the lad has a home with the circus then. There's just another thing I've been wondering about. Did you believe all that about John and the female circus performer?'

****

This unusual case was reported in the Evening Post June 2nd 1919, page 8. A longer version was written in New Zealand Times 3 June 1919, page 3 under the title, Short Married Life. The actual circumstances are lost in the mists of time and this is a fictional account of the court case. Private John Payne was in all probability suffering from Post-Traumatic Stress Disorder (PSTD), known as shell shock in the First World War. John, as part of the Baker circus family would have been able to stay with them. Interestingly enough, John and his wife, Rheta were reunited later on, married again, and I have written Rheta's story in Going Home.

Private John Payne
NZ Army Canterbury Infantry Regiment
From a family collection

THE CIRCUS

The circus in the nineteenth and early twentieth century provided great entertainment for all the family. It was in North Queensland that the Baker Paragon Circus[21] became well known as the circus that brought in the crowds due in part to the showmanship and enterprise of one William John Baker, known to all as Jerry.

The Bakers' Circus
From the photographic collection held at the State Library of Queensland

How Irishman, Jerry Baker was able to finance such an enterprise is unknown. How he came to the circus world is also something of a mystery. Horses seem to have featured

[21] The Northern Miner 1899 28th February, page 1

prominently in his life and we can only assume that he was an accomplished equestrian and this talent had been nurtured in Ireland. Jerry was the eldest of eight children born to John Baker and Henrietta Thomasina Casey who were married in Kilfinnane, County Limerick on 8th November 1866. Jerry was born on 29th January 1868. As he was the eldest son, it appears that he may have been the first in his family to leave Ireland bound for a new life in Australia.

Ireland at that time was still suffering from the ravages of famine and colonial oppression and the vision of starting a new life in Australia must have been an attractive one. No doubt if Jerry had made the journey first, he would have written home to his parents about the prospect of a better life in Australia. As so many of his fellow countrymen and women were also leaving Ireland bound for America and the British colonies, news that their eldest son was making a name for himself in Australia and North Queensland in particular, must have hastened the Baker family's decision to leave also. Jerry may well have established the circus by the time of the arrival of the rest of his family. Records show that Jerry's mother, Henrietta and some of her children arrived in Brisbane on board the *Jumna* on 18th January 1898 having left London on 3rd November 1897[22] Whether Henrietta's husband, John was on board is something of a mystery as he is not mentioned. Given that John Baker is such a common name, it can be difficult to verify by the records. Whatever happened, the whole Baker clan eventually settled in Queensland.

---

[22] Queensland, Australia, Immigration Records, Passengers and Crew, 1852 - 1899

Photograph by the Author

The first mention of the Baker Circus was reported in *The Northern Miner* on Wednesday 1st March 1899 when it was stated that '*12 Lady and Gentlemen Artistes*' were to appear nightly for a short season. *The Baker Family in their great acrobatic Feats, Wire Walking and Pedestal Contortionists* were top of the billing. Mention was made of *Baby Kathleen in her Great Hurdle Act* and *Miss Cissy Baker, in her Great Hurricane Act and Trapeze Performer*. It is evident from this that the younger members of the Baker family were already gaining recognition as impressive equestrians, acrobats, trapeze artists and contortionists. There is no mention in the report of any animals in the menagerie nor anything of the horses and ponies. The great equestrian acts were certainly the beginning of the success of the circus. The horses and their acrobatic artists must have provided great entertainment for country folk who were often isolated by distance and hindered from travelling due to poor roads and unpredictable weather. Life in North Queensland at that time must have been somewhat remote and the arrival of the circus would have been seen as a welcome relief from the isolation that would have beset the early white settlers to Australia.

Bakers' Paragon Circus, Georgetown, 1905
State Library of Queensland

This photograph taken of the Baker Circus and held in the State Library of Queensland illustrates clearly that there were a lot of horses, ponies and people involved with the circus and the size of the circus tent is impressive, to say the least.

Managing and maintaining a circus troupe with the menagerie and all the equipment needed to put on a show must have been a remarkable feat of organisation as the Baker Circus travelled extensively. Nightly shows and matinees were the order of the day. Although most newspaper articles from the early 1900s place the Baker Circus in North Queensland, it appears that they did venture south.

In March 1906 they were in Inverell, a country town in Northern New South Wales, not far from the Queensland border. Here, as reported in the *Inverell Times*[23] the circus played to a packed house. Notable performer was Miss Kathleen Baker, wire-walker. *The Baker family startles the audience with contortion acts and tumbling of a sort not seen here before.* Various other artistes are mentioned and the tricks done by the horses and the high-jumping dog seem to have captured the reporter's imagination.

The *Morning Bulletin* from Rockhampton in central Queensland lists the number of animals in the menagerie [24] *as small, but good and includes a dozen tigers, a lion, a leopard, monkeys, emus and cassowary's.* This is the first report that mentions the menagerie in detail so it has to be assumed that Jerry Baker was already expanding the circus to include a variety of captive wild animals and birds that were to become so much a feature of the shows. Of particular reference is to the performing black bear which presumably had been acquired after the circus moved back to North Queensland. Again, Miss Kathleen Baker as well as her brothers, Frank and Willie and sister, Babs are praised for their remarkable equestrian and tumbling acts.

By 1910 we find the circus back in North Queensland in Cairns with the Baker family given accolades for their acrobatic and equestrian stunts[25] This time Mr Frank Baker went through some very clever feats of horsemanship, his perfect tumbling, balancing etc., being suggestive of long training and careful practice with his horse while little Miss Baker, better known as 'Babs', astonished the audience with her wonderful contortionist feats, and her tumbling was decidedly clever.

---

[23] Inverell Times, Saturday 3rd March 1906, page 7
[24] Morning Bulletin, Wednesday 28th October 1908, page 4
[25] Cairns Post 23rd December 1910, page 5

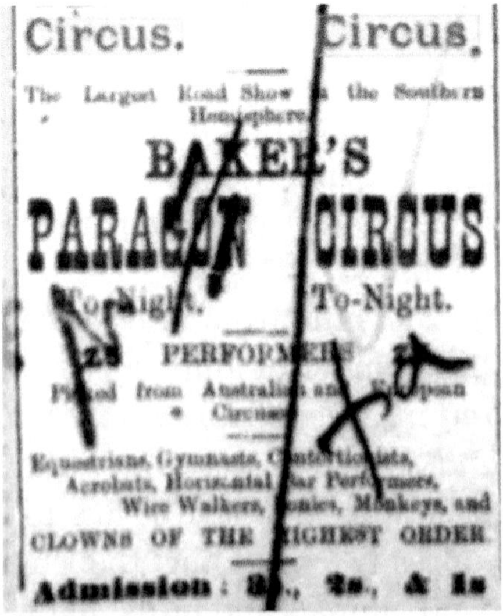

Advertisement from *Mackay Mercury*
2nd April 1903, page 3

It must have been quite an event when the circus arrived in country towns where not much happened. Just the sight and sounds of so many wild animals, never seen before, must have excited and intrigued the locals. The arrival of the circus in town was often accompanied by a band of musicians playing popular tunes of the day. The band would play again when the big tent was erected and the show began. To further bring in the crowds, who by now would be anticipating a great entertainment that evening; acrobatic performers, notably the Baker family members, somersaulted along the dusty main streets whilst the clowns, dressed up in their costumes delighted the children with their antics. The ringmaster cracked his whip. Drum beats and the brass band and the circus had arrived. The Baker circus was so popular that people would come from miles around, the distance between the towns in Australia never being a reason not to travel. The show would be the subject of conversation long after the circus had left. Jerry Baker knew how to bring in a crowd.

In January and February 1907, the Baker Circus combined with the Kirkpatrick Circus to perform in Sydney at Wonderland City where people could take the tram to Bondi. It is believed that over forty thousand people attended the shows.

Newspaper reports[26] and advertisements suggest that by 1909 the Baker Circus was back in familiar territory in North Queensland. No doubt the fame of performing in Sydney was well advertised as noted in this article: *It may be mentioned that this circus is the same which appeared at Wonderland City, Sydney for five months before audiences of from 1,000 to 40,000 nightly*[27].

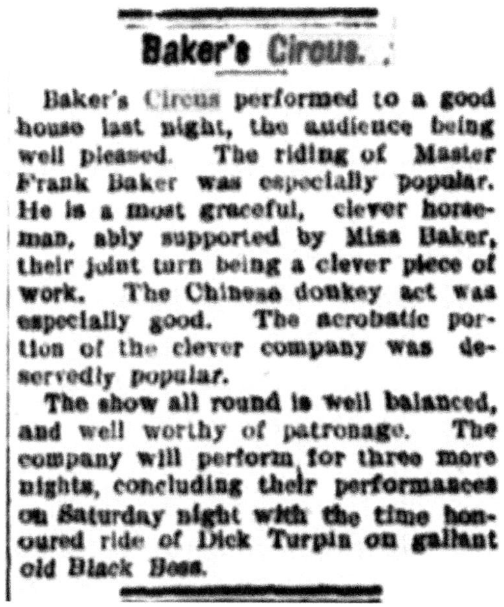

Baker's Circus.

Baker's Circus performed to a good house last night, the audience being well pleased. The riding of Master Frank Baker was especially popular. He is a most graceful, clever horseman, ably supported by Miss Baker, their joint turn being a clever piece of work. The Chinese donkey act was especially good. The acrobatic portion of the clever company was deservedly popular.

The show all round is well balanced, and well worthy of patronage. The company will perform for three more nights, concluding their performances on Saturday night with the time honoured ride of Dick Turpin on gallant old Black Bess.

The Northern Miner, 6th April, 1911, page 5

According to the census records, Jerry's brothers and sisters must have joined the circus at various times. Margaret, Jerry's younger sister listed her occupation as *a circus performer* and

[26] The Daily Telegraph, Sydney Thursday 10th January 1907, page 2 and Monday 4th February, page 6

[27] Daily Mercury, Mackay 28th December 1909, page 4

her place of residence as *the circus tent* in 1903. Alice Adeline, Jerry's youngest sister, who would have been eighteen years old at the time, has her occupation as domestic duties and the same place of residence as her sister, Margaret. The census was taken at Mackay in North Queensland and there is a record of Jerry Baker (William John) being there at the same time. He recorded his occupation as a circus proprietor and his place of residence is *the circus tent* as well. I have not been able to find any other record of other members of the Baker clan on the census list. Presumably, they were there, however, and enjoying their transient way of life.

For reasons we will never know the next momentous decision that occurred in the world of the Baker circus was the move from Australia to New Zealand. We only imagine what sort of logistic undertaking that must have been to transport a menagerie of wild animals, their cages and food, plus all the paraphernalia which goes with a circus, across the Tasman Sea, a sea journey of three or four days.

In 1912 the circus was in Wanganui on the North Island and it was here that Babs (Babarina) Baker diced with death by falling from the high wire[28]. The injury must not have caused too much disruption, however, for the next newspaper article advertises the show coming by rail and road to New Plymouth[29] with the Baker family, ten in number listed as arriving direct from the Dublin Hippodrome which raises some questions for which we will never know the answer. Perhaps, the reporter thought it made for better publicity to mention Dublin rather than Australia given that the bonds between Australia and New Zealand and the Old Country would have been closer than the present day. At New Plymouth, the Baker Circus was joined with the Barton Circus with forty-star artistes and seventy horses,

---

[28] Wanganui Chronicle, 16th November 1912

[29] Taranaki Daily News, 28th November 1912, page 1

ponies, mules and donkeys making it, according to the advertisement, *the most expensive show that has travelled the Dominion.*

When World War One broke out the Bakers donated money to the war effort. They had shown their altruistic side before in North Queensland because on occasion they had donated money raised from the shows to various good causes, notably the Ambulance fund.

Here, in New Zealand, that same generosity applied. The Stratford Evening Post reported that half the takings from the Baker circus that evening were given to the Wounded Soldiers' Fund[30]. The circus played to a packed tent wherever they performed as they moved around both the North and South Islands and it must have provided fascinating entertainment for a war-weary population.

---

[30] Stratford Evening Post 6th May 1916, page 3

From this advertisement in the Stratford Evening Post 25th November 1919, p 1, it can be noted that the Baker circus had plenty of competition and it must have taken a lot of entrepreneurial skill on the part of Jerry to keep attracting the crowds. This would also indicate why various members of the Baker clan often moved between circuses and at times, circuses combined to put on an even bigger show!

By 1918, the First World War was over and the Baker family continued to help their relatives. A war-damaged Private John Payne, William's nephew travelled with the circus for a time. What work he was able to do is unknown but a newspaper article[31] suggests that he was not paid for his services. The magistrate on this occasion appeared to be somewhat sceptical about John Payne and the circus connection as he probably regarded circus folk with a somewhat prejudicial point of view which was possibly the order of the day at that time. However, it seems that the Baker family unit was strong and compassionate enough to care for their own.

The world of the Baker Circus changed dramatically on 12th October 1925. That day, Jerry Baker died of a heart attack while travelling by train between Ohakune and Wairmarino. He was just fifty-six years of age.

Alice, Jerry's widow struggled as best she could. Her son, Frank took over the managerial role from his late father but it seems that the momentum was lost without guidance from Jerry. It is also possible that the circus was losing its popularity amongst the public as new forms of entertainment arrived. No doubt the Great Depression of the early 1920's meant that money wasn't quite so abundant for the average family. With the loss of their lions and disputes about payment to their entertainers, the writing was on the wall. All these factors

[31] New Zealand Times 3rd June, page 3, Magistrate's Court

probably were responsible for the ultimate winding up of the Baker Circus.

A newspaper article from New Zealand [32]reports that Babarina and Lorenz found work in the United States and Canada.

> According to "The Billboard," an American theatrical review, two Australian girls, Barbarina and Lorenz Baker, daughters of William Baker, a circus owner, well-known in Australia, have made good in the "big time" vaudeville circuits in America. Barbarina is a gifted singer and Lorenz a daring trapeze artist. Last month they were due to return to London, merely to have their passports extended, to allow them to fulfil other engagements in the United States.

Their Uncle Michael had already left Australia for America. The census record of 1920 lists him living with his wife, Margaret and their two children in San Mateo, California and his occupation as a lorry driver.

Barbarina must have continued working and travelling for many years. As late as 1941 there is a record of her crossing into the United States accompanied by her mother, Alice. She states that her occupation is an acrobatic dancer and her destination is the Capitol Theatre, Portland, Oregon (Eastern Vaudeville Circuit). Interestingly, she lists a relative, her Uncle Patrick Baker, whose place of residence is Red Hill in Brisbane as her contact name in Australia[33]. Also, at some point, Babarina married Clarence Oswald, an American and the marriage ended in a divorce.

---

[32] Timaru Herald, 26th May 1928, page13

[33] Manifest Blane, Washington 27th April 1941

PASSING BY: Bar[illegible] Baker. Vaudevillian. She has a clever dog act. Uses only pomeranians. Many people claim the fox terrier is best for dog acts but Miss Baker says it isn't the breed of dog that counts for cleverness in doing tricks. It is the way they are trained . . . Helen O'Connell. Band Canary. She popularized that catchy ditty "Six Lessons from Madame Lzsonga." Helen is a turf enthusiast. In wagering she uses what is known as "the Chinese system."

The Boston American, June 22nd 1943
Suffolk County, Massachusetts

It seems that Babarina had many talents and as she aged she entertained in a variety of ways. Whether her brothers and sisters continued to work in the circus world is unknown but in their day the Baker family were certainly a class act and their combined talents would have provided wonderful entertainment bringing pleasure to hundreds, if not thousands of people, the like of which we will never see again.

FULLER FAMILY

ORIGINS OF THE FAMILY NAME FULLER

This surname is derived from an occupation: the fuller, the cloth bleacher or felter.

A NEW LIFE

The *Palmyra* had left London bound for New South Wales on a cold January day and I, for one, was ever fearful of the journey. Us poor Irish were crowded below decks like so many herded cattle, confined together with hardly a space to breathe whilst all the time the constant rocking of the ship, the never-ending creaking of the wooden boards and the disgusting odour all around made me think we had indeed entered Hell. I think I must have cried buckets those first few days. The memory of leaving my poor sad mother behind in Tipperary, her face worn out and aged beyond her years, would stay with me for the rest of my life. No wonder I cried.

I think I first caught sight of Margaret Maher as the *Palmyra* battled the rolling seas around the Bay of Biscay. At least that's where we thought we were, but no one was too sure. We could have been anywhere. The ocean was so vast and the horizon in front of us was just a fleeting line ahead covered in mist. The *Palmyra* ploughed on with white sails flapping through the fierce wind, and me heaving and feeling as if all the saints had deserted me, and there was Margaret next to me, her face against the wind with a smile on her lips.

As I clung, fearful and nauseous to the railing I was certain that any moment my life was about to end and that was when Margaret took hold of my arm. Her presence seemed to steady me for I stopped trembling when I heard her voice.

'Will ye just look at them seas. 'Tis a far cry from Tipperary, ain't it now?'

I didn't reply for at that moment the sway of the ship caused me to slip and fall, rather unladylike, onto the deck.

'Take hold of me hand an' hang on tight. There's another wave comin' at a fair speed.' And Margaret's hand was strong. I managed to stand upright and held her hand as the next wave came and the spray showered my face and hair. Margaret was jubilant.

'There's nothin' to fear, dearie,' she said. 'We're off to a better life, ye see, an' the Holy Mother is lookin' down on us poor Irish sinners an' we'll be safe. Our time's not up yet. Sure, I've just had me eighteenth birthday an' we're young. How old are ye, dearie?'

'Sixteen.'

'There ye are. We've our whole life ahead of us an' mark me words, a new life it will be. Just ye wait an' see. This old ship'll get us there with a few Hail Marys thrown in for good measure,' Margaret laughed.

This time when the spray splashed my face once again, I laughed too. On this wretched sea journey, I had found a friend.

****

Margaret was fearless. She was short and plump with brown eyes and a fierce temper. Everything I was not. I was thin and scrawny and I must say, timid. At least that's what the nuns were forever telling me, *Ye'll never amount to anything, Bridget O'Reilly, yer a scaredy cat.* After a while, I believed them until one day the opportunity arose for me to prove them wrong and that's why I made up my mind to emigrate. Australia sounded like a heaven on earth and I would be away from all the ridicule and the name-calling that had been with me all my life, even if it meant leaving my poor blessed mother to look after my younger siblings. I was one of twelve. I'd be hardly missed. One less mouth to feed.

When I told Margaret I was travelling alone she was full of kindness.

'Sure, Bridget, I'll look after ye,' she said. 'An' there's Philip and John, me brothers, we'll see no harm comes to ye though I don't see much of the boys, pretty much on me own as well. Them's in the single men's quarters an' it's frowned upon if us girlies venture down there. Wouldn't ye just know it?' She giggled.

Margaret and I became inseparable. She seemed to enjoy mothering me and I was happy to have her around me especially when the deckhands called out to us and made lewd remarks.

'Take no heed of them buggers,' Margaret reassured me. 'I'll give 'em what for if they lay a finger on ye.'

I believed her. Margaret was a match for any man. When any of the men tried to provoke her, she responded with the banter that would send them away, and no harm came to her. 'That's some lass, that short Irish one,' one was heard to say after a particularly ribald encounter. 'Pity the man that gets her.' I was inclined to agree.

When the *Palmyra* reached the Cape, we disembarked. By then, I had got somewhat used to the roll of the ship but I was glad to be on dry land again even though my legs felt like jelly and that peculiar sensation made me walk as if I was still on board. Margaret and I giggled like schoolgirls then.

Cape Town was a magical place for us girls. We had become used to the intense cloudless blue sky when the weather was fine. On those days it was fun to be aboard the *Palmyra* as we sailed along the coast of Africa but neither of us had seen anything like the vegetation and the tropical fruits of the Cape. Monkeys and baboons wandered freely around the dusty streets and these animals intrigued me the most. I was somewhat nervous about the black men who stared at us from street corners. They gathered together in small groups and seemed intrigued by the sight of white women. Margaret and I crossed the road to avoid their stares.

'Just keep walking, Bridie. They mean us no harm. Guess they've never seen so many white women before,' reassured Margaret and she took hold of my arm. 'Remember, they're men, whatever the colour. What do you think of that big one with those bulging arm muscles? Fancy him?'

Margaret giggled. I tried not to look towards the men but

kept my eyes away from them. I was unsure of men. My own father had been a brute and my mother and my brothers and sisters suffered from his drunken rages. I was glad I had Margaret beside me. She was so bold. I could imagine that she would stand up to any man, black or white.

When the *Palmyra* sailed from Cape Town and its magnificent mountain so much like a tabletop disappeared into the distance, I must say I was relieved. The memory of the black men stayed with me for days after. One night I dreamed of the man with the muscles that Margaret had teased me about and I awoke shivering and frightened. I wondered what it would be like to be with a man and whether Margaret knew anything of men. She was just eighteen and a Convent girl but she had such a spirit of adventure, I couldn't help but ponder this interesting fact. I was to find out a bit more about Margaret and men as the journey continued towards Sydney Town.

****

It was noticeable even to me that when the *Palmyra* rounded the Cape and sailed into the Indian Ocean she picked up some speed. It was a deckhand who had befriended us and told us all about the roaring forties, those strong westerly winds that occur in the southern latitudes and caused the sailing ships to plough through the seas at such a pace. The deckhand's name was George and he was English. He was also a handsome lad with fair complexion and light brown hair and he liked to flirt with the girls, especially Margaret.

'When we get to Sydney Town, I'm jumpin' ship', I'm tellin' ye now. I'm no sailor. More fool me for thinkin' I'd like the sea. How about ye come with me, Margaret me girl, an' we'll set up home together in Australia an' make lots of babies?'

But Margaret wasn't impressed.

'Why do ye think I would want to settle down with ye? I ain't come all this way to saddle meself with a man and all that brings. We're free spirits, ain't we now, Bridie, an' no need of a man?'

I blushed. Margaret was always so straight-talking that she sometimes embarrassed me, and anyway, I rather liked George and wouldn't have minded settling down with him but he hardly noticed me.

'Well, if ye change yer mind, me girl, I'll be waitin' for ye. She don't know what she's missin', now does she?' George winked at me and I felt my face under the freckles growing redder. He had such devilish blue eyes I barely could look at him when he spoke to me. But then he would turn his attention to Margaret and I could study him more closely. I wished I could flirt like Margaret. Then he might notice me.

I must say I forgot about George when I first caught sight of our new life when we sailed alongside the Great Australian Bight and I glimpsed the never-ending sameness of the desert-like coastline. The seas were choppy there but the sway and roll of the *Palmyra* hardly had any effect on me. Margaret and I giggled as we held onto the railings. Now when the spray hit my face, I almost enjoyed the taste of the salt water. I had indeed got my sea legs and the adventure of my life was about to begin.

The *Palmyra* approached Sydney Town, rolled and swayed through the swell at the Heads and entered the harbour, and I was in awe at the sight before me. Four months ago we had left a cold miserable London January day and here on this May day was sunshine, blue sky, and hope. The sunlight shimmered on the azure blue water like a million sparkling jewels. Gone was the roll of the ship. The *Palmyra* sailed over a calm sea. I had thought Cape Town was magnificent. It was nothing to compare to this beautiful harbour with its inlets and odd-looking trees growing along the shoreline. We passed the small island of Fort Denison where the hardened convicts had been housed to weight anchor beside other similar vessels. Excitement took hold of me. The deck was full of chattering passengers, weary from the long journey but possessed with the same sense of anticipation and wonder as myself. This was to be our new home and our new life. I would stay with Margaret until I could find employment and then, what lay ahead?

****

Margaret and I stood in line as our names were checked off a list by a bored official. Margaret's two brothers had joined us and I felt safe standing with the little family. Margaret and I had decided that we would stay together in Sydney Town until we worked out what to do next. Surely all the saints in heaven would look kindly on two Irish girls, we thought. Then we would each find our way but we would always be friends. When my name appeared on the list, I was certain that it would be ticked off the same as Margaret and her brothers had been and we four would be free to go.

'Bridget O'Reilly,' the man glanced at me and then he wrote something besides my name. 'You're to go to Norfolk Island,' he said. 'They need some domestic help and you look the type to do the job. Stand over there beside those folk. They're to board another vessel bound for Norfolk Island today. Next.'

I couldn't quite take in what he was saying.

'There must be some mistake... ,' I blurted out.

'No mistake. Move along please.'

I could feel tears welling up behind my eyes. How could this be happening to me? I had heard a rumour that there were a small group of emigrants on board the *Palmyra* who had been selected to go to Norfolk Island to assist the Pitcairn Islanders in several handicrafts that these people lacked but I had thought it was just a rumour. I had no idea where Norfolk Island was or what was there. It could have been the moon for all I knew.

'Help me Margaret, what can I do? I don't want to leave you.' I started to cry.

How could my destiny be changed with hardly a murmur because of some bored official ticking names off a list? But Margaret had already been pushed aside by the next family anxious to set foot on this new land and I was left alone.

I saw George scuttling away and merging into the crowd but he didn't notice me. He had his bag over his shoulder and a look of determination on his face and then he disappeared. The last sight I had of Margaret was the back of her stout body. Soon she, too, vanished into the crowd.

'Come along, Miss,' I heard a kind voice. 'They tell us that we're to sail to Norfolk Island today. I hear that it's a beautiful place where there are dozens of pine trees growing and it's nothing like we've left behind in England. Don't fancy another few days at sea but it's a new life, ain't it now, wherever we are?'

****

The 1859 passenger list for the Palmyra includes Margaret Maher and her brothers, John and Philip as being assisted emigrants. I have created a fictional character, Bridget O'Reilly, aged sixteen to befriend Margaret. Young single women did emigrate to Australia at that time, often unaccompanied. The fictional Bridget being sent to Norfolk Island is based on fact as written in the Freeman's Journal Sat 7th May 1859, page 3. Specially selected emigrants were sent to Norfolk Island from Sydney to assist the Pitcairn Islanders in several handicrafts which these emigrants possessed. Norfolk Island had housed the most dangerous convicts and was known for its brutality.

There was an apprentice on board the Palmyra named George Hutchinson who did abscond when the ship arrived in Sydney. State Records Authority of New South Wales: Shipping Master's Office; Passengers Arriving 1855 – 1922; NRS13278 [X98 – 102] reel 406-40 (Transcribed by Margaret Smith, 2005). A reward of £2 was issued for his apprehension. Whether he and Margaret became friends on board is fiction.

Margaret's occupation was listed as a general servant of the Roman Catholic faith.

She married Henry Fuller in Tenterfield, NSW in 1860.

Margaret Maher (née Fuller)
From the family collection of Carolyn Tweedie

'Ye an' yer man are nothin' but cheatin' bloody exploiters of us God fearin', hard workin' folk. An' ye, Mrs bloody Cavanagh, count yeself lucky, I don't come round to that fancy establishment ye call a dressmaker's shop, an' rip all the garments off the shelves for what ye and yer man 'ave done to me poor daughter, Juliet. Why, me lass ain't learned nothin' from ye since she's been with ye, an' me tryin' to do me best for her. Thought she'd make a good dressmaker that's why me Henry found the money so she could be learned the trade. But no. Yer a feckin' lyin' bitch for all yer high and mighty ways an' I'm tellin' anyone what listens, that's what I think of ye.'

Margaret Fuller was panting so hard that she had to pause for breath but not for long. A few seconds later the expletives grew more and more colourful while the object of her anger, Mrs Cavanagh tried to distance herself from her accuser as best she could.

'Really, Mrs Fuller,' she said, 'there is no need to speak like that to me. My husband and I have done our best for both your daughters but you know that the matter of payment for their apprenticeship has not been forthcoming.'

'Me Henry explained all that to yer husband 'bout our circumstances. I tell ye, exploiters ye are of the workin' class. Not a penny in wages has me poor girl received from ye for eighteen weeks hard work but the likes of ye don't think twice about that. Takers, not givers. I tell ye, for all ye fancy clothes, ye are nothin' but a filthy whore.'

'Mrs Fuller. I don't have to listen to this. I would ask you to refrain from this language. I have a good mind to call Sergeant Rafferty.'

'Aye, ye do that. I'm no friend o' the constabulary but the law this time is on me side, ye feckin' bitch.'

The raised voices had drawn a small crowd and it wasn't long before Sergeant Rafferty arrived on the scene. He recognised both women. He had heard the language coming from Margaret Fuller and it was indecent to his way of thinking. No self-respecting woman would speak like that but then, Margaret was Irish with a temper to match, and she had a reputation. Sergeant Rafferty knew that the Inspector was friendly with the Cavanaghs and that had to be taken into consideration. He decided to tread carefully and try to diffuse the situation as best he could but then, he hadn't counted on the wrath of Margaret Fuller.

'Now, ladies,' he said, although he thought 'ladies' was not the most appropriate word to use, given the circumstances, 'what's all this here fuss about? Good day to you, Mrs Cavanagh.'

'Ah!' shrieked Margaret. 'That's ye, Sergeant Rafferty, always on the side of the gentry. I tell ye, this here woman is nothin' but a thievin', cheatin', piece o' shit. How would ye like to not be paid for yer work for eighteen bloody weeks? Well, that's what them Cavanaghs 'ave done to me poor daughter. Not a penny has she got from them, an' she workin' all the God givin' hours, so she has.'

'Mrs Fuller that is a matter between you and Mr and Mrs Cavanagh. There is no need to use such language in a public place. The law forbids it, you know, and I must say, it's not very becoming for a woman to speak like that.'

'Feck ye, Sergeant Rafferty. I'll speak how I like. I always say what I mean and I tells the truth in what I say. And the fact remains, me daughter has not been paid for her work by this here woman. Get that, everyone? Bloody disgrace it is.'

Margaret turned to the small group of about ten men and women who had gathered, with some amusement it has to be said, to witness the altercation. One of the women cupped her hands around the ears of her small boy. Another woman shielded her daughter's eyes as if the sight of the angry and diminutive Margaret was just too much for her child to witness.

'Please, Mrs Fuller. Mind your language or I'll have to take action.'

'Is that a threat, Sergeant? I don't much take heed of any threats 'specially when I have right on my side. And this time, I have. By all that's holy and on me mother's grave, I'll take no intimidation from the constabulary.'

'Mrs Fuller. This is a caution, not a threat.'

'Call it what ye may. To me mind, it's a threat an' I'll speak how I like to this bloody woman. I've never been one for takin' things lyin' down.'

Hearing these words, one of the men in the crowd gave a cheer.

'That's tellin' you, Rafferty,' another was heard to mumble.

Sergeant Rafferty was nervous. The tide of public opinion seemed to have turned in Margaret Fuller's direction, despite her use of profane language. Threatening Mrs Cavanagh had also become an issue and, although no blows had been struck, the atmosphere was tense. It was his duty to maintain law and order and he decided he needed to act quickly to diffuse the situation. He positioned himself between the two women and blew his whistle for reinforcements. His action provoked more mumblings from the small crowd. Seeing the crowd and the policeman more men and women were joining the group. The sergeant calculated that there were now about fifteen or sixteen people, curious bystanders but it would just take a remark from either woman to cause an explosion.

'Mrs Fuller,' the sergeant took hold of Margaret's right arm. 'I am warning you this time, leave this place and go about your business. If you continue, I will have to charge you with a public order offence.'

Margaret, by now, was incensed and her keen observation gauged that the crowd was on her side and if the sergeant continued to try his strong-arm tactics, there could be a riot.

'Take yer filthy hands off me.' She wrestled her arm from the sergeant's grasp which took some doing but she had caught him unawares. A small boy about ten, no doubt encouraged by his father, kicked some pebbles in the direction of the sergeant. One of the pebbles caught the sergeant on his shin and he let out a curse.

'Ah,' cried Margaret, 'whose usin' bad language now?'

And the assembled onlookers started to clap. A woman, about forty years of age, yelled, 'You tell him, Margaret. Ain't no way to handle a woman, usin' brute force like that. You coppers are all the same.'

This was too much for Sergeant Rafferty. By now, he was red in the face, humiliated, and angry.

'This is an order,' he barked. 'Disperse now, all of youse, or you'll be spendin' the rest of the day in the gaol.' And he blew his whistle again.

Seeing that the sergeant meant business, the crowd shuffled away but not before another pebble was thrown towards the policeman. This pebble missed its target and rolled into the gutter.

'Mrs Fuller. Mrs Cavanagh. I will see you both before the magistrate to clear this unfortunate matter up, once and for all. Now, both of youse, go about your business and I'll do the same.'

This remark was met with no enthusiasm whatsoever. The two women glared at each other but they did go their separate ways, in the opposite direction.

****

Nine days later Mrs Fuller and Mrs Cavanagh faced each other once again. The argument between the two women had caused a good deal of interest in the small town. Various versions were banded about and the courthouse was full. The magistrate considered that the case was a small matter indeed as no blows had been struck but he was duty bound to listen to the evidence. Mr Proctor stood up for the defence and stated that Mr Fuller had deemed it unnecessary to attend the court. His wife was only expressing an opinion and had meant no harm to Mrs Cavanagh.

'In this case, your Honour,' intoned Mr Proctor, 'Mrs Cavanagh should have herself handed my client over to the police, if there had been sufficient merit to do so.'

Mr Blythe, for the police interjected, 'Your Honour, it is my considered opinion that Sergeant Rafferty was indeed justified in laying the information.'

Mr Blythe quoted Section Five of the Public Order Act. Mr Proctor countered with Section Six. Not to be outdone, Mr Blythe returned to Section Five. It looked as if it was a contest of wills between the two lawyers. Neither appeared to want to concede defeat but when Mrs Cavanagh gave evidence to the fact that the strong language had caused her unnecessary pain and the public humiliation in front of so many witnesses, it appeared to the magistrate that there was a strong case for the police.

'Mr Proctor, you may cross-examine the witness.'

The tide seemed to turn when Mr Proctor gave a powerful speech after he called another witness to the stand. This was the same woman who had cheered Margaret on.

'Your Honour,' intoned Mr Proctor, 'this has been a case of misdirection. My client did not at any time physically threaten Mrs Cavanagh. The language that was used was inappropriate, I grant you that, but it is my considered opinion that Mrs Fuller had some justification for tackling Mrs Cavanagh. Mrs Fuller's daughter has not been paid for eighteen weeks of work and the family were in dire straits because of the lack of income coming into the household. Mr Fuller is a miller and he has not been employed for many weeks due to the drought and the lack of enough water to power the mill. Mrs Fuller was distraught at the prospect of the family going hungry and it appears that when she saw Mrs Cavanagh in the street, she allowed her frustrations about the matter to explode. The language used was regrettable but understandable. Sergeant Rafferty is to be commended for not allowing the situation to escalate.'

The magistrate listened carefully to both sides of the argument.

'It is the opinion of the bench,' he said after about ten minutes deliberation, 'that the objections voiced by Mr Proctor are sufficient to dismiss the case. Court adjoined.'

****

'Thank ye indeed, Mr Proctor, sir, for all ye did for me in clearin' me good name. Now, there's just one last thing I need to do afore this sorry mess is sorted out. I want to say one last word to Mrs Cavanagh.'

'Would that be wise, Mrs Fuller?'

'Aye. Needs to be done.'

Mrs Cavanagh had hurried away from the courthouse after the case had been dismissed. She had no wish to be seen anywhere near Mrs Fuller but Margaret had other ideas. Margaret, being short and stout, was panting by the time she caught up with Mrs Cavanagh. The two women faced each other like two angry lionesses.

'I have somethin' to say to ye, Mrs Cavanagh... '

Mrs Cavanagh drew herself up to her full height. Her nostrils appeared to inflate and she took a deep breath.

'We have nothing to say to each other, Mrs Fuller.'

'Oh aye, that we do. Just like ye to know by all that's holy... that ye are still a feckin' bitch... '

And with that, Margaret turned around and strode off in the opposite direction. A passer-by was certain that he heard her mumble that Mary and Joseph and all the saints in heaven had looked down on her today, but we will never know.

****

I have included this story in the collection as an example of the social morals which were prevalent at the time. According to police reports Margaret Fuller did confront Mrs Cavanagh and used indecent language towards her. The Armidale Express and New England General Advertiser dated Friday 31 January 1879 p.6 reported in great detail that the confrontation took place. The objections raised by Margaret Fuller's lawyer, Mr Proctor, were sufficient to warrant dismissing the case. Whether Margaret confronted Mrs Cavanagh after the court case is unknown but given Margaret's feisty character, it is more than possible that she did so.

THE MILLER'S TALE

With Apologies to Chaucer

It was well-known that Henry was a man who liked to talk a lot. He also liked to drink a lot and the local hostelry was a second home to him. The more he talked, the drunker he became until not one of his fellow drinkers knew what he was on about and none of them, often as drunk as he, even cared. Then the publican nine times out of ten would tell Henry to leave and to return when he was sober, which was usually the very next night.

Unfortunately for his wife, Margaret, all this was such a regular occurrence that in her mind the drinking and the talking were synonymous. Henry was forever dreaming up new plans which would turn him into a rich man so that he and Margaret and their six children would be able to retire and live off the earnings. Margaret, an Irishwoman, was both straight-talking and fierce. She was the power in her household and woe betide anyone who crossed her. Even Henry would cease his constant chattering whenever Margaret's temper was up.

Although Henry could neither read nor write, he did not see this as a disadvantage, even though his wife, Margaret was literate and could outsmart him at every opportunity, he was certain that he could make his way in the world come what may, and despite his wife's reading and writing ability. After all, most times he was able to find enough work to keep a roof over the families' heads, and reading and writing wasn't much use when you were wielding a pickaxe on a dusty road. However, it was Margaret who had the best ideas and Henry, deep down, knew that. He wasn't too fond of the labouring side of things and it was Margaret who first suggested that he find work at the flour mill for after all wasn't he a miller and had worked in England at that trade?. Being a miller sounded better than mere labourer, she said. And Henry agreed.

Henry rather liked being a miller. There was something altogether satisfying seeing grains of wheat ground between the giant granite wheels, to emerge into flour. Being a miller was certainly easier than labouring under the hot Australian sun. The camaraderie between the workers at the mill was good and Henry very soon became liked for his banter, even though his wild schemes were looked upon as just that, and unlikely to amount to anything. Henry was a bit of a dreamer after all.

When he returned home after a day's work at the mill he was covered in flour and full of talk.

'Will ye just quit yer gabbin', man,' Margaret would say to him but it made no earthly difference.

'I like the mill, Margaret,' Henry said to her one day, 'but I've plans afoot in me head. Don't want to be a miller all me life.'

'It's a job, Henry.'

'Aye. But I tell ye I didn't come all this way from Sussex, stuck for weeks an' weeks aboard that wretched vessel, *Irene*, to spend the rest of me life here, labourin' away an' me lungs full o' the dust from the mill. No, I have plans, ye see. I want a better life. That's what they said to us when we left Liverpool. Milk an' honey, Australia was, they said. Milk an' honey.'

Henry shook his head. The vision of what he had thought would be his life and what it had turned out to be was different.

'I could 'ave stayed in England.' He was now in full flow. 'Labourin' away, just the same as I'm doin' here. Aye, bein' a miller is better than labourin', I'll grant ye that, Margaret, but I 'ave plans, ye just wait an' see.'

'Aye, I'll wait an' see, Henry Fuller. I'll wait an' see but I won't hold my breath.'

His wife's scepticism meant nothing to Henry. It was doubtful if he ever took much notice and the only time he noticed was when Margaret raised her voice above his. Then he would cease talking and wait until the fury had passed, to resume again a few minutes later. Henry had plans, you see.

They would move from Armidale that would be the first step, for Henry had decided that another flour mill in another town would increase the family fortunes. They would cross the border into Queensland and make their fortune there. Whether Margaret agreed was doubtful for she had been witness to many of Henry's fanciful schemes. This latest venture seemed just as foolhardy as the one before. Margaret was right. The new location at Warwick proved to be as she had thought. Henry soon tired of the mill. The family moved once more and back to the flour mills in northern New South Wales but this time the mill owner wasn't quite so keen to employ Henry.

'If I can't get work in the mill,' Henry informed Margaret, 'best I try me hand at the carpentry. I've enough to go on with, been doin' odd carpentry jobs all me life. I'll start me own business. You can do the writin' and the readin' an' we'll make ourselves a fortune, mark my words. People are always lookin' for someone to make things out o' wood an' fix carts and the like.'

'How do ye propose to go about it, then?' retorted the ever-practical Margaret.

'Just you wait and see, wife o' mine. I 'ave meself an 'ammer, a saw an' me chisels. What more does a carpenter want? All I need is a good word here an' there an' the name o' Henry Fuller will be heard far an' wide as the best carpenter in the whole of New South Wales.'

'Well, ye wait and see, Henry Fuller. Ye didn't last long at the mill.'

'Truth be told, I was findin' all that fine flour dust was gettin' into me lungs so 'twas time to move on. A miller's life was not for me. I'm on the right track with the carpentry. Now, I'm off to 'ave a drink an' put the word out that any carpentry work to be done, I'm yer man.'

With that Henry put on his old tweed jacket and cap and

strode out the door. He had plans, you see.

The very next day Henry, despite his sore head from the night's visit to the hostelry which had ended somewhat unceremoniously when the publican had ushered the inebriated ex-miller to the door and given him a warning, was up and about at an earlier time than was usual much to the surprise of Margaret and their now almost grown up six children.

'I met a fella last night who is in need of some carpentry work. There's a dray to be fixed up, he says. Out Uralla way. I'll be off, then, to see what needs to be done.'

'How will ye get there? It's twenty miles or so from here.'

'It's this side of Uralla an' I'll get a lift along the way, me old darlin'. People know me. Never let it be said that Henry Fuller couldn't find work or get a lift when needed. This joker and me agreed to a price an' he'll pay me when the works done.'

'Well, we'll wait and see,' was the reply.

When Henry arrived at the farm where the dray was to be fixed it was well past midday and the farmer wasn't too pleased.

'Thought you said you'd be here early morning,' he grumbled.

'Now, my good sir,' replied the ever loquacious Henry. 'I'll 'ave yer dray fixed up in no time at all. And would I be troublin' yer good lady for a drink for I'm sure parched with the thirst after walkin' all this way? It sure is a hot day to be out an' about an' them bloody flies are gettin' into me eyes. Sure, I've never seen so many of the little blighters hangin' around me face. If I could just 'ave a drink first. Ye know, I've heard if ye take a glass of beer, them flies just disappear. Don't like the smell of the liquor. Did you know that? Beer and flies don't mix, 'cept if one of them buggers land in yer glass.'

Henry hardly paused for breath before he was on to the next subject.

'Now this here dray. You'll need some amount of work to be done on it. There might be a bit more costs involved than I first thought. I know we discussed a price last night and shook hands on it but you didn't tell me the shaft needed fixin' as well as the bottom of the dray. The sides look in a sorry state as well.'

Henry took some tobacco from a leather pouch on his belt and lit his pipe.

'See here,' he said and pointed to a joint along the side of the dray. 'This here bit's rotted right away. Will need to be replaced. Some of the holes along the side I could fix with glue and sawdust once it's cleaned out. It's about a week's work all told. Can't be done in a day. No, sir, no way.'

He shook his head. By this time the farmer was beginning to lose patience with the talkative Henry.

'I suppose you're saying a week but it's probably going to be more like two.'

'Now, sir. If I says a week, a week it'll be. I'll 'ave yer dray fixed up like new but I need some cash aforehand to get me started. Need to get some wood and glue. An' I sure am parched. My throat's as rough as the bottom of a cocky's cage. Can I trouble ye for a beer afore I set off to get the materials?'

The farmer, who was also fond of a drink, nodded his head.

'Come over to the farmhouse an' meet the missus,' he said.

The farm kitchen was dark after the bright sunshine outside and Henry had difficulty focusing on the farmer's wife. He blinked and took off his cap.

'This here's Henry Fuller,' the farmer said to his wife. 'He's here to fix the old dray I've been on about. He'd like a beer to be gettin' on with and I'll take one too. Can't have ye drinkin' alone, can we, Henry?'

'No sir. It's awfully good of ye. Glad to make your acquaintance,' Henry said to the wife. 'It sure is a hot one out there today. I was sayin' to yer man how the flies followed me from Armidale. Ye know I walked most of the way an' it bein' so bloody hot, pardon my French, Missus, but a man gets up a thirst in this here heat.'

All this time, the farmer's wife stared at Henry as he continued to gabble on. After a few moments, she poured both men a beer and set the glasses down on the pine kitchen table.

'Did you say your name was Henry Fuller?' she asked when the men had finished drinking. She poured them both another glass of the amber liquid.

'I am indeed,' answered Henry, somewhat surprised.

'I know your wife, Margaret.'

Oh dear, thought Henry.

'You say you are a carpenter and can fix our dray.'

'That I can, Madam. That I can. I met your husband last night an' we got to talkin' an' he mentioned that he needed a good carpenter an' we agreed, I'm your man. I've done a lot of carpentry in me life, I says to him, an' that's when we decided I should fix the dray. Shook hands on it. It'll be like new when I'm finished with it, mark me words.'

'Oh!'

For a moment Henry was silent which was unusual. He didn't like the sound of the ominous 'Oh'.

The farmer's wife fixed him with such a gaze that it reminded him of Margaret when his wife was in one of her moods.

'Henry Fuller. Now I thought you was a miller at the flour mill. At least that's what Margaret told me. She was right proud of you and said you were the best miller around. Said nothin' about you being a carpenter.'

'I am a miller as well,' replied the ever-resourceful Henry, 'an' I like the job. Bein' a miller is something to be proud of right enough. But,' he hesitated, 'you know, I can turn me hand to most things an' I'm a carpenter too. Have fixed up a few things at the mill with me hammer and chisel. Margaret must 'ave forgot to mention this fact when you and she was talkin'. She does forget things sometimes. But just you wait an' see. I 'ave plans, you know. Did Margaret tell ye anything of me plans?'

****

Although this story is fiction it is based on fact. Henry Fuller was a miller and a carpenter. His business enterprise as a carpenter ended up in the court as reported in The Armidale Express and New England General Advertiser Friday 16th May 1879, page 5. He appeared in the Uralla Police Court on Monday 19th May 1879 and he was declared Insolvent. His Liabilities were £123 and his assets £10.

A QUESTION OF LEGALITY

It had been a simple matter at first. Juliet and Ann would be taught to be dressmakers and, if all went well, the two sisters would find work later on for people always needed a dressmaker. With four daughters in the family, what else could be done with them until they could find suitable husbands? Margaret and Rachael might join their older sisters in due course. By then, Juliet and Ann hopefully would have found the suitable husbands and Mr Cavanagh would be able to employ the other two Fuller girls.

Mr Cavanagh's dressmaking business was the place to go to for all this training for he and his wife had built up a good reputation for the finest work around. Not only would Juliet and Ann be taught the trade but they would learn how to mend garments, make hats and how to use the sewing machine. All that was needed was to approach Mr Cavanagh with the proposal and sign some agreement or other between both parties. Problems arose almost as soon as the decision was made.

First and foremost, Mr Cavanagh agreed to employ both the Fuller girls once their father had paid twenty pounds for the girls to be apprenticed and taught the trade of dressmaking. For the work the girls would do they would be paid a wage of eight shillings a week but nothing could be done until the fee of twenty pounds was paid.

'Well, now, Mr Cavanagh,' announced Henry Fuller and he filled his pipe with tobacco and lit it, blowing some of the smoke in Mr Cavanagh's direction which caused Mr Cavanagh to cough slightly and clear his throat. 'Well, Mr Cavanagh,' continued Henry, 'we have a slight problem here, I 'ave to say at the outset that my two eldest daughters are hardworkin' and honest lassies an' they will be an asset to your business, of that I'm certain.

Mrs Fuller and meself 'ave brought them up to be honourable an' they will do their best, I'm sure given the wonderful opportunity that you and your good lady are about to bestow on them. But it has to be said that it is with some difficulty that I would be able to pay the twenty pounds needed for both my two girls at the present moment in time. Could we perhaps come to some agreement about the initial payment?'

Henry, who was known far and wide for his garrulous nature, paused and fixed Mr Cavanagh with such an eye that slightly unnerved the usual astute businessman.

'I see,' Mr Cavanagh replied. 'What are you suggesting, Mr Fuller? A legal agreement is a legal agreement and it is the law that an apprenticeship must be paid before employment can be made. I would be loath to employ your two girls without payment in advance.'

'I understand what ye are sayin', sir, an' this is my proposal which I hope will meet with your approval. Times are hard, ye see. Times are hard. Why, the work at the mill is not all that secure for meself given the drought has caused the waterwheels not to produce as much water to power the mill. Combined with all that, the farmers haven't been able to produce the full quota of wheat this year to keep things goin'. As I say, I 'ave to turn me hand to the carpentry to make ends meet and me good wife has plans to open a shop on Beardy Street. It is to be hoped that our combined enterprise will bring in the necessaries. We have many expenses, you know, an' us doin' our best to keep a roof over the families' heads so when I heard on the grapevine that you and Mrs Cavanagh were lookin' for some honest lassies to be apprenticed to the dressmaking trade, I says to me wife, "Margaret, Juliet and Ann would do well to become dressmakers and milliners. Then we'll be able to make some money what with their wages comin' in on a regular basis." And Margaret agreed that it would be the best course of action to approach yer good self but I 'ave to say, no one informed me that we would need to pay ye such a large amount before all this could begin. I might be able, however, to scrape enough cash together to pay five pounds for Ann but I can't see my way clear to pay another fifteen at this present time. Times are hard, Mr Cavanagh. Times are hard.'

'It is the law, Mr Fuller.'

'I agree. The law is the law an' must be obeyed.' This was said with some degree of scepticism but Mr Cavanagh decided to overlook the remark.

'What do you propose then, Mr Fuller?'

'Ah, now we are beginning to understand each other an' I promise you that ye 'ave made the right decision to employ me two girls... '

'Get to the point, Mr Fuller. I'm a busy man.'

'I know ye are, sir, an' this here is my proposal which I hope will meet with your approval. I will pay ye five pounds firstly, once we sign the agreement, an' I promise ye I'll pay the rest when I can get some work for meself. As I said, the mill isn't payin' much these days but once we get the rains again, I'll be back there, workin' all the hours God gave me. There's another thing to be said about all this. I 'ave to tell ye, Mr Cavanagh, that Mrs Fuller will need to sign on my behalf as I 'ave hurt me hand somethin' bad at the mill an' I'm not able to write but I trust this would meet with the approval of all concerned an' it would then be a legal matter between us an' me two girls can start work straight away.'

'It is highly irregular, Mr Fuller. Apprenticeships require full payment. As for your wife signing for you, this is a matter between gentlemen. Women normally aren't involved in such matters.'

'I understand, Mr Cavanagh, but to the matter of my wife signing for me, I could put a cross beside her signature to note that I agree. My poor hand cannot write anything more than a cross, I'm sorry to say. As for payment, I would like to do the honourable thing. I ’ave some fowls I am willin’ to give ye as a token of my sincerity in this matter. And this might help ye until I can get the rest of the money together.’

‘How many fowls, Mr Fuller?’

‘I can spare about a dozen. Good layers they are, too, an’ good for the pot.’

By now Mr Cavanagh was in somewhat of a dilemma. His business required some good hardworking girls. The Cavanaghs were highly respected in the community and more and more people were coming to the dressmaking shop. As the orders increased he sometimes had to turn customers away. The lead time for completing orders was becoming something of a nightmare. He decided, somewhat reluctantly, to agree to Henry’s proposal. At least, the girls could be set to work immediately to clear the backlog of work.

Henry continued to smoke his pipe while Mr Cavanagh thought over the matter. After a few more minutes contemplating his next move, Mr Cavanagh made his decision. He held out his hand.

‘Very well, Mr Fuller,’ he said, ‘I’ll see that the documents are drawn up and once they are signed by yourself and Mrs Fuller, we will bring your two daughters into work. The sooner they get started, the better for all concerned.’

‘You won’t regret this, Mr Cavanagh. My girls won’t let ye down. Good lassies they are, an’ then there’s Margaret and Rachael to be considered as well. Both are good needlewomen like their elder sisters. When the time comes, ye might like to consider them as apprentices to the trade?’

Mr Cavanagh did not reply. He thought it best to see how the two elder Fuller girls shaped up before engaging any more potential recruits.

‘I will take your fowls, too, Mr Fuller. We do need some more poultry. The fox got into the coop the other day and left a few corpses around. A dozen more would come in handy. And…’

The two men stared at each other. Henry was pleased how the meeting had gone but he was anxious to depart. He had a terrible thirst on him that needed to be satisfied.

'And,' Mr Cavanagh continued, 'I expect the remaining fifteen pounds to be paid as promptly as you can.'

'Rest assured, Mr Cavanagh, 'when the mill starts working again, you will 'ave your money.'

Henry was already at the door as he spoke the words.

****

Juliet and Ann proved to be good needlewomen and it all looked as though everything would work out to the mutual benefit of all concerned. Mrs Cavanagh was a strict disciplinarian and expected the girls to meet her high standards. Juliet and Ann did not disappoint. At least, for the first few months. Then, things began to change.

'When can we expect your father to be bringing in payment for your apprenticeship, Miss Fuller? It is long overdue,' asked Mr Cavanagh to Juliet one day at the end of their work.

'I do not know, Mr Cavanagh,' was the reply. 'He has been out of work these past few weeks and we are in sore circumstances.'

'I expect you will inform him of my concern, Miss Fuller. I would like the matter settled as agreed. Also, your father promised to gift me a dozen fowl as a gesture of goodwill between us but to date, I have not seen so much as a feather.'

'I know nothing of the fowls, sir.'

'Be that as it may, but I trust you will inform your father of my concern about payment for you and your sister's apprenticeship. I cannot afford to train you both in the fine art of dressmaking if the monies are not paid in advance. That is the law and that was our agreement.'

'I will tell him, Mr Cavanagh,' answered Juliet and she lowered her eyes to avoid the gaze of her employer. Her father had not been seen for the last few days and when he did return, as he always did, she doubted if the matter of paying Mr Cavanagh would be of any interest to him.

****

It was when Juliet started work on the sewing machine that the trouble started. As she attempted to sew a straight line along a piece of fine linen, her foot slipped off the treadle and the needle came down on her finger. In the panic, she twisted her foot. Mortified at seeing her blood staining the piece of fabric that Mrs Cavanagh had already told her was worth more than her wages, Juliet tried to hide both the fabric and the bloodied finger but the sharp eye of her employer saw all of this.

'You foolish girl,' she admonished the distraught Juliet. 'Now you will have to have that finger seen too or you will be wasting more of the material. Whatever, were you thinking?'

'I'm sorry, Mrs Cavanagh. My foot slipped.'

'You weren't thinking of what you were doing. Your head away in the clouds, not concentrating on your work as usual. Now, because of your foolishness, you've ruined the garment.'

Juliet started to cry. Some of her tears dripped down onto the offending piece of linen and spread the blood even further.

'You will need to get the finger seen to by the Chinese doctor,' Mrs Cavanagh said abruptly. 'Mr Cavanagh will not be pleased.'

Juliet, holding a cloth over her bloodied finger, hobbled to the door, not looking back to see what her sister was doing or whether Mr Cavanagh was anywhere to be seen. With a bit of luck, the Chinese doctor might say she couldn't work for a few weeks and she would be spared Mrs Cavanagh's wrath. She wondered who would pay the Chinese doctor to fix her finger. It certainly wouldn't be her father. The Cavanaghs would have to settle the bill. With that thought, her finger didn't throb quite as much.

****

The weeks passed by and no payment was made from Henry to

Mr Cavanagh for Juliet's apprenticeship. Now Henry found himself in somewhat of a predicament. At first, he had thought that Juliet and Ann would be able to supplement the income coming into the household but that had proved to be unlikely, given the acrimony that now existed between the Fullers and the Cavanaghs.

'I am off to see Cavanagh,' he told his wife. 'This state of affairs cannot go on. Juliet hasn't been paid for eighteen weeks. I will take the girls away. We'll settle the matter in court if needs be.'

'Them Cavanaghs have a lot to answer for, Henry,' replied Margaret. 'Why, Juliet's finger hasn't healed up proper even now. Aye, ye go an' 'ave it out with him. An' the other matter, 'bout the fowls. Thought the agreement was that Cavanagh paid for them 'afore delivery? No payment for them either an' ye told me that was what was agreed between the two of ye. Thievin' beggars, the lot o' them.'

This was all the encouragement Henry needed although he had neglected to tell his wife that he said he would give the fowls to Cavanagh. Henry had thought that the gift might placate Cavanagh and the matter of the apprenticeship money might somehow be forgotten. He set off the very next day to tackle Mr Cavanagh.

When Henry arrived at the dressmaker's shop, he was surprised to find that Juliet wasn't working at the sewing machine but had been taken on as a cook.

'This isn't right, Mr Cavanagh. My girl was to be learned the trade of dressmaker, not a cook.'

Both Mr and Mrs Cavanagh faced Henry.

'See here, Mr Fuller,' said Mr Cavanagh, 'your girl injured herself and we paid the bill from the Chinese doctor to fix her injury. Paid ten shillings out of my pocket, so I did.'

'That was generous of ye to be sure, Mr Cavanagh, but the injury occurred whilst she was workin' at your place of employment, and the law would say that it was your duty to do so.'

'Be that as it may, the money for the doctor has been paid. However, I am still awaiting the fifteen pounds owed for your two daughter's apprenticeship. As we discussed, and you agreed, we had a new agreement drawn up, which you signed with an "X" that allowed you more time to settle. That was months ago now.'

Henry chose to ignore this remark and decided to try a new tactic as he had not a penny of the fifteen pounds owed.

'Where is Juliet's wages? Eighteen weeks it is now an' not a penny 'ave I seen.'

'Mr Fuller, Mrs Cavanagh and myself have been more than generous with goods given to your girls. Our patience is wearing thin with all this.'

'Mine, too, Mr Cavanagh. Ye leave me no other course of action but to take me girls away from here. I will see ye in court, Mr Cavanagh.'

Henry drew himself up to his full height which wasn't very high, he being just five foot eight inches from head to toe. Mr Cavanagh was taller and more threatening but Henry felt he had right on his side. There was the matter of lost wages and the much-disputed fowls. The court would surely settle in his favour. With a bit of luck, Cavanagh would have to pay the court costs and Henry might be in pocket to the tune of twenty pounds. Henry was the eternal optimist.

****

The small court was buzzing with people interested to see what the magistrate would make of the Fuller case against the Cavanaghs. Mr Proctor had decided to take on the case for the Fullers. He was keen to pit his wits against Mr Mitchell who appeared for the defendant. Mr Cavanagh was respected in the district but in Mr Proctor's mind, Juliet Fuller had a good chance of winning. It was a trumpery case, he decided and would require some amount of persuasion to convince the magistrate that Juliet's circumstances were such that she should have been paid for her work.

'Your Honour,' Mr Proctor cleared his throat, 'my client was apprenticed to Mr Cavanagh to learn the fine art of dressmaking and her father was duty bound to pay the twenty pounds for his daughters, Juliet and Ann. Mr Fuller, in good faith has paid five pounds but because of his strained circumstances he deferred payment for remainder. This deferment was agreed by both parties and an agreement was signed by both parties to this effect. However, wages set at eight shillings per week have not been paid to Juliet and this is for eighteen weeks of work. This is a clear misdirection and in my mind, an exploitation by Mr Cavanagh towards my client.'

'Objection', interjected Mr Mitchell. 'The full facts of this case have not been given by my learned colleague.'

'Objection overruled,' replied the magistrate. 'Continue, Mr Proctor, but please keep to the facts.'

'Thank you, Your Honour. Whilst my client was employed by Mr Cavanagh she performed some other duties, not connected to the dressmaking trade because a servant had left the employment of Mr and Mrs Cavanagh. This, given the circumstances, seemed highly irregular.'

Mr Proctor was enjoying himself. He was certain that he would win the case and Mr Mitchell would stand him a drink in the bar afterwards. The two men had something of a bet between themselves as to who would win this particular case.

'Another unfortunate incident occurred whereby my client injured her finger and sustained an injury to her foot whilst working on the sewing machine. This meant that she was unable to perform any work connected to her dressmaking apprenticeship. I rest my case.'

When Mr Mitchell stood up to speak the courtroom came alive. Known for his flamboyant nature, it was always entertaining to watch him cross-examine the witnesses who often became flustered and walked straight into the verbal trap that the lawyer set. This time, Mr Mitchell did not disappoint and Juliet, standing in the witness box became increasingly confused, but it was when her father was questioned about the remaining money which was yet to be paid to the Cavanaghs for her apprenticeship, and the fact that Henry had taken his daughters away from their employment after signing the apprenticeship agreement, meant that the contract between them was broken. At this point, Mr Mitchell tasted blood. He became more and more theatrical.

'My client,' boomed Mr Mitchell, and he waved his hand in the air, 'in the goodness of his heart and at his own expense paid the defendant in goods alone. It has to be pointed out that he also kept her in his employment even though she was unable to continue with the dressmaking work because of her injury. Her father was somewhat neglectful in all his dealings with my client. His tardiness in refusing to pay the rest of the monies owed for his two daughters' apprenticeship is of the most concern. Indeed, as the court has heard Mr Fuller has to date, only paid five pounds out of the twenty pounds agreed. My client's generosity in not pursuing this matter to the full would compensate for any wages not paid.'

'I object, Your Honour,' interjected Mr Proctor, somewhat flustered, 'Mr Fuller had no recourse but to remove both his daughters from the Cavanagh establishment given that wages were not paid. My client's father has already explained that he was unable to pay the full amount because of the lack of work at the flour mill.'

This was a long case and much evidence was given. The magistrate, however, had met Mr and Mrs Cavanagh on numerous social occasions. The Fullers were by reputation and by gossip a well-known family in the small town, and this was something to be considered but the magistrate would not allow that to colour his judgement. All the facts had to be argued by both parties before a decision could be made. He was a fair-minded man but he was also hungry. It was way past lunchtime and he wanted the case rounded up as soon as possible.

'I have considered the case in question and I rule in favour of the defendant,' and he brought the gavel down hard onto the bench.

****

'This is not the end of it,' announced Henry to his wife and Juliet a few days later. 'We'll take Cavanagh to court again. He's not going to get away with it next time. I will see Mr Proctor tomorrow.'

'Ye do that, Henry. 'Bout time them Cavanaghs had to pay up. Ye tell him 'bout the fowls too, won't ye?' Henry had Margaret's blessing and he was more than ready for the fight. He had rather enjoyed the previous courtroom drama and he was sure that this time, he had right on his side.

But when Henry visited Mr Proctor, the lawyer was sympathetic but not all that enthusiastic about another round against Mr Mitchell. Although he and Mitchell were arch-rivals in the court room, socially they were friends and visited each other's homes on occasion. This time Mr Proctor told Henry he would take on the case again but he would instruct Mr O'Connor for the defence.

'An able man, Mr O'Connor,' reassured Mr Proctor, 'he'll do the best for you, you have my word.'

'I 'ave every faith in yer judgement in this matter, Mr Proctor, sir. If ye say that Mr O'Connor will win the case for me, I'll 'ave no objection to him standin' in for yer good self. But let me say again Mr Cavanagh has treated meself and me two hard workin' daughters in a dishonourable way. There is the matter of the fowls to be considered as well. I gave them to the Cavanaghs as a gift. I did not expect payment for them an' I told him that at the time but it seems the fowls 'ave become somethin' of an issue in this here case. And another thing, I took me girls away from the dressmakin' establishment because there was no way they was gettin' the trainin' me and Mrs Fuller expected when we signed the agreement. Juliet workin' as a cook was the last straw an' Ann tells me Mrs Cavanagh can be a hard taskmaster an' nothin' is ever done to her satisfaction...'

'Very well, Mr Fuller,' interjected Mr Proctor, hoping to usher him to the door, for once his client starting talking, there was no way he could be stopped.

'We will put the case together and we will see you in court. However, I don't know when a date can be arranged for the magistrate to arrive as there's been heavy rain to the south and his Honour might find getting here difficult. I'll be in touch when we have a date.'

'The rains sure 'ave been needed, Mr Proctor, for we 'ave had such a drought in this here part of the country, haven't we now? They tell me the mills will be startin' to work again soon once the water starts flowin' an' I'll be off there again to do me work. Ye will get yer fee, Mr Proctor, ye 'ave my word an' I'll be makin' plans for Juliet and Ann to continue doin' their dressmakin' so as they can earn a bit of money until they can find themselves some suitable husbands... an' another thing...'

'Very well, Mr Fuller. Good day to you.'

Mr Proctor steered Henry towards the door. He had doubts that his Honour would take too kindly to listening to Henry Fuller in the witness box again but the man did pay him last time so he should perhaps give him one more chance. Henry Fuller was an entertainment, it had to be said. Mr Proctor closed the door as Henry continued to gabble. Passers-by heard Henry's mutterings as he walked along the street but he was oblivious to their amusement. He was already plotting a course of action against the Cavanaghs and he hoped Mr Proctor would instruct Mr O'Connor on the best way to win the case this time.

****

The magistrate was in a bad mood which didn't bode well for Henry. The normally dusty track was now a muddy road thanks to the heavy rain, and the magistrate was late getting to the courthouse. The driver had had to coax two weary horses to pull themselves through the mire which resulted in an irritable driver and an equally irritable magistrate. When the magistrate found that the case in question was Henry Fuller versus A. J. Cavanagh, his mood darkened.

'The defence will amend the complaint,' he bellowed. 'It is too vague.'

Mr O'Connor shuffled the papers in front of him and apologised to the bench. Henry looked confused.

When Mr Mitchell stood up for the plaintiff, it was obvious to the magistrate that this was much the same complaint as he had previously had to listen to just a few weeks previously. This made him even more annoyed. He wanted the whole thing wound up as soon as possible. The heavy rain would mean that he might have to stay overnight in Armidale, a prospect that did not meet with much enthusiasm.

'I rule in favour of the plaintiff,' he said after all the evidence had been given.

'Mr Fuller, the court instructs you to pay Mr Cavanagh six pounds and I do not want to see you in this court again. Case dismissed.'

As everyone in the court stood up as the magistrate left the room, Henry Fuller was heard to mutter, 'You'll see me again, Your Honour, mark me words, and next time by all that is holy, I'll win.'

****

This story is based on two court cases: Juliet Fuller versus A. J. Cavanagh The Armidale Express and New England General Advertiser Friday 7th February 1879, page 6, and A. J. Cavanagh versus Henry Fuller The Armidale Express and New England General Advertiser Friday 21st February 1879. Both were complicated cases and the details even then were unclear. However, I have attempted to weave a story about the events and to also provide an insight into the social values of the time as well as providing a fictionalised account of the character of the protagonists.

Juliet and Ann did find 'suitable' husbands. Juliet married Alexander Symington and she had ten children. Ann's marriage produced four children. That's another story.

ON BEARDY STREET

When Henry and Margaret took a lease to open a wine shop on Beardy Street, both decided that this was to be a new beginning for them. This time Henry was certain that their fortunes would be made and he would no longer have to try to make ends meet by toiling away at the flour mill or when times were hard, turning his hand to carpentry. A wine shop offered a lot of possibilities. The premises being situated in Beardy Street and conveniently positioned opposite the Tattersall's Hotel, well, it couldn't fail, he told his wife.

Beardy Street was the main street in the northern New South Wales town of Armidale and it was named by two men who both sported impressive beards. There hadn't been much imagination at play with the naming it has to be said but the wine shop located where it was couldn't have been sited better. At least, that's what Margaret thought when the lease was signed. Her only reservation was the fact that it was a wine shop and Henry had a liking for the drink. She decided to keep a tight lookout for any discrepancies in the takings or any disappearance of the wine bottles.

But as usual, Henry was full of enthusiasm for the project.

'We'll make our fortune this time, Margaret me girl,' he said. 'When the punters come out of the Tattersalls they'll still be thirsty an' will be wantin' to keep on with the drinkin'. Where else to go but to the wine shop opposite to replenish their thirst?'

Margaret was wise.

'I'll take on the running of the shop, Henry an' I'll make sure all payments are made on time. I'm not givin' no credit and that goes for all yer drinkin' mates, Henry Fuller. Yer not goin' to be the big man and' give out free drinks to all an' sundry.'

'As if I'd do that, Margaret, me love. I'm more than happy

that the wine shop be your enterprise and yours alone. This time we'll make our fortune an' ye can be the grand lady an' be countin' yer takings every day. And the first thing I'm goin' to buy ye when we make a profit is a new bonnet. That's me word.'

Margaret had wanted a new bonnet for some time. She nodded her head but she wasn't convinced. She would keep the key to the till on a string around her neck at all times, just for insurance.

Everything went well for a little while. Margaret kept her eagle eye on the takings and made sure the number of bottles in the shop was accounted for, and Henry was true to his word, at least for a month or two. She bolted the door with two heavy brass keys at closing times and wouldn't let any latecomers in to buy a bottle or two after hours. She was ever mindful of the law in this case. She kept a wary eye on the local constabulary for she knew they watched her and the Fullers with much the same interest. This time, she decided, everything had to be above board.

'We'll close when we say we'll close, Henry, that's my final word. An' I'll not listen to any amount of persuasion by yer drinkin' mates to sell 'em a sly bottle or two after hours. No, we're not havin' the constabulary sniffing about ready to pounce on us an' shut us down. Sure we'd be up afore the court again an' that would be the end of our enterprise in this here town. There's certain folk here who would just delight in hearin' that the Fullers had been caught out again. This time we'll obey the law by all that's holy but I must say, if any of yer mates want to come round to the house, I'll 'ave a few bottles there for the buyin'. No credit given though, ye tell 'em that. I'm not runnin' a charity for yer drinkin' pals,' she added darkly.

Henry was used to his wife's persuasive powers and knew how to get his way with her, even when she was in a temper. He had helped himself to a bottle or two when Margaret wasn't looking. The least he could hope for was that the slight discrepancy would not be spotted and he would be able to continue this altogether agreeable misdemeanour. After all, he reasoned, Margaret was intent on making a profit and a few missing bottles could easily be explained, he thought with hope in his heart.

They had taken out a lease for a year with an option to renew for another two years. The shop was owned by the Campbell Brothers with John Moore acting as their agent. There had been a little bit of caution on the part of the Campbells in signing the premises over to the Fullers, given Henry's reputation, but as usual, Henry had been persuasive and in the end, it was decided by them that a bird in the hand was preferable to one in the bush and no one else had taken much interest in the shop as it had needed some repair. Henry assured everyone that with his carpentry skills he could fix the place up in no time. It was a win-win situation all around, he told the agent.

All went well for six months. The shop began to make a profit. Until one day, things took a turn for the worse. Margaret caught Henry helping himself to a bottle of a particularly fine Chardonnay.

'What's this then?' she roared. It was said later that her voice could be heard right up Beardy Street.

Henry, caught out, tried to hide the bottle behind his back.

'What's what, love?' he murmured.

'Ye know very well what's up, Henry Fuller. That's a bottle of the finest wine ye 'ave hidin' behind yer back, an' it just so happens, I had that particular one marked for Mr Proctor, our solicitor if ye remember him. Him bein' the one that looks after us in the courthouse. An' keeps ye out of the gaol.'

'Now, now, Margaret, me girl. I'm sure we can find another one just as good an' Mr Proctor will be none the wiser.'

'Ye think so, do ye? Well, Mr Proctor was in the shop a day or two ago an' he spies this here bottle on the shelf an' he says to me, “Mrs Fuller, my wife and I have asked Mr Campbell and his wife to dine with us this coming weekend. Mr Campbell has a fine palate and a particular liking for a well-rounded Chardonnay. Could you put that bottle aside for us, please and I’ll collect it this coming Friday?” It’s Thursday now and ye ’ave that same bottle behind yer back.’

‘He’ll never know the difference. We’ll find another one. Must be another bottle ’round here somewhere of the same vintage.’

‘There ain’t.’

Henry started to inch his way towards the door with the disputed bottle still held behind his back. This was too much for Margaret. She let out a shriek that all the banshees in faraway Ireland could have heard.

‘Give me that bloody bottle! Now!’

She charged at Henry. Her object was to wrestle the bottle from Henry’s grasp but he had slid out the door before she managed to get hold of him, or the bottle, and he skedaddled along Beardy Street. Margaret let out a yell.

Henry by now was further along Beardy Street. He collided with a woman wheeling a pram, apologised, and shot off the pavement to run along the main road where he nearly got run over by a horse and cart and was cursed by the driver. All the time Margaret was behind him. With one hand she hitched up her skirt so she could run faster which was somewhat awkward for her as she had short legs and was not built for running. However, she was so angry that her only thought was to stop her wayward husband in his tracks and retrieve the bottle. Even if the contents of it were drunk.

‘Ye come back here, Henry Fuller,’ she shouted.

But Henry kept running. When he reached the corner of Beardy and Faulkner Streets, he turned, and with a devilish grin, he waved the half-empty bottle of Chardonnay at Margaret. A second later he disappeared.

Margaret, in her haste to catch Henry, had forgotten that she had left the wine shop open to all and sundry and panting now, she, too, arrived at the corner of the two streets to be greeted by the familiar face of Sergeant Rafferty.

'Here, here, Mrs Fuller. What's all this goin' on?' He managed to take hold of Margaret's arms to restrain her. She was by now red-faced, out of breath and very angry.

'Don't ye dare touch me. It ain't nothin' to do with the constabulary. This here is between me husband and meself. I'm after catchin' the waster. Leave me be.'

Sergeant Rafferty loosened his grip on Margaret's arms. She had a valid point. It could be harassment if he grabbed her too hard. The next thing the Fullers and he would be in the police court again and this time the magistrate might not be so lenient with either party. He could lose his job or at the very least, be demoted to constable. The humiliation would be too much for him.

'Very well, Mrs Fuller,' he said after a few moments. 'Just this once. I would caution you, however, about causing a disturbance by running up Beardy Street at such a pace.'

He had expected an angry reply but Margaret surprised him. She took a deep breath and still panting, replied,

'Aye, ye are right, Sergeant Rafferty. My Henry ain't worth the trouble an' it's no way to behave, I grant ye that. I'll go back to the shop right now an' see if the customers haven't purloined all the stock while I've been away. But,' she added, 'if by chance ye see me Henry an' he has a bottle of the finest Chardonnay with him, I would ask ye to take the bottle from him an' return it to the shop. Ye could bring Henry back while ye are at it. I'll be waitin'.'

She turned and proceeded to walk at a much slower pace along Beardy Street.

****

Mr Proctor was somewhat annoyed when he arrived at the

Fuller's wine shop a few days later to hear that his much desired vintage Chardonnay was nowhere to be seen.

'But, Mrs Fuller,' he said, 'I thought ye were keeping the bottle for me. We agreed, didn't we?'

'I know, Mr Proctor but we have had an unfortunate accident with that particular bottle. It was not up to standard for various reasons. However, as ye are a good customer of this here establishment, I 'ave managed to obtain a much better wine from the Hunter Valley for ye good self. It's a much older vintage an' I am sure that ye an' Mr Campbell will enjoy it even more. This here Shirez has cost me twice as much as the Chardonnay but I am willin' to sell it to you at the same price.'

What else could Mr Proctor do but agree?

Henry arrived back a few days later, minus the bottle but with a new bonnet for his wife.

What else could Margaret do but accept?

****

Details of Margaret opening a wine shop are correct. A lease was granted to Henry Fuller from December 1st 1879 to December 1st 1880. Reports in the 'The Armidale Express and New England General Advertiser', Friday 18th February 1881, p.5, suggests that Margaret was advertising for a tenant to take over the lease. By February 1883 there appears to have been an argument about the lease of the premises: The Armidale Express and New England General Advertiser Friday 6th April 1883 p.4. This newspaper report states that Henry Fuller had gone missing from Armidale about 15th August 1882. It is probable that Henry had already left Margaret before that date. He had been declared insolvent in 1879. Given Henry's weakness for alcohol it is indeed possible that he drank the proceeds and Margaret had no recourse but to advertise for a new tenant to take over Henry's lease. The actual story is fiction but not beyond the realm of possibility.

GONE MISSING

It had been a quiet morning at the No. 2 Police Station on the corner of Pitt and George Streets and the constable at the front desk was rather bored. He had spent his time trying to look busy whenever the sergeant was in the vicinity but with just an early morning robbery down at the docks to report, he was rather at a loss as to what to do next, so that when he saw the short, stocky woman hurtle towards him with fiery eyes and the look of a temper to match, he straightened up and knew that he was in for some entertainment.

'What can I do for you, Madam?' he asked, trying to suppress a smirk for the woman looked as if she was about to hammer him with her umbrella. It had been raining all morning and her shoes and skirt were wet through.

'Ye can find that waster of a husband, so ye can.'

This time the constable couldn't resist the smirk. He covered his mouth with his hand to prevent the woman in front of him from seeing his amusement but he was thinking that, with a woman like her, no wonder the husband cleared off, but he kept quiet and opened the incident book.

'Now, Madam,' he said after a few moments and after he had cleared his throat. 'Can you give me a description of the missing person?' He added, 'We do get a lot of men deserting their wives, you know, and it can be difficult to track the men in question down.'

The remark did not seem to please the woman. Instead, she shook her head and rested her arms on the desk in just a slightly intimidating manner. She was now just inches away from the constable's face and he took a step backwards to avoid such proximity. He decided that her demeanour suggested that she was none too fond of the constabulary and had made her way to the police station as a last resort. By her accent, he judged that she was Irish and his opinion was that she would be trouble. He decided to tread carefully. He cleared his throat again.

'Well, Madam.' He thought that he would follow the procedure to the letter in this case. Anything else might lead to a physical confrontation between the two of them. Although she was short and stocky, he was wary of the wet umbrella. It had come perilously close to his head and water from it had dripped onto his desk. Some droplets had fallen onto the opened incident book.

'What is your name, Madam?'

'Margaret Fuller.'

The constable wrote the name in copperplate writing. He prided himself on his handwriting and it was well known at No 2 Police Station that his reports were always legible. He did take a lot of time to write the words though and this often led to frustration with his fellow officers, especially when the police station was busy.

'And your husband's name?'

'By all that is holy an' I often ask meself why did I marry him? It was a sad day when he came a courtin' but then me own father was no better.'

The constable cleared his throat again and coughed. The morning wasn't going particularly well, and this Irishwoman with the fiery eyes wasn't helping one bit.

'Madam, I just want to know the name of your husband?'

'Henry Fuller.'

'And his age?'

'Fifty-five years of age, God help him. Been missin' since July.'

It was now January.

'And you have had no contact since then?' The constable asked. In his head, he was trying to picture the relationship between the husband and wife.

'That's why I'm here! Don't ye know? I've six childers an'

not a penny have I got from him since he went missin' an' that's why I've walked from Erskinville to here in the rain. Can't afford the tram.'

The constable nodded his head and attempted to look sympathetic. If the man had indeed been missing for six months without any contact, it would have been hard for the woman to manage. Anything could have happened. Her husband could be dead or just disappeared into the great outback, never to be seen again. There had been plenty of incidents like this. If he had stayed in Sydney, there might be a chance of tracking him down but if he had headed west, over the Blue Mountains, he would melt into the vast unending plains and the chances of finding him would be remote.

'Can you give me a description of your husband please?'

'He talks a lot. That's what attracted me to him in the first place. Full of plans he was for us. He's English, ye know, and he has the gift of the blarney, that's why I liked him, at first. That is, till I got to know the bugger better, more fool me.'

'I just want a physical description, Madam.'

Mrs Fuller didn't answer. She seemed to be away with her thoughts and the constable had to ask the question again.

'He's got sandy whiskers that are turnin' grey. As I told ye, he's fifty-five years of age though he looks older. He likes to think he's a dapper dresser an' he's generally wearin' tweeds. Thinks he's a country gent he does.'

The constable wrote all this down except the bit about being a country gent. This particular description wouldn't look good on the report and the sergeant was a stickler for facts, not suppositions.

'Anything else you can think of which could help us track him down?'

'Tell him he'll see the back of me tongue when I sees him an' his life won't be worth livin', so help me God.'

'I mean, physical description, Mrs Fuller.'

'He's short like me. About five foot eight inches.'

'And?'

'Likes to drink. When he has the drink in him it's all how he'll make money an' live the life of the gentry. More fool me for believin' him. 'Cos nothin' ever comes of it, just the hangover.'

'What work does he do?'

This remark seemed to amuse the woman. She laughed.

'Work! Doesn't know the meanin' of the word. He's a miller an' when he gets fired from that or sick of it, he tries a bit of carpentry.' She was thoughtful. 'We've turned our hand to a few things over the years, mind, to make ends meet. It's not easy with six mouths to feed, ye know.'

'Have you any idea where he might go?' asked the constable. He wondered what sort of things the woman had done to make ends meet but he thought it best not to pursue that particular line of enquiry.

'Well, we lived up Armidale way for most of our time together. We was wed in Tenterfield. He was working as a miller over the border in Queensland for a while... near Warwick,' she added. 'But doubt he'd head back there. Too many folk up there chasin' him for money owed. I tell ye, I'd like to give him a piece of me mind if I catch him. Just took off one night, never to be seen again. 'Cause I got used to his drinkin' an' expected him back, like, all contrite, but no sign of the bugger since.' She sniffed, took out a handkerchief from her pocket and blew her nose. The memory of the many nights of dealing with a drunken husband seemed to be an emotional one, and for the first time, the constable felt a bit sorry for her.

'Is there anything else you could tell us to help?'

'Aye. I'd heard that he was seen near Hartley but no one was sure it was him. Although he'd be hard to miss, with all that blarney.'

Hartley was a small township west of Sydney. And over the Blue Mountains. Maybe Henry had travelled there headed for who knows where? Finding him would be almost impossible but the constable dutifully wrote *may have gone to Hartley* in his copperplate handwriting.

'Well, Mrs Fuller, we'll see what we can do for you.'

'I tell ye if I had me life over again, I'd run a mile from Henry Fuller. I was just a lassie, ye know, an' findin' a husband seemed to be the best option. He couldn't read or write when I met him. I taught him as best I could. I'm able to read and write meself.'

The constable smiled for the first time.

'I can see ye have good handwriting, Constable. I admire folk that can write like that. 'Cos Henry was jealous of anyone who could write. Didn't like that I could read either.'

The constable closed the incident book. The police station was filling up with an assortment of men and women of various ages and attire. A man of about fifty years of age dressed in a faded blue shirt and worn brown trousers with a cigarette hanging from his lips like a toddler's dummy was standing just a few feet behind Mrs Fuller. He was already making impatient mumblings. The constable decided that it was time for Margaret Fuller and her sorry tale about an errant husband to go. However, Mrs Fuller showed no signs of moving. Although she had seemed reticent at first to be in a police station, she seemed to have warmed to the constable and continued to brattle about copperplate writing and the benefits of being able to read and write.

'We'll see what we can do for you, Mrs Fuller,' the constable said kindly. 'We'll notify the Hartley police and the station in Bathurst but I can't promise that we'll be able to locate your husband. As I said, he could be anywhere and if he's headed out west, it makes it so much harder. You know what the distances are like out there. You can go for miles and not see a living soul.'

'Aye. If ye tell them coppers out there to take a look in the pubs, there's a good chance he will be in one of them. Couldn't go past a pub, that one.'

'We'll see what we can do, Mrs Fuller. Now, I think the matter is in hand and there's a few people behind you needing attention...'

It seemed to amuse Mrs Fuller that the motley crew behind her were waiting to see the constable.

'Constable,' she said and she leaned closer to him so that their eyes met. 'It took me some time to come here... I'm no friend of the constabulary, you know. But I must say, ye have been a true gentleman throughout. Why, if anyone could find me Henry, it'd be ye.'

'That's very kind of you, Mrs Fuller, but as I said, it's like looking for a needle in a haystack but we'll do what we can do. Sometimes, we manage to locate wayward husbands and reunite them with their wives. What happens between them after that is anyone's guess.'

The constable smiled. He was a kind man and even if he had seen the worst of humanity in his job, he was an optimist at heart. Most people were not that bad really and everyone deserved a second chance, even Henry Fuller.

'Thank ye indeed, Constable, an' I just want to tell ye somethin' afore I leave this here establishment. I know I said a lot of things about Henry an' most of them are true. He wasn't much of a husband, I'll grant ye that, but he was mine after all an' for better or worse, so help me God, I still 'ave feelin's for the old bugger.'

And with that, Margaret Fuller shook her now almost dry umbrella, and strode out of the No2 Police Station with her head held high, not looking left or right, but with just the slightest smile on her lips and the hint of a twinkle in her brown eyes.

****

In the Police Gazette dated 28th January 1884 Henry Fuller was listed as a missing person and any information about his whereabouts was to be conveyed to Mrs Fuller, No 2 Police Station, Sydney. The conversation between Margaret Fuller and the constable described in my story is fiction. However, the fact is Henry Fuller did disappear, never to be seen again as there is no record of his death.

In 1857 Henry Fuller, aged thirty-three years, boarded the *Irene* bound for Australia. He appears to have travelled alone as he is listed as a single male travelling without families.[34] Henry was a miller with carpentry skills. He, however, stated that his occupation was a labourer on the passenger list. This was not an uncommon practice at the time. Labourers were more likely to be needed in the colony than millers and Henry probably thought that by stating that his occupation was a labourer, he would have been more likely to be granted assisted passage. It appeared to have worked.

Henry stated on the shipping list that he was not literate. This throws up an interesting mystery as his grandfather was the Reverend Andrew Fuller. It seems unlikely that his grandson would not have been able to read or write. Perhaps Henry thought that it would be more advantageous to say he was illiterate given that is occupation was a labourer? Again, an unknown story.

The *Irene* arrived at Moreton Bay on 11th February 1858[35] The voyage of one hundred and nine days from London via Plymouth was an uneventful one and the passengers and crew arrived in good health. The *Irene* was to continue her journey to Sydney and South Australia. It appears from the ship's record that Henry disembarked at Moreton Bay. The passengers and crew had to wait a few days on board because of a difficulty in procuring river steamers to take them further up the river to the town to what is now the city of Brisbane.

It seems that Henry left Brisbane at some stage and travelled to the New England district of northern New South

---

34 New South Wales, Assisted Immigrant Passenger Lists, 1828 – 1896.

35 The Sydney Morning Herald Fri 19 Feb 1858, page 2, Moreton Bay

Wales. Queensland, as we now know it, was a part of New South Wales until 1859 when it became a separate state. Possibly Henry left Brisbane in search of work as a miller.

The New England Tablelands were one part of the interior of New South Wales where water-powered flourmills were constructed during the nineteenth century. The geography of this area is characterised by a consistently high altitude above sea level and a relatively high rainfall. However, it took the settlers sometime time to realise that, although relatively high, the rainfall could also be highly variable, consequently rendering the flow of the rivers and streams unreliable for supplying water to power the mills. This lesson is borne out in the histories of the watermills constructed there.[36]

How long Henry was in the New England area is unknown but it is here that he met Margaret Maher or Meagher. The couple were married on 4th September 1860 in Tenterfield.

Margaret had emigrated from Ireland with her two brothers, Phillip and John on board the *Palmyra* which left Plymouth on 13th February 1859 and arrived in Sydney on 27th May 1859 after one hundred and five days at sea. Both brothers are recorded as farm labourers. Phillip, aged twenty-one could read and write and John, aged twenty-one, was illiterate. Margaret could read and write. Margaret was born circa 1841 in North Tipperary, Ireland. On the passenger list, her religion was recorded as Roman Catholic and her occupation was a general domestic servant.[37] Again, it is unknown how she came to be living in the New England area. Possibly as she was a domestic servant there was a place of employment offered to her there.

---

[36] Pearson, Warwick, Water-Powered Flour milling in the New England Tablelands of New South Wales,
Australasian Historical Archaeology 16, 1998, page 32

[37] New South Wales, Assisted Immigrant Passenger Lists, 1828 -1896

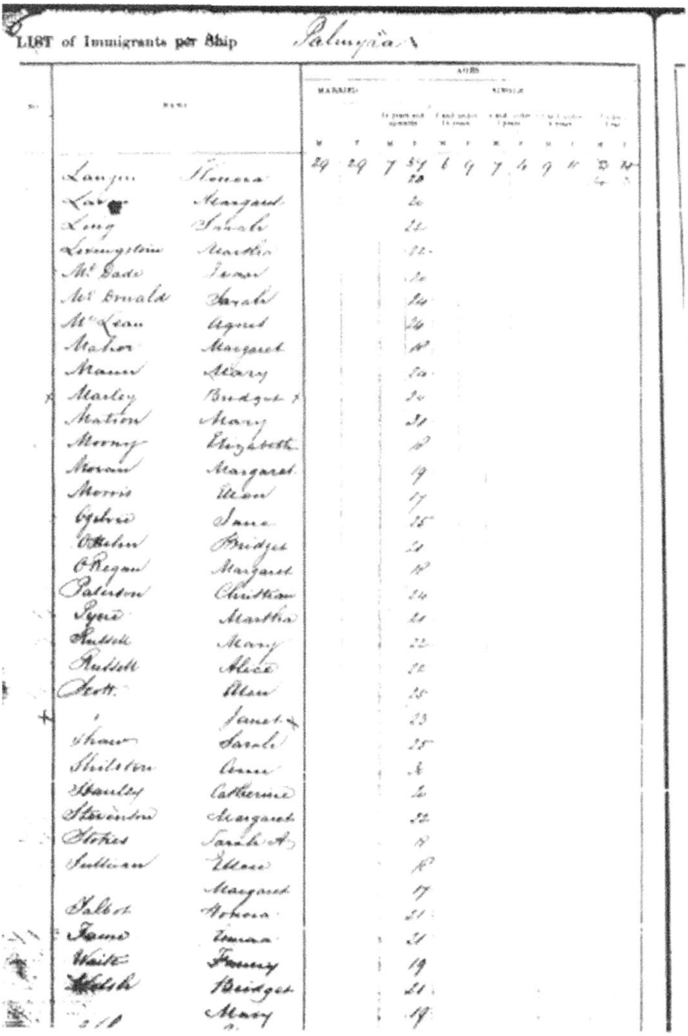

LIST of Immigrants per Ship Palmyra

Surname	Name	Age
Langan	Honora	20
Lawlor	Margaret	20
Long	Sarah	22
Livingstone	Martha	22
McDade	Susan	20
McDonald	Sarah	24
McLean	Agnes	24
Maher	Margaret	18
Mann	Mary	20
Marley	Bridget	20
Mahon	Mary	21
Morony	Elizabeth	18
Moran	Margaret	19
Morris	Ellen	17
Ogilvie	Jane	25
O'Hehir	Bridget	21
O'Regan	Margaret	18
Paterson	Christina	24
Pyne	Martha	21
Russell	Mary	22
Russell	Alice	20
Scott	Ellen	25
	Janet	23
Shaw	Sarah	25
Shilston	Anne	[illegible]
Stanley	Catherine	20
Stevenson	Margaret	32
Stokes	Sarah A.	18
Sullivan	Ellen	18
	Margaret	17
Talbot	Honora	21
[illegible]	Emma	21
Waite	Fanny	19
Walsh	Bridget	21
	Mary	19

Margaret Maher listed on Immigrant ship, Palymra, 1859

Present day view of the Armidale area, New England, New South Wales
Photograph by the Author

The couple were to produce seven children. Juliet, sometimes named Juliette, the eldest was born in 1861. She was to marry Alexander Thomas Symington in Armidale and give birth to ten children. Annie came next. Two more daughters were born, Margaret, and then Rachael who married Henry Price. Rachael was to have ten children. William, Herbert and Arthur completed the family. All the children of Henry and Margaret increased the family and all those children had more children.

Henry and Margaret seemed to have had a rather interesting marriage to say the least. Henry was somewhat addicted to alcohol and he would disappear for days. He worked mainly as a miller however. Birth certificates for all his children list his occupation as “Miller”. Between court cases, business enterprises and a growing family, Henry and Margaret managed to stay together for approximately twenty-four years. Things must have become difficult for Margaret with Henry's frequent absences. On 28th January 1884 she reported him missing to the police in Sydney.[38]

It is challenging to find any records as to whether he was ever found or where he was buried. Australia is a vast country, and at that time communications were not what they are in the twenty-first century. It is more than likely that Henry disappeared into the bush, never to be seen again.

What happened after that is lost in the mists of time. The date Margaret died is unknown. She seems to have moved from the Armidale area at some point possibly to be closer to her married daughters in Sydney. When she reported Henry missing her address then was listed as Erskinville, now an inner city suburb of Sydney.

The Fuller descendants of Henry and Margaret are many. They settled in various parts of Australia and New Zealand and some ventured further afield. The New England area was a strong location for the first generation with some of them migrating to Sydney. Like all families everywhere, they had their challenges to face. Henry and Margaret would, no doubt, be surprised at the number of their descendants. These descendants have made their lives in a country so far from England and Ireland. We can only wonder if Henry and Margaret ever had any regrets about emigrating. That too, is an unknown.

---

[38] NSW Police Gazette 28th January 1884

PRICE FAMILY

ORIGIN OF THE FAMILY NAME

Price is a patronymic surname derived from the Welsh *apRhys,* meaning "son of Rhys." The given name Rhys means "enthusiasm" in Welsh.

A TERRIBLE SEA JOURNEY

I think I fell in love with Thomas the moment I first looked into his eyes. He was a shy sort of fellow but it was the rhythm of his Welsh voice that captivated me. I'm a London girl, born in Lambeth and Thomas was the first Welshman I had ever met. It wasn't long before he proposed marriage. It looked to be ideal except for one small fact.

'I'm happy to marry Thomas,' I told my friend, Elsie, 'except I don't like his smell.'

'Shush, Sarah,' Elsie said, 'for he can't help that. He's a tanner and a hard worker. That's all you need to know. In time, you'll get used to the smell.'

'I wonder,' I replied for I still had my doubts.

We were married at St James Church in Bermondsey on a cold November day. Thomas put a cross on the marriage certificate but I had learned to read and write and I signed my name. Thomas said he was pleased that I could read and write. I decided that I would teach him as best I could one day.

We were very happy those first few years living in Mill Road. Our little girl, Mary Ann, came first and four years later we had a son, Robert. Baby Henry arrived just two years after Robert. My friend, Elsie's words proved to be true, Thomas was indeed a hard worker and a good provider. I couldn't have wished for a kinder husband.

One day Thomas arrived home and he was in a state of some excitement for he had learned something at the tannery which was to change all our lives.

'Sarah, dear wife,' he said, 'I have been aware for a long time that we can better ourselves and as luck would have it, today I met up with a fine young fellow. He's a tanner like me. Well, he and his family have decided to immigrate to Australia and they have been accepted for an assisted passage to New South

Wales.'

I guessed what was coming next.

'I think we should apply as well. We would have a new beginning in Australia and I hear there's plenty of work for a tanner out there so I'm told. Would you be agreeable, my dear?'

I thought for a few moments. London was where I was born but there was no one here for me, except Thomas and our three children. My poor mother died giving birth to me and my father had passed away some years later. It had been a great sadness for me that neither of my parents had lived to see me married to such a good man. Thomas's parents and siblings were all in Wales and far enough away. But to travel halfway around the world?

'It's a new country, Sarah, and there's plenty of space not like crowded London.'

'And no fog?' I hated the damp and the cold winters.

'No fog.' Thomas smiled.

'There's nothing here for me, Thomas. I am happy to leave.'

'Well, that's settled then. I will apply for an assisted passage for the five of us tomorrow. I hear families wishing to emigrate are well received by the authorities.'

That night I dreamed that I was flying through a forest and when I came down to earth I entered a log cabin surrounded by odd-looking trees. I awoke from the dream in the early morning and I knew then what we were doing was the right decision for us all.

****

The *Devonport* was anchored on the Thames and what a fine vessel she was. I had seen the tall ships coming and going but I had never been so close to one of them before. When we shuffled our way up the gangplank, I could not imagine how a ship this size could sail so far and undertake the many journeys. We held tight to our few possessions and found our way below decks to the area assigned to married couples. These cramped quarters would be our home for nearly four months. I had never been to sea before and I began to have some doubts as to whether I should have agreed so readily to Thomas's decision but it was too late for any regrets as the sails were unfurled and I heard the chains holding the anchor lifting.

'Let's go on deck and say goodbye to old London Town,' Thomas said and we joined the other passengers who were no doubt all thinking the same. A grey mist lay like a cloud over the docks and a fine rain wet our faces. I shivered with the cold. I was with child again but in all the excitement of departure, I forgot my weariness and held little Henry's hand tight.

'Where are we going?' Henry asked and his five-year-old self looked puzzled.

'To a new life, son. Now, hang on tight to your mother. There'll be a swell as the ship leaves the Thames and puts out to the open sea.'

'I don't like this ship,' cried Mary Ann. She was just eleven years old and a frail child. I feared that the voyage might prove difficult for her.

'I do!' announced Robert. He was always taking charge of Mary Ann and Henry. Although he had no conception of the journey ahead, he was a strong lad and a determined one. I was sure he would prosper in New South Wales and I hoped and prayed we would all do the same.

****

The *Devonport* rose and fell when we sailed into the open sea and set course through the English Channel and I felt as if my stomach had risen to my mouth when the nausea hit me hard. There was a gale blowing from the west and the ship ploughed through heavy seas. We were below decks and the constant movement set pans and bedding rolling from side to side. We could hardly stand up straight and Mary Ann vomited all over her pinafore. The wind was savage and the conditions so critical that Captain Kennedy had no recourse but to weigh anchor in

Portsmouth Harbour and wait until the worst of the weather subsided. It was with some relief not to endure the constant rolling but the waves even in the harbour meant that the ship still swayed, and somewhat dangerously to my mind. I became fearful of the constant creaking of the wooden boards all about us. If this was the start of our journey, what would it be like for another three months or so?

There were twenty married couples on board and I found solace in talking to another two women from London, both as fearful as I was about the journey ahead.

'I see ye are in the family way, dearie,' one of the women said to me.

'Not the best situation to be in,' the other woman said to me and she shrugged her shoulders. 'Men!'

She had a head of red hair and smoked a pipe. I liked her immediately.

'You'll be alright, Luv. We'll look after ye when your time comes. Looks like this 'un will be born at sea. Poor wee mite. What a place to come into the world.'

I couldn't have agreed more.

'I've heard there's a Matron on board, dearie. Believe she's emigratin' as well. Between us all, we'll keep ye safe. Here's to be hopin' that this here boat ain't swayin' like it's been when yer baby decides to come out or it'll find itself on the other side of deck afore ye know it,' chuckled the other woman. She looked worn out already. Her brood numbered six.

'An' ye along with it,' concluded red head.

Their humour lifted my spirits somewhat and I must say it was a relief to have met them. We were all destined for Sydney Town and a new life. My baby would most certainly be born at sea but this one would never know England. If we survived the journey, I decided that might be a good thing.

Our fortunes did not improve as we sailed past the Iberian Peninsula for a fierce storm ripped apart one of the sails. Panic set in below decks when word of this reached us but in truth, we were all so intent on hanging on to anything that would steady us from the constant rolling and heaving that we scarcely had time to contemplate what was happening. Our lives were in danger as many a ship had sunk in seas less choppy. I feared the worst. When we heard that the gallant sailors had climbed the rigging to secure the sail risking their lives in the process, we were relieved beyond words. I began to wish most fervently that I had not agreed to this journey.

Another problem was the constant sickening smell all about us. Try as I could, I found it nauseating and as my belly grew larger, I had to spend more time lying down on the rough bedding for I was not able to venture above our deck even when the weather calmed down a bit. I had complained about the odour from my dear Thomas when he returned from work at the tannery, now that smell was perfume to my nostrils compared to the stench around me.

When we reached the coast of Africa, the storms abated to be replaced by an intense heat and I thought we would die from being cooped up with such high temperatures. I had never experienced heat like it. My thick woollen dress and heavy petticoat clung to my body. Modesty prevented me from removing any of my undergarments but I would have gladly flung them away and run naked around the deck. I kept this thought from Thomas but my two women friends did agree with me and our giggling gave us some relief I must declare.

As the days grew longer we began to find it easier to move about as our bodies adapted somewhat to the constant roll of the ship but not so my poor wee Mary Ann. Our sweet little daughter was very precious to both Thomas and me as she was our firstborn. We had been married for about three years before Mary Ann arrived and both of us had begun to fear that we would be childless so her arrival was a blessing and we viewed her birth as a gift from God. But Mary Ann was a frail child and prone to coughs and sneezes. She was sick from the moment the *Devonport* left London. I found it difficult to tend to her as well as look after my two boys whilst all the time, I was suffering greatly with my latest pregnancy.

'I'm worried about Mary Ann,' I whispered to Thomas one evening when we were alone. 'I fear that this journey has been too much for her.'

'We must pray that she will survive, my dear. I believe that we will soon be at the Cape of Good Hope and then the Roaring Forties will speed up our journey across the ocean.'

'I hope you are right, Thomas. Her coughing seems worse today. I think we should ask advice from the ship's doctor.'

'I will see to that.' Thomas replied but I knew from his face that he was as troubled as I was.

The *Devonport* did indeed pick up speed once we reached the Indian Ocean. Our spirits lifted somewhat with the prospect that our journey would soon be over and we would once again walk on dry land. I tried to comfort Mary Ann with this thought but the poor child showed no interest in what was happening about her.

One evening about an hour after we had eaten our meagre rations, we had all adjoined to the upper deck to enjoy the unexpectedly calm sea and marvel at a pod of dolphins swimming so close to the bow, Mary Ann complained of a sore stomach. A few seconds later, the poor child grasped her hands over her abdomen and screamed. The memory of that cry would remain with me for the rest of my life.

'Whatever's wrong, Mary Ann?' I asked.

'My belly hurts.'

'Where?'

'All over.'

'We'd best get ye below decks to your bed and your father will summon Doctor Sanger.'

But Mary Ann could not walk. Still grasping her stomach

she bent over and a few seconds later she fell to the deck, unconscious. Thomas scooped up the pitiable child in his strong arms and cried out,

'We need help here. Someone call for the doctor.'

I heard a man shout. Then I heard someone say that Captain Kennedy was needed and the situation was urgent. A child had been taken ill.

Mary Ann was put to rest on her bed below decks. I held her hand and wiped her brow with my handkerchief. She did not regain consciousness.

To lose a child in such circumstances is a dreadful thing. I was not able to weep for Mary Ann. The shock was so acute that it seemed all my feelings had disappeared with her, and I feared I might never recover from the loss of someone so precious to me.

Captain Kennedy summoned Thomas and me to his quarters the next day. He was brusque but sympathetic. Mary Ann would have to be buried at sea. I knew in my heart that this had to be so but in truth I did not want it to happen this way. My dear daughter had hated the sea journey from the moment of our departure. It was sad to think that these waters would be her last resting place but Thomas assured me that she would be at peace at the bottom of the sea. With tears behind my eyes, I had to agree and the arrangements were made.

The seas were choppy the morning we stood in silence whilst the prayers were said and then Thomas and three sailors lowered Mary Ann into the deep dark ocean. As her body disappeared beneath the waves, I saw the albatross fly overhead. It was like an omen that I needed for the mystery of those wonderful birds with their majestic wings heralded a new beginning. An hour later my waters broke and I knew that soon a new life would come to me.

This labour was hard. My red-haired London friend wiped my brow and I gripped her hand so tightly that my nails dug into her skin causing bleeding. Throughout the ordeal Matron kept telling me to work harder as if I wasn't doing just that. I yelled like a woman possessed with the pain. Twenty hours later I held a small infant in my arms, a boy. We would call him Frederick Kennedy. It seemed only right that Captain Kennedy should be acknowledged for he had been kind to us in our grief.

Our fortunes did not improve as the *Devonport* navigated the seas between Van Diemen's Land and the mainland of that vast continent. At times I thought that the ship would go down this time and that we had come all this way to end our lives at the bottom of the ocean, to join Mary Ann there, and be devoured by the sea creatures. We survived.

The first sight of Port Jackson was one of wonder and relief for us all. It was raining the day we weighed anchor and we could barely make out the sights of the settlement except that there appeared to be a lot of activity on the shoreline. We had left England eighty-nine long days ago and it had been raining then but the light was different here. Even through the rain, the atmosphere was brighter. We had left the grey light of London behind us to find this other world.

Anchored beside the *Devonport* were two tall ships and we spied passengers being lowered to the waiting small boats from one of them. I must confess for the first time I felt excited that we, too, would soon be standing on dry land. It was not to be. Because several of the passengers on the *Devonport* had contracted an infectious disease it was deemed necessary that we were to be quarantined for forty-one days. I had endured much suffering throughout this journey. The *Devonport* had become a kind of home for me, and although many times I had feared for my life, being on board the ship was a sanctuary of sorts. What would life be like in this unknown place when we finally were allowed to leave the old vessel? I stood with Thomas and our two boys on the deck trying to understand what had gone before and what was yet to be. Cradling my new baby boy in my arms, I whispered to Thomas,

'Were we right to leave home?'

'Time will tell, my dear,' was his reply and that was comfort enough for me.

****

This story is based on fact. It was a difficult voyage partly due to storms but also because of an uneven distribution of iron and cement which caused the Devonport to roll 'frightfully'. This was reported in The Sydney Morning Herald 12th August 1868, page 8. Although some of the characters are fiction, the main events did take place. Mary Ann, the eldest daughter of Thomas and Sarah died of mesenteric disease and was buried at sea. This was recorded in the ship's journal. Captain Kennedy and Doctor Sanger were real characters. Sarah did give birth to a son, Frederick Kennedy on board. According to the report given by Superintendent Carroll the ship was quarantined at Sydney Cove for ten days for the ship and forty-one days for infected passengers. This account was written by Foley (p69 – 70) and further details are held in the Manly Library (Local Studies).

Sarah Price (née Jarvis)

SETTLING IN

Those first few years were hard. I often wonder how we survived in such an unforgiving place for the country we had travelled to was such a different world from the London I knew. Thomas and I had so much hope when we left England bound for New South Wales, and after our terrible sea journey, we prayed that we would find peace and prosperity in this new land for we knew that there was no way back to our old world.

I think Thomas adjusted better to our life in Australia than I did. We moved to Penrith, thirty miles west of Sydney Town. There were seven tanneries in the area and work was plentiful with tanners being much in demand. The tanneries had been sited there because of the ready supply of water. Thomas earned more than he ever could have done had we stayed in England. We moved into a small but comfortable dwelling with a corrugated iron roof and timber frame. There was a tiny veranda in the front and an outhouse at the back. We had a garden and room for some chickens. Our neighbours were friendly and on Sundays, after church, we would often take our picnic baskets and venture to the river. The Nepean was a mighty river and the children loved to play beside it. I marvelled at the birds, so different from the ones in England. No sweet sounds of the nightingale here. The raucous shrieks of the colourful parrots intrigued us. Flocks of small green birds called budgerigars often ventured to the river. They would swoop down, and then in the twinkling of an eye, they were gone.

I remember the first time that we saw kangaroos and it was a wonder to me that such a strange creature could exist. The boys laughed and tried to chase them away and the animals hopped at speed and soon disappeared into the bush. How we enjoyed that day.

I admit that I struggled the first year. The heat was a

monster that sapped my energy. There seemed no way to escape from it. The sun rose in the morning and by midday, like some fire god of old, it scorched the earth below, seeking vengeance. With no rain the ground laid bare, brown and dry, and the emaciated cattle, their ribs protruding through their spent bodies, began to die. The farmers despaired, and there were prayers said for rain at the churches. But the cloudless sky above gave no hint that soon there would be any relief, and the roads turned into dusty tracks. The dust got into your nose and stung your eyes. It was then that I longed for the fog of London and the soft rain of England.

The children developed heat rashes and blisters. Their white skin was no match for the intense summer heat. Seeing their blistered skin, children who had lived longer in the town pointed, giggling at the pale bodies clothed in such unsuitable attire. I wore long skirts and covered my arms so that I could save myself from being burnt but to no avail. I, too, found my skin browning despite all my precautions. There was no respite from it. That first year no rain fell for six months and the water in the creeks began to dry up making life even more difficult for us all.

As the days went by and the drought showed no sign of breaking, water became scarce and men began to be laid off at the tannery and the other factories in the town. I feared that Thomas would suffer the same fate and we would be penniless in this difficult land. He told me that the dry conditions had made the supply of cattle hides less suitable for leather and the tannery owner had refused to pay the farmers. All these problems added to our anxiety as we tried our best to settle in. With no way back to England, and fearful if we stayed, it seemed to me that our decision to travel halfway around the world had indeed been a foolish one and not such a well-thought-out plan.

I think my worst encounter that first year was with the red-bellied black snake. Neighbours had warned us of the ever-present danger of the snakes and the venomous spiders, and although on one occasion I had disturbed a funnel-webbed spider that had been hiding under a log, I had not seen any snakes. The spider had frightened me. It rose onto its hind legs and displayed its fangs. Glossy and dark and alien-looking, this small creature was deadly and I had quickly left it to its own devices. After that encounter, I warned my boys to be careful moving any logs but I was unprepared for the snake.

It was morning and the heat was already intense. Baby Frederick had fallen asleep in his cradle and Robert and Henry were busy playing soldiers in the back garden. Thomas had left early that morning for the tannery and I had been outside trying to collect some rather sad-looking runner beans for our supper. The result of the dry conditions and lack of sufficient water meant that there was very little to eat from our garden. When I entered our house my eyes were dimmed from being outside and it was then that I felt something slide over my shoe. When I looked down I saw a black shape. I knew at once what it was. I dropped my basket filled with a few wrinkled beans, and I screamed. Frederick woke and started to cry. As my eyes adjusted to the light I could see the snake more clearly. I suspected it had entered the house to find some sanctuary from the heat and perhaps capture a stray rodent. Instead of sliding away, the creature half coiled around, facing me and all the time I could see its forked tongue and the black eyes. Now I could make out the vibrant red of its belly and the black scales upon its back. The scales glistened in the half-light. It was a small snake, probably a young one, but venomous. I wondered what I could find to kill it but my legs had turned to jelly so I stood motionless, unable to move or to think what to do next. A few seconds passed. It seemed like an hour, and before I could make any decision, the snake slithered away towards the open door, to disappear into the dry grasses next to the iron water tank. I cradled Frederick in my arms and I started to cry.

Perhaps that was the moment that I realised that my life from now on would be forever connected to this vast land and its inhabitants. Certainly, it was not the same world as the one I had known and I had often felt fear. Living here was not without its challenges but there was space to breathe. I was with child again and this child would be born here and never know anything about the old country. Somehow, I found that to be reassuring and a cause for optimism. I confess that I had panicked when I saw the red-bellied snake in my kitchen but snakes lived here and had done so for millenniums, we were newcomers. Surely with care, we could all live together.

That night the air cooled. We lay in our beds and wondered at the peculiar night sounds we could hear. At dawn, we heard the hammering on the iron roof and woke in the morning to a torrent of water. The drought had broken.

The rains brought all manner of new things. The dusty road outside our home became a muddy track and the horses and carts struggled to get through. I heard the men curse as often both cart and horse became stuck in the mud. Most times help was at hand and the situation was resolved soon enough but I began to wonder how we had gone from lack of water to a deluge. Was this what happened in this country? I doubted that we would ever get used to the constant battle with the weather. At least my vegetable garden came alive again and we had plenty to eat once more. I kept an eye out for my red-bellied black snake but I never did see it again and I began to lose my fear of the creatures. The floods often washed them away. I fantasised that my particular snake had met that same fate.

Christmas came and with it all sorts of memories. I remembered the snowy days and nights of London, how we had to huddle beside the fire to keep warm, and the way people greeted you on Christmas Day. That first Christmas in Australia the sky was so bright. There wasn't a cloud to be seen and the rains had stopped. It was a beautiful day but it felt odd for

Thomas and me to be here in the heat of summer, not winter. When we ventured outside the neighbours greeted us with as much warmth as people had done on winter's days at home. It gave me some hope that there is human kindness evident wherever you might find yourself in this world. Here we were in this land, struggling along beset with our problems but I believe that this was where we were meant to be and it was in Australia that we would make a home for us and for the generations to come.

My optimism returned with the coming of the New Year and the birth of my daughter, Emily Louisa. She arrived in the world without fuss and I felt God had given me a new beginning. I had mourned the loss of my dear daughter, Mary Ann, on board the *Devonport* for many a year and now here was a beautiful little girl so like her dead sister. I must admit I cried like a baby when I held this child to my breast.

Six years later, George Vere was born. Thomas prospered so much working in the tannery that he and a partner decided to make a move from Penrith to northern New South Wales to establish a tannery there at a place called Walcha. Our world had entered a new phase and I, at last, was no longer a stranger in this far distant land of droughts and floods and magical creatures. I had indeed made my home here.

****

Although the character of Sarah Price is unknown her story would have been a familiar one to hundreds of pioneer women in nineteenth century Australia. The events described are based on fact, the story is fiction. However, I believe that these pioneer women would have faced a hostile environment at times and also been subject to a myriad of problems, the weather conditions and the unfamiliar native creatures being just two of many.

IN THE BLINK OF AN EYE

Thomas dressed early that March day. The sky was clear and although a light wind from the east had brought an early morning chill to the air, it was the sort of day that made a man feel happy to be alive, thought Thomas. He was fifty-one years of age and he showed no signs of slowing down. Since setting up his tannery business in Walcha with his partner, he was fitter than ever. He viewed their move from Penrith as a new beginning and life could only get better from now on. All the previous years of toil spent working for various bosses were behind him, and all to the good. He and his wife would make their fortune in this sleepy little northern New South Wales town with its four blacksmiths and two flour mills. Thomas owned the only tannery.

Walcha was an ideal place for a tannery with its rivers and tumbling waterfalls and a ready supply of cattle for the hides. Thomas was a skilled and hard worker. He was a sturdy man and he could lift piles of hides with ease. Something that younger men often struggled with but Thomas had worked as a tanner all his life and was as strong as the proverbial ox. Hard physical work was in Thomas's blood. His father had laboured in Abergavenny. Although Abergavenny and Wales was now a faraway place in the mind of Thomas he remembered how his father had come home from work, tired and worn out but without a word of complaint for he had a family to feed.

The tannery was situated just fifty yards from the slab-built home that he shared with his wife, Sarah. Living so near to the tannery meant a watchful eye could be kept on the comings and goings. Thomas was all too aware that leather had sometimes gone missing from other tanneries where he had worked. He was determined that no such thing would happen at his tannery. He and his partner had been able to afford to employ a few men to help with the workload. Two fleshers spent the day scraping the flesh and fat off the hides. These two were hard workers and Thomas was pleased with them. Another two were employed placing the animal hides into the various tanks that would convert the hide into leather.

All these men were good workers but he was a little unsure of the man they employed as the engine driver. This man often stopped work for no apparent reason to have a smoke. He wasn't a shirker but Thomas kept a close eye on him. Employing men has its problems, he thought as he passed by the water and lime tanks towards the office. The stench from the vats greeted him. After a lifetime of breathing in the smells from the skins of the cattle, Thomas barely noticed. He was puzzled when people moaned about the tannery and its particular odour. For him, it was the familiar aroma of work.

There were two aspects of the tanning process that Thomas enjoyed. One was working on the bark-crushing machine. He had managed through some bargaining to source a ready supply of black wattle barks from a local farmer. Other trees that grew in the area including oak and stringy bark were sometimes used as well but he preferred the tannins from the black wattle for the tanning process. All this he had learned since living in Australia. In England he had worked with oak bark but here in the hotter climate, the wattle bark was more suitable for leather as it was softer and more pliable. He had recently acquired a bark-crushing machine. Powered by steam from the water mill, this machine had become an integral part of the tannery and Thomas soon became a skilled operator.

The other part of the tannery process that Thomas liked was the final result. The age-old process of turning animal hides into leather which could be used for boots and saddles and all manner of clothing was to him one of the wonders of human ingenuity and the sight of a good leather hide filled him with pride. The leather from his tannery fetched a good price and life was looking good that March day.

He whistled as he passed by the bark store. A frilly-necked lizard basked in the early morning sun on top of the stack of bark but it didn't move when it heard Thomas. Instead, the lizard balanced on three legs, stretched its front leg and lifted its head to capture the sun's rays. He heard the laugh of the kookaburra perched on a branch of the stringy bark tree at the side of the tannery. This was a welcome sound that Thomas had grown to love to hear. He watched as the bird swooped towards him to land on a beam in the shed. The bird cackled again, and hearing this, the lizard scampered away and disappeared towards the leaching pits. The kookaburra had just missed out on a meal for its lethal beak could dismember snakes and a lizard could be despatched in the same dramatic way.

'Better not fall in there, Frilly,' Thomas thought as his eyes followed the fleeing reptile. 'Lizard hide won't produce much leather.'

The morning just got better as the sun rose in a cloudless blue sky. The clock struck seven. Thomas always made a point of greeting his men as they arrived for their day's work. Bosses he had worked for had thought their employees were just workhorses to be exploited but Thomas was more generous. In his mind, a boss should be firm but understanding. His workers had families to feed as he had. The men were cheerful and they set about their tasks with plenty of banter between them all. Thomas positioned himself at the bark crushing machine and shouted to the engine driver to start up the steam to power the machine.

'I'll be workin' on here today, Bert,' he said. 'Just keep the steam comin' till smoko.'

'Sure thing, Boss.' Bert spat a strand of tobacco onto the ground and the bark crusher roared into life like some primeval monster. Thomas put on his leather gloves to protect his hands from the splinters. The work began.

After the smoko, the men returned to their work in the afternoon. The sun was beginning to make its descent towards the western skies when Thomas began to feel weary. He had stood at the bark-crushing machine all day, feeding the bark through the teeth wheels and always careful to protect his hands from the deadly blades. He was pleased with his day's work. He had managed to convert about half a ton of bark into pulp. It was nearly knock-off time when the crushing machine suddenly lost power.

Thomas, unaware that the steam had been shut off, pushed the last few sticks of bark through the teeth of the machine. The next moment the unthinkable happened. The machine propelled by its momentum and gradually slackening speed caught Thomas's right hand between its revolving teeth. Horrified, he endeavoured to pull his hand away but the machine kept moving. As he saw his hand and then his right arm disappearing, he tried to call out to the engine driver who was responsible for keeping the steam going to power the machine. The man was unaware of what was happening. He had stopped the machine to have a smoke.

The machine kept moving until Thomas's shoulder was drawn into its teeth. Then it stopped. A terrible silence descended upon the tannery. The engine driver, the cigarette hanging from his bottom lip, heard the weak cry of Thomas. When he saw what had happened he nearly fainted. Blood had spilled onto the machine and the ground below and hand, arm and shoulder were now reduced to a pulp. Thomas's head lay on top of the machine. The teeth of the machine had caused his back and chest to be horribly slashed.

The men managed somehow to extricate Thomas from the machine and wrap blankets around his body. He was confused and tried to push them away. He was in shock and he fell.

'Get the doctor,' he heard one of the men cry. 'Take the horse and ride into town, for Chrissake.'

'Boss, just sit down. We'll get help.'

But Thomas was having none of it. He stood up, stumbled and almost fell again. His body was numb. His heart pounded like a drum in his chest. His skin felt cold and moist and he gasped for air. But this strong man had just one thought in his head. Sarah.

Fifty yards was fifty miles. Thomas tried to hold the two blankets with his left hand to stem the flow of blood as he stumbled towards the house. But he had no strength left in his torn body and one of the blankets fell to the ground. He felt dizziness pass through him from head to toe and he staggered, dropping to his knees. The tough grasses would have hurt him under different conditions but the pain from his injury was so fierce that he hardly noticed their spiky leaves. His blood was now on the grass. He was close to his home. If he had strength left, he must call for Sarah.

Two of his men tried to hold him, to restrain him, but he was unaware that they were even beside him. He was conscious enough to wonder with one part of his brain if his hand and arm were attached to his body. Part of his shoulder had been crushed to a pulp but he didn't believe his mind. His mind said that hand and arm were still there, joined to his shoulder. If he had the energy he would argue that they were. Then he saw Sarah, her long dark hair held with a red ribbon and tied in a bun on the top of her head, and he called her name with all the strength he could muster. For that precious moment, she was there beside him and then he passed out.

****

This terrible accident happened on Wednesday 20th March 1884. Thomas died from the injuries sustained two days later on Friday 23rd March. In the nineteenth century no safety mechanisms were in place and accidents involving machines would have been all too common. The Newcastle Morning Herald and Miners Advocate Tuesday 4th April, page 3, reported This terrible accident happened on Wednesday 20th March 1884. Thomas died from the injuries sustained two days later on Friday 23rd March. In the nineteenth century no safety mechanisms were in place and accidents involving machines would have been all too common.

COURAGE, THY NAME IS WOMAN
The Story of Sarah Jarvis

I'm an old woman now. I have seen great changes in my life. I'm coming up to my eighty-ninth year. The folk around me tell me that I'm a grand old lady. It's as if they are preparing themselves for when I am no longer here.

Another life ago I was a girl in England, a wife and mother here in New South Wales and twice a widow. Here is my story.

My father was a bedstead maker. It was an honourable occupation to have for don't we all need a bed to sleep in? I can't remember my mother. She died in childbirth having me. My father did not recover from his loss and I guess you could say he died a few years later of a broken heart. Sometimes I try to imagine what he looked like for I only have my memory of him and what people had told me. Truth to say, I see my early life in England through a mist. I was a different person then.

Marriage seemed the only option for a woman in my position and I must say I was indeed fortunate when I met Thomas Price. He was a kind man. When Thomas suggested that we emigrate to find a better life for ourselves and our children, I agreed. There was nothing in England for me. Australia seemed to me to be an exotic and exciting place to be. I was as excited as Thomas was. We would find a new beginning for ourselves and our children at the other end of the earth.

The sea journey aboard the *Devonport* was horrific. How I cursed the vessel. Eighty-nine days we were at sea, and every day I prayed that we would soon reach our destination and be released from the constant rocking and rolling of the ship. The journey strengthened my resolve to succeed in Australia as great misfortune had been visited upon us when our eldest child and only daughter, Mary Ann succumbed to a dreadful illness and died on board that ship. How I wept for her. Life seemed cruel then. It was as if I was being punished for some long-forgotten sin. Despair visited me and I wondered if I had the will to keep going.

When new life came to me with the arrival of Frederick Kennedy, born on board that cursed ship, I knew that I must not give in to despair, that my grief would lessen but would never be forgotten. This I learned. Time is indeed a great healer, and there was much to do.

Those first years in our new country were difficult. It was a struggle sometimes to have food on the table but we were young and we were so determined to overcome everything that was sent to try us. There was much that I despaired about and much that I feared. It was the weather that affected me the most during those first few years. The heat of the summer was so intense that at times I wished I could escape the merciless sun and plunge into cool water or feel the rain wetting my skin. Days and weeks brought no relief but when the droughts broke, as they always do, the intense heat was replaced with a deluge and the parched earth became a flood plain. Then we struggled through the mud and cursed the weather even more.

I have learned some shadows and joys come into all our lives. When the floods subsided and the sun shone again, the countryside came alive. The brown grasses turned to green and everyone was cheerful once again. Then we felt that we were indeed fortunate to live in our new home.

I remember the evenings that Thomas and I shared. Married for years, we could always find time to talk to each other. These memories are precious to me, even now if I shut my eyes, I can hear his voice. He had such plans for us, you see. He worked hard in the tannery. That was his trade. We lived in Penrith, some thirty miles west of Sydney. There were seven tanneries in the area and work was plentiful for skilled tanners and Thomas was one of the best. I must say I worked hard as well. It was not easy sometimes to keep the family together. Our two youngest, Emily and George were born in Penrith. They would never know the Old Country nor would our older boys remember anything of it. When I had time to think about this, I knew I had no regrets. Despite the climate that I hated and the snakes that I had feared, this was a magic place to be. In time, I learned to accept both.

When Thomas and his partner established the tannery at Walcha some three hundred miles or so away north of Sydney, it seemed like a dream come true. Our slab-built house was comfortable and there was more space around us. In Penrith, we had lived side by side with our neighbours. Here in Walcha, I grew melons the size of footballs. I could never have imagined that I could have such a huge vegetable garden. We had food a plenty. Life was good then.

Even to this day, I find it hard to talk about what happened in Walcha that terrible day when Thomas had his accident at the tannery. How he managed somehow to walk those fifty yards to be with me even though his arm and shoulder had been crushed in that fearsome machine is still a mystery. I saw him, the blood soaking the blankets his men had thrown over his poor damaged body, and I froze.

My mind could not comprehend what had happened. He had left me in the morning to go to his work. He had been so full of good cheer and optimism then. It took me a few seconds to realise that he no longer had a hand or an arm. His shoulder had been torn asunder. One of the sodden blankets, now red with blood fell at his feet. He held his left hand out for me. Those few seconds of disbelief remain with me to this day, and even though it happened a long time ago now, sometimes it seems to me that it was yesterday, and the pain is still there. Part of me died with Thomas that day.

A few seconds later, I ran and threw my arms around him. I remember his blood flowed so freely that it drenched my white blouse. Two days later he died in my arms and the very next day, I burnt the white blouse.

We had very little money after Thomas died and I had to find work to support the two youngest in the family. Robert and Henry were married by then and Frederick was just sixteen. Thomas's partner took charge of the tannery but I wanted nothing more to do with it.

I moved into Armidale with Emily and George and I found work as a housekeeper at one of the hotels. It was here that my life changed once again.

Folk had told me about John McAllister, the Scottish seaman who had turned farmer and whose wife had left him in mysterious circumstances. I took no notice of their gossip for I did not need any man. I was married to Thomas for twenty-two years and had he not suffered the horrific accident, I would still be his wife. I doubted that I could love again, certainly not such a man as John McAllister whose harsh behaviour towards his sons was the subject of much talk. Thomas had been firm but fair with his boys. Never once had he taken the whip to them. From all accounts, John McAllister had no such scruples. I had no desire to saddle myself with such a man.

Life has many twists and turns and this I was to learn when I was introduced to John. My first impression was that he was different from what I had imagined him to be. His bushy beard covered half his face. He had piercing blue eyes that seemed to bore right into your soul and a Scottish accent that was quite delightful to hear. It soon became evident that he intended to court me and would not take no for an answer.

We were married at the Presbyterian Church in Armidale and I moved to John's farm at Daisy Hill with Emily and George. My eldest boys, Robert and Henry would help out whenever they could even though both were married and had families of their own to look after. John believed that a family should work together and unfortunately, he was as hard on my boys as he had been with his children. That was when the trouble began. Neither boy had wanted me to marry John but I had made up my mind. John had means and would provide for us. I respected him although I doubted I would ever have the love for him as I had for Thomas, but I was no longer a girl. The arrangement suited us both.

John and my boys argued constantly. Henry had a temper on him. He and his stepfather were close to blows many a time. It all became too much for Robert and he left, with his wife, Rosabell and baby Ella, for Western Australia. I missed Robert. He was a good son. Henry stayed around with Rachel but he wasn't such a good boy. I sensed there was trouble between Rachel and Henry right from the start but a mother doesn't like to interfere with matters such as this. I kept my counsel.

I was pleased when Emily married John Savage. The family stayed nearby. That was a blessing to me. I missed them and the children when they moved to Melbourne to start a shoe-making business. Emily always had a liking for leather like her father. These things must be passed on from generation to generation I think. I remember how Thomas had talked to her about the tanning process and she had loved the feel of the leather hides. The boys weren't interested at all which had been some disappointment to their father. That's families, I guess.

George moved away too. As soon as he was able he joined his brother in Western Australia to work with him as a miner. It was in Western Australia that he married a girl he met there, Margaret. A few years later they moved to New Zealand where he did very well for himself. My children have wandered around just like Thomas and I did.

As the years went by, John and I became more comfortable with each other and I grew to be fond of him. We had been together for twenty years and I thought we would just grow old together and that would be that. It was not to be. I'll never forget the moment I heard about his accident. I've always loved my vegetable garden and I was enjoying just sitting there on a bench that sunny day thinking about what next to plant when I heard one of the farmhands call out my name. The man was in such a state, I remember. I tried to calm him but he kept babbling on about a sulky overturning and the poor spent horse pulling so hard to be free. He thought that a man had been trapped underneath.

I felt the cold fear of a memory. I asked the farmhand who the man was. He took off his brown leather hat and lowered his head so he wouldn't have to look into my eyes. I always remember that moment. The fingers on my hands turned white even though it was a warm day and the sun was shining. Beads of sweat settled on my brow. I brushed them away with an icy hand. My mind was aware of what was coming before he spoke and I knew that history was about to repeat itself on another sunny day. The farmhand told me it was John who was trapped underneath the sulky. A few men had managed to free him but it was too late. John was dead.

That was a long time ago now. I like living at Daisy Hill. It has been my home now for nigh on thirty-five years. I've so many grandchildren to come after me. That's good to know. Life goes on. Whether I will join John in the afterlife, I don't know.

All those memories. I'm tired now. Think I'll just close my eyes and have a little nap here on the veranda at Daisy Hill. I've had a good life, all things considered.

****

John and Sarah McAllister
Photograph in the family collection of Dorothy Griffey

****

The facts about Sarah's life are recorded. I have allowed myself some writer's imagination to bring her story to life. Sarah, like so many pioneer women, was a true hero. I am reminded of the fine words written by the Australian poet, George Essex Evans:

For them no trumpet sounds the call, no poet plies his arts,
They only hear the beating of their gallant, loving hearts.
But they have sung with silent lives the song all songs above?
The holiness of sacrifice, the dignity of love.

Well have we held our fathers creed. No call has passed us by.
We faced and fought the wilderness, we sent our sons to die.
And we have hearts to do and dare, and yet, o'er all the rest,
The hearts that made the Nation were the Women of the West.

This surely was Sarah.

DIGGING FOR GOLD

'I'm off to find me some gold,' announced Henry. He had a pick, a shovel and a lot of hope.

To be certain gold was out there and from all accounts it was to found everywhere.

'They say there's more gold in northern New South Wales than Ballarat and Bendigo. People will be flockin' here from everywhere, mark my words. Gold will put Hillgrove on the map and we just happen to be livin' here. I reckon we're sittin' on top of a goldmine. We just need to get out there an' start diggin' before the place is overrun with prospectors.'

Henry was undeterred by doubts the rest of his family had. They thought that the likelihood of Henry finding gold and growing rich was just a pipe dream. After all, Henry had not shown any capacity for hard work in his nineteen years. Fossicking meant hard physical work in all weathers. The heat alone in the summer would do for most men and the difficult terrain made matters worse. Rumour had it that gold had been discovered at Baker's Creek but it was located at the bottom of a gorge. Hard toil would be required to dig it out from there. They had discovered lodes of antimony in the area a few years before. Finding gold would spark a much more exciting challenge and Henry was right, miners would come from everywhere to dig it out. Gold is an addiction without a cure. But would Henry have the strength of character to keep going or would he fall victim to that very addiction? His family doubted that he would stick at it. After a few weeks of hard graft, and finding nothing, he would be back with his tail between his legs.

'I'm off then,' said Henry. 'Me and Charlie are headin' for Baker's Creek. When you see me next, I'll be a rich man.'

Henry had enlisted the aid of his mate, Charlie, who was thought to be just as unreliable as Henry. Both of them are adverse to work,' his father said. 'Tipping at windmills,' his mother said.

****

Henry and Charlie walked to Baker's Creek from Hillgrove with their meagre possessions wrapped up in hessian bags and slung over their shoulders. The hot summer made the going difficult and the rough terrain of the New England area meant that they could only walk so far before they would have to stop and seek shade under a eucalyptus tree. To quench their thirst they drank from the creeks, filling their water bottles afterwards. They trudged on, undeterred. They slept on the rough ground and covered their bodies with coarse woollen blankets. The world was full of wonder for them at night. They gazed at the trillions of stars above, talked of how they would find gold and what they would do with the riches the gold would bring.

'I'll head to Sydney,' Charlie said, 'an' stay in the finest hotel there an' fill meself up with the most expensive grub around. The Sydney oysters are the best in the world, so they say. Then I'll get meself a tailored made suit an' find me some girls for company. The more the merrier. They'll flock to me when they know what a filthy rich bloke I am.'

'Yeah,' replied Henry. He already had plans to spend his newfound wealth. 'I'm goin' to first buy the butcher's shop in Hillgrove, an' then I'm off to the big smoke too. I'll meet you in King's Cross an' we'll get drunk for a week. Let's shake on it, mate.'

The two boys shook hands and vowed to keep to their plan. Henry had been working in a butcher's shop of late. He wasn't on good terms with the owner and his plan was to buy the man out, just for spite. With his newfound wealth he had already decided that he would be quite happy to give up being a butcher but he relished the thought that his employer would have to pay him rent for the shop in the future.

With their heads full of hope and dreaming of riches, the

boys settled down for the night under the stars.

A day later they arrived at the site of the mine. Sunk deep in the gorge, it was already the scene of human activity and the boys were somewhat at a loss as to what to do next. Their plan had been to stake a claim, dig a shaft and fossick for the elusive gold themselves. They were certain that the gold was there. They just hadn't reckoned on digging out gold for a boss.

'Looks like we'll have to move further along the gorge and away from the mine here,' said Charlie. 'I sure as hell don't fancy spendin' all me time underground workin' for the mining company, do you?'

'No way, mate,' was Henry's reply.

To say that Henry and Charlie were optimists at this time in the lives would be a fact. The youthful vigour was there and no way were they about to give up. They hoisted the hessian bags over their shoulders and headed further up the gorge avoiding the boulders and the occasional snake.

Two days later they came to an open clearing and it was there that they decided to stake their claim. Neither of them had any knowledge of the geology of the area or the best possible place to find gold. All they had was blind faith and optimism in equal measure.

For days they toiled under the hot sun. They cut timbers for a makeshift shaft and started digging. Food became scarce. One day they managed to shoot some rabbits that had been brought into the country by the white man. The rabbits were plentiful, increasing their numbers by the hour and already becoming something of an ecological disaster but the boys were just grateful to eat them. They still had not found any gold.

'I dunno about you, Charlie,' Henry said one evening as they sat by the fire, weary after a hard day's hard graft that had yielded nothing, 'but I reckon this digging for gold is a fool's game. They said we'd just trip over gold nuggets without the diggin'.

'Yeah. Bloody fools, aren't we, mate?'

Henry didn't reply. Instead, he rolled a cigarette and lit it with a stick from the fire. He was tired, fed up and ready to give up.

'Should we go back to the mining company and ask for a job?' Charlie asked. 'They must be gettin' gold out the number of men that were round there.'

He was as fed up as Henry and every day his dreams of being a rich man seemed to be disappearing. There was also the matter of whether to pay money for a claim or not, or just pack up and go, telling no one. It was an empty sort of place, anyhow. They could vanish into thin air and who would ever know they had sunk a shaft here? There were plenty of empty shafts around. Had all these blokes staked a claim and paid to be there? He doubted it.

'I reckon we should sleep on it,' Henry said after a few moments of deep thought. 'We'll give it one more day before we quit. Agreed?'

Charlie grunted a reply which could have been 'yes' or possibly 'no'. All he wanted to do was sleep.

During the night it rained.

They had erected a canvas canopy for shelter and strung ropes to nearby trees. It had kept the moisture off them on the hot nights but it was no use with the rain. Water accumulated in the middle of the canvas and the weight had caused the ropes to break free. The result was that in the middle of the night they had been drenched.

They were hungry, angry and wet through. They argued.

'I'm not givin' it another day,' Charlie grumbled. 'Let's pack up and get the hell out of here.'

Henry, by this time, was in much the same frame of mind as his friend. It had stopped raining and the early morning air was clear. Their spirits lifted a little when they heard the tinkle of the bellbirds followed by the cackle of a kookaburra.

'Yeah,' said Henry. 'We'll pack up and head off home.'

'Glad you've seen sense, mate. Should we ask for a job at the mining company? We might find some gold after all.'

'I'm fed up with all of it,' replied Henry. 'Guess I'm stuck with butcherin' for a while longer. You can stay here and look for a job at the minin' company if you like but I'm headin' home.'

They packed up and retraced their steps towards the big mine in silence.

They kept walking. That night the boys slept under the stars again. They woke to another clear day that promised to turn into a hot one.

It was at midday that Henry tripped over a small misshapen rock. He was tired of walking and in a fit of rage he kicked the rock with his boot. It rolled a few yards in front of him and landed upside down. He bent down to pick it up, and when he saw what was there, he let out a yell so loud that it disturbed a flock of parrots. The birds flew from the trees but Henry wasn't looking at the birds.

'Bloody hell, Charlie. Look at this.'

Specks of gold were visible and embedded in the rock.

'That's gold, mate. You've found gold!'

Charlie picked up another rock and sure enough it, too, contained specks of gold.

'Looks like we've found gold here after all. Let's start digging!'

That evening they sat by the fire again. Now all talk was about what they would do with the gold they had found by accident and without much effort.

'I've been thinkin', said Henry. 'I reckon I'll head for Sydney now. I sort of fancy turnin' a bit of this here gold into a ring. Some of those fancy jewellers down there will do a good job.'

'Why a ring?'

'I dunno, Charlie. Just an idea. Get some cash for the gold

first... an' keep a bit for a ring. Yeah, that's what I'll do.'

****

I have included this story in the collection because both the Price and Fuller families lived in an area of northern New South Wales named New England where gold had been discovered. The gold deposits here were vast. The story of Henry Price who discovered enough gold to get a ring made is based on a fact. How he came to find the gold, however, is pure fiction as is the name of Henry's mate.

Henry was always known as Harry within his family but for the sake of consistency, I have decided to keep to his baptismal name.

Photograph taken by Schoolmaster Henry Tonkin 1888 from the book, *New England from Old Photographs* by Lionel Gilbert, page 102. Held by the Armidale Heritage Centre.

THE SADDEST STORY

The boy wailed all night. He had a fever and his small, freckled face was soaked with sweat. When he coughed it seemed that some evil demon had taken hold of his frail body and he trembled all over. He complained that his head ached, and then he coughed again. This time small droplets of blood appeared on his hand. He tried to cover his mouth.

'My throat hurts, Mumma.'

The mother tried her best to comfort him but she was wracked with pain as well. Her throat burned and her breath was a sickening, sweet and putrid odour when she held her boy in her arms. Her whole body felt exhausted, what with trying to look after the other three children, and now she was pregnant again. What a life, she thought and at that moment death would have been a happy release but her poor William started to cough again and Rachael wept with him. William, her firstborn, now six years of age had been playing near the water source, and unbeknown to any of them, had tripped and fallen face down into a puddle of water. As he lay there under the cloudless blue sky some of the rancid water dribbled into his mouth. It was here that the waste from the abattoir was allowed to flow unhindered and so close to the town. The water tasted horrible and William spat it out. A few days later William complained of stomach pain. No one took any notice until he started to cough.

His father was not impressed with his son.

'Can't you stop that boy from coughin', woman? I've work to do in the mornin' an' I need me sleep?'

But no amount of comfort from the mother stopped the boy. His coughing kept everyone awake and Rachael coughed too. William shared his bed with his siblings, Herbert, just four, Alice two, and baby Percy, just one year old. William's coughing kept them all awake and in the morning, his temperature rose and the coughing increased.

'We'll need to get the doctor to him, Henry.' Rachael pleaded, but her husband was against any medical help.

'We can't afford the doctor. All the boy needs is to get himself out of his bed and into the fresh air. He's a strong lad. You fuss too much.'

But Rachael knew that no amount of fresh air would cure her son.

The next evening Rachael suffered. The weariness that had engulfed her whole body meant that even a simple task was a painful one. Thirsty, she poured herself a drink of tea and lifted the cup to her lips, but this ordinary task seemed to take an age so great was her fatigue. She found it difficult to swallow the tea for her throat hurt so much. Even the thought of food made her feel nauseous. Added to this was the worry that both she and William might succumb to the fever and her husband would be left a widower with all the responsibilities of the family heaped onto his not-so-strong shoulders. While the demands of the young children distracted her she longed to lie down beside William, close her eyes and drift into some sort of sleep, but that was impossible for every few moments she would cough again and what little energy she could muster would disappear as she felt even more pain in her stomach. She feared she would not see the dawn of a new day.

The situation continued for a few more days and neither Rachael nor William showed any signs of beating the fever. William was losing his battle for life. A doctor had to be called for now his mother feared that she would lose her boy. She doubted if William would live through the night.

'What have you done to yourself, my poor Willie?' she whispered into his ear. 'Your father will call for the doctor now... Doctor Gorrick will make things better for you, just wait and see.'

Then William looked into his mother's eyes. She saw no fear

there, just acceptance of what was to be. William tried hard to grasp his mother's hand but he was so weak that he could not raise his small hand. The hand of this poor child, covered in droplets of sweat, and positioned so neatly there on top of the bed sheet, could become stiff that night for death was near. Tears filled his mother's eyes.

****

Doctor Gorrick, who was also the Government Medical Officer, was not impressed with what he saw.

'Your boy is very ill,' he told Henry. 'You must prepare yourself for the worst.'

But his father would not hear of it.

'He's a strong lad,' he said. 'We'll just have to wait and see what tomorrow brings.'

'Your wife is ill as well. She has caught the fever from your boy.' The doctor was anxious that Henry realised the seriousness of the matter. 'Here's praying that the other children don't succumb.'

'My wife will rally round. Mark my words,' Henry said and shrugged his shoulders.

But the next day brought no change for Rachael. She became breathless with any exertion and the constant coughing began to take its toll on her. She struggled, and even if she tried her best to go about the everyday tasks it became evident that she was losing the battle to survive. Doctor Gorrick wondered if Rachael would give in to the disease before her son. Something had to be done about the sanitation in the town or even more people would become infected. He was a worried man. He knew that it was now a matter of extreme urgency and that the authorities had to inspect the source and supply of water to the town as soon as possible to prevent the epidemic from spreading. If Rachael Price died, others would follow.

To everyone's surprise, William was alive in the morning but the spectre of death was all around them. For the poor boy, it was just a matter of time.

****

When Doctor Gorrick and the other members of the local Progress Committee inspected the water it was discovered that the spot where the local carriers obtained their supply was infected, orders were given immediately that no water should be taken from that spot but that the water should be brought into the town from the reserve, a mile higher upstream. This might just reduce the risk that the epidemic would spread further into the town. This would mean that lives would be saved. Much to the dismay of Doctor Gorrick, it was also discovered that the local butchers had been somewhat lax in disposing of the waste from the abattoir. It was decided that a new site had to be found as early as possible but here the authorities encountered a problem. The site that was decided upon was surrounded by land which was owned by a rather obstinate individual who refused to allow any traffic through his property. A new road had to be created, and quickly, and notice was given to that effect. In the meantime, the public school was closed and people were cautioned about drinking any of the water from the contaminated site. There had already been a few cases of diphtheria and typhoid reported to the authorities but it was the sad story of William and Rachael that hastened the decisions to try to stop the spread of these deadly diseases. During the critical weeks that followed Doctor Gorrick acted in an exemplary manner and later on, he was viewed as something of a hero.

****

"I'm dyin', ain't I, Mumma?' What could Rachel say to her boy that would reassure him for in her heart she knew that the question he asked was a truthful one and any denial would be false? If there had been any way that she could have taken his place, she would have, for a mother's love is strong and unflinching in its intensity. She placed her hand as gently as she could onto his wet brow and with her other hand she stroked his hair. All the while she murmured words of comfort.

'You're a brave boy, my dearest Willie,' she whispered. 'I love you.'

'I love you too, Mumma.'

William smiled and closed both his eyes. The moment passed as all moments did leaving his mother with eyes full of tears and the terrible ache of sadness in her heart.

They laid William to rest under the pepperina tree where he used to play because they thought that that was where he would like to be. Rachael did not speak to anyone about her loss but went about her day's work as best she could. Exhausted, she began to fear the worst for herself until one morning she woke to find that the swelling in her neck glands had all but disappeared and the painful throat she had endured for days had disappeared. She felt better and she coughed less.

'You are making good progress Mrs Price,' Doctor Gorrick told her. 'You will be pleased to know that the committee have made great progress in containing the epidemic. The road to the new water source has been approved by the government and this should allay all fears that there might be another outbreak. There have been some notifications sent to the guilty parties regarding hygiene laws in the town you'll be happy to hear. Here's hoping that there won't be a reoccurrence of the deadly disease.'

Rachael nodded her head. She did feel a lot stronger and she was grateful for the good doctor's words.

Doctor Gorrick closed his black bag and said,

'It has indeed been a tragedy for you and your husband to lose such a fine young boy in such difficult circumstances. My sympathies are with you both. But it's been a blessing that your other children haven't caught the disease and you, yourself, are looking a lot better. Given your family circumstances, I will waive my fee this time.'

This was indeed good news for Rachel. In life, there is much goodness and people can often be surprised that in the face of suffering, hope prevails. The next day Rachael picked some wildflowers and laid them on the mound of dirt where her William lay. Then she carried on.

****

Before immunisation typhoid and diphtheria were prevalent in the nineteenth century. This story is based on a newspaper article from The Armidale Express and New England Advertiser Tue 24th September 1889, page 8. Although the actual account of Rachael and Doctor Gorrick is fictionalised as we have no way of knowing if the doctor did treat the family. William, the eldest of the Price children, did die from the disease and Rachael herself came close to death. However, she gave birth to ten children and lived to the age of eighty-seven.

ON A FOREIGN SHORE

Nurse Sullivan was becoming rather fond of the Australian soldiers. And there was an entire battalion of them stationed just over the hill from the military hospital where she worked. Vi Sullivan wasn't an actual fully fledged nurse but she had answered the call when the word went out that nurses were needed to tend to the wounded and the war-damaged. Vi passed her Red Cross qualification with the minimum of effort and was soon put to work on the wards as an auxiliary nurse. She looked smart in her white uniform which stretched right to her ankles. Her curly hair was covered by the linen veil and secured with just one plain safety pin over the folds. The Matron, a rather dour Army personality, nodded her approval when she inspected the uniform and the unstarched veil. Then she told Vi that she did have an aptitude for nursing and she should pursue a career later on when all this wretched business was over. Vi was just eighteen years of age and it was all rather exciting to have all these young men around. The Australian soldiers seemed so different from the boys she had known in the quiet village where she had lived all her life. These lads came from the other end of the earth, thought Vi. She wondered what life must be like in faraway Australia. She had only travelled a mere twenty miles from her village.

Vi had bright blue eyes. The boys all thought she was a good looker but most of all, Vi had a kind heart. She cried after her first day on the wards. This was a place where life and death sat side by side, and more often than not, death held the upper hand. The boys brought home from the Front were much the same age as Vi. Had it been another time, she would have been flirting with them. Now all she saw were boys lying in the wards with limbs gone, and wounds that left scars that might never heal the body or the soul. Those first few weeks she wondered whether she was able to do her bit to help the war effort in this way. Maybe it all had been a mistake to volunteer to nurse these boy soldiers but her friends from the village were all lining up to go to the hospital and she hadn't wanted to be left behind. It was much more exciting than domestic service after all. Who knows what would happen to be amongst all those young men?

The village girls who worked in the hospital were full of tales about the Australians and what a great lot of fellows they were. One of the girls had already formed an attachment to a young soldier who had been badly wounded at the Front, and if it was to be believed, the boy had proposed marriage. So Vi had volunteered thinking how exciting it would be to meet someone like that.

Learning how to bandage and apply pressure to wounds had been interesting but that training had all been done on dummies, not the real thing. One day, Betsy, Vi's best friend from the village, found her crying in the room where they kept the bed linen.

'Why, Vi,' she said, 'whatever's the matter?'

Between sobs, Vi told Betsy that the sight of all the sick and wounded lads was just too much for her. She wanted to run away from all this misery. Betsy put a comforting arm around Vi's shoulders.

'I was just the same at first,' she said. 'Don't give up, Vi. You're a good nurse, better than me. No one can bandage as good as you.'

'If it wasn't so real,' Vi sobbed.

'Aye, I know. It's hard to see them with half their limbs away and God knows what else. But did you know there's a young lad who has his eye on you, Vi? He's caught bronchitis and it's not looking so good for him.'

This cheered Vi up a bit. She wiped her eyes and asked Betsy who it could be.

'The lad in the bed nearest the door in Ward 6. He's the one who coughs all the time. Well, they all do but I think it's gone down to his chest. He's finding it harder and harder to breathe. Don't think he's seen any action yet though. Told me he just started training a month ago and came down with the bronchitis. It's the damp, you see. They're not used to the cold, poor blighters.'

'How do you know he likes me?'

'You silly goose. He told me. Tells me he noticed you running up and down the ward.'

'How will I know which lad he is?' asked Vi. Her curiosity had been aroused and she wiped the tears from her eyes.

'Just walk up and down and keep your eye out for him. Unless they've moved him, he was in the third bed from the door... on the right going in. He's poorly though. Prepare for the worst.'

'What do I say to him?'

'Oh, Vi, for heaven's sake... just give him your best smile and put on your nurse's look. They love it when you do that. Makes life a bit more bearable for them... feel they're back to normal, I guess.'

The very next day Vi made a point of ensuring that she was on the same bronchitis ward. Beds here were arranged in such a way that any privacy the men might have wished for was gone. They were packed close together for the wounded just kept coming. It was a busy day on the bronchitis ward. Nurses and doctors were doing their best to restrain one of the patients. This young fellow, cursing profusely between bouts of coughing, and minus an arm, had somehow managed to climb out of his bed threatening to punch another soldier. In the commotion that ensured, Vi was able to glide along the length of the ward without anyone paying any attention to her. She planned to appear that she wasn't looking for one particular soldier. Her presence was greeted with a few saucy words but, in truth, all attention was focused on the altercation between the two boys at the far end of the ward. It looked as though a serious injury might take place if things weren't brought under control. Fights, both verbal and physical often occurred on the wards. It was as if all the pent-up anger that had lain dormant in the young men's minds would surface and even though they were sick, wounded and some of them dying, often an ill-spoken word would cause the mayhem.

Vi put on her professional demeanour as best she could and avoided going anywhere near the two angry soldiers. She was about to give up looking for her admirer when she spied Betsy.

'C'mon, Vi. Let's introduce yourself to him.' Betsy giggled and Vi felt her face redden as the two nurses made their way to the soldier's bed. Then Betsy left Vi standing there looking at a young man with fair hair and blue eyes. On his right arm there was a tattoo of a bunch of flowers and he had a scar on his right forearm and elbow. Vi wondered how he had got the scar. He did look very ill.

'What's your name?' he asked between coughs.

'Violet. But my friends call me Vi.'

'Well, Vi, I'm William George but my friends call me George.'

He coughed again, spitting out some green mucus into a bowl at the side of his bed. When he sank back onto the pillow he looked so ill. Vi glanced at the notes at the end of the bed. George was just twenty-two years and ten months old. He hadn't seen any action. He had disembarked at Devonport at the end of January and had been training with the 30th A.I.F. Battalion for a month when the disease struck him.

'What was the commotion about between those two chaps?' she asked to make some conversation. The older nurses had told her that this was just what some of the boys needed, just a kind word and nothing about the war.

'Oh, those two blokes are always at each other's throats. The bloke with one arm thinks the other one cheated at two-up.

Both of 'em have been to France though. Not like me.' George wheezed. His breathing was so laboured now Vi wondered if she should call for a doctor.

'What's two-up?'

'A nice girl like you, don't want to know. It's a gambling game us Aussies play, a man's game. Women not allowed.'

'Doesn't seem to have done either of them any good then,' Vi sniffed.

George smiled.

'Will you come and see me again, Vi?' he asked. He held out his hand and Vi placed her small hand into his. Surely no one would notice. Her hand felt safe in his. She didn't want to let go.

'I'll have to leave you now, George,' she whispered. 'I'm wanted on the pneumonia ward. This is a better ward, I think.'

'Guess it's 'cos I'm here!'

'Cheeky bugger.'

'You'll come tomorrow, won't you? I'm not going away.'

'Of course I will.'

The Vi did something that she never thought she would. Without hesitating, and still holding his hand, she kissed him.

His cheek felt cold and clammy.

The next moment she hurried from his bed, her cheeks a deep red, while emotions ran through her like a torrent of pure clear water; all the while conscious of the sudden power of love for a young man, so far from home, for whom she had suddenly and completely out of the blue, fallen in love with. Later that evening she would be embarrassed, mortified at her action but for now all she wanted to do was to see him again and hold his hand.

The next day she kept away from his bronchitis ward and it was only at the end of her shift that she took the courage to return. He had worsened during the night. She asked the Staff Nurse whether she could talk to him for a little while, to somehow ease his suffering. The Staff Nurse was a kindly soul.

With so much death and pain all about her, she could sense the triumph of love in this young woman's eyes. She nodded her head and watched as Vi made her way to the soldier's bed to hold his hand.

'I've come back, George,' Vi said.

'I hoped you would. You're so beautiful, Vi. What's your hair like under the veil?' he asked.

'Red,' she said. 'I get teased about that. Carrot-top, they call me.'

'Can I have a peek? No one's looking.'

'Well... ?'

She lifted the edge of the white veil. A tiny curly red strand of hair appeared. George grinned between a cough.

'Wish I could see some more,' he said.

Vi smiled. He really was such a tease. Another time, they would be stepping out together with their future stretching before them, predictable and peaceful.

'Stay with me for a while, Vi.'

She perched on the side of the bed and held his hand. The soldier next to him moaned and called a nurse to bring a glass of water.

'He's not going to make it,' George said matter-of-factly. 'He's just nineteen and a country boy like me. What are we doing here, Vi?'

'I don't know. It's all so horrible.'

'Maybe it'll be over soon and we can be together.'

'Is that a proposal?'

George grinned. 'Could be,' he said and squeezed her hand.

****

The next few days she was once again assigned to Ward Six, his ward. Although she tried hard to hide her emotions when she was near him, it failed for word soon got around that George had found himself a sweetheart and a right good looker this one was. When they got the chance, they talked, whispering so as not to let others into their secret conversations for there was much to discuss and plans to be made. George told her about Australia, how the distances there were so vast and nothing like England; about his mother but never a mention of his father; of his many brothers and sisters, and what work he did there, labouring and horse driving, all these things but not a word about the war or what others had told him to expect when he finally got over to the Front. He whispered that he had gone AWOL twice a few weeks after he enlisted and been reprimanded for that with just a fine both times. The other blokes were doing the same. He wondered what sort of soldier he wanted to be.

Two weeks passed by. Every moment Vi spent with George was precious for all the time the terrible uncertainty of the war hung there, worrying them. Any moment he could be taken away from her and ordered to pack for the Front. Who knows if she would ever see him again?

On the days that Vi wasn't assigned to George's bronchitis ward, she made a point of looking in on him after her shift. One evening she returned to the bronchitis ward to find another soldier in her lover's bed. The kindly Staff Nurse was there at her desk, writing notes.

'Sister,' Vi asked her and her voice trembled as she spoke, 'where's Private Price... George?'

The nurse looked up at the young woman before her. This was war after all and there was much to face and harder words to say.

'Vi, my dear,' she replied. This young nurse was the same age as her daughter. 'I'm so very sorry. There is no easy way to tell you. George passed away this morning, just before noon. There was nothing we could do. This wretched disease has taken so many young men from us.' She added, 'I know you had become very fond of him, dear. He looked out for you too. The doctor told me he whispered your name. These were his last words, Vi. Whatever happens, remember that, my dear.'

****

Vi Sullivan is a fictional character. So also is the romance between Vi and George. Romance did occur between the soldiers and the nurses. One such incident has been recorded which resulted in marriage. The military facts are correct, however. Army records show that Private William George Price died from bronchitis at Fovant Military Hospital, near Salisbury in 1917 having only been stationed a month in England. The Fovant Military Hospital consisted of six hundred beds and I am certain there would have been more than one ward with bronchitis patients.

Grave of Private William George Price
St Editha Churchyard, Baverstock
Wiltshire, Unitary Authority, Wiltshire, England

JUSTICE

The tomahawk was the last straw. He threatened to split her in two with it.

A few minutes before, he had grabbed her shoulders and shook them so fiercely that she felt her small frame would not be able to recover this time. A thought crossed her mind that this might be the end. She might indeed die there in front of her children in the small kitchen that should have been the safe refuge people called home. But he hadn't finished yet. The next second after, he punched her face with such force that she did collapse and stumbled, falling at his feet. She tried to cover her bleeding face with her hands. The boys had brought the tomahawk into the kitchen and had laid it besides some kindling for the fire. In a mindless rage, he grabbed the tomahawk, swung it so close to her body that the tip of it grazed her arm and drew blood but she hardly registered the pain, so great was her fear now. Five times he swung the tomahawk like this and every time he shouted words of abuse. He uttered the filthy words that had no justification whilst all through this nightmare, a maniacal glee revealed, in his eyes, the power that this man she had lived with on and off for twenty-six torturous years, had over her. Five times she feared for her life.

The horror of it all was the fear; that terrifying chill that the next minute in time might be the last and that her three youngest little children, clinging to one another, fearful and cowering in the corner of the room, might be witness to the absolute and unbelievable horror that their mother was killed by the man they knew to be their father.

****

It hadn't started like this. Rachael was just seventeen when she married Henry. He was a handsome sort of fellow with a thin moustache, brown eyes and a gift for flattery that made her blush. Her father had assured her that Henry had good prospects and would make a fine husband. 'Give him time,' her father said, for Henry was young, too. Twenty years of age. It wouldn't be quite a match made in heaven but life could be hard sometimes and everyone had to learn to take the rough with the smooth. Had Rachael been able to glimpse the future, she would have seen that the roughness far outweighed the smoothness with her life with Henry. But she believed her father.

Of course her mother was fair against the marriage right from the start but this had more to do with religion than character. Henry insisted they marry in the Wesleyan Chapel as this was the faith of his family and all his forebears before him but to her mother's eyes that would mean the marriage would be declared null and void for her Irish mother, as fiery as she was, was a staunch believer in the Roman Catholic Church. There was no way out for Rachael. She was pregnant, and for the sake of the unborn child, it would be far better to have a ring on her finger than to be fearful of what the church might dictate and excommunicate her. So Henry and Rachael were married in the heathen church, as her mother called it. His brother, Robert, and her sister, Juliet, witnessed their signatures. Her mother refused to enter the chapel. She stood outside in the rain, holding her umbrella above her head and with a face like a thundercloud.

****

The courtroom was crowded that Monday morning in June when Henry and Rachael faced themselves once again. This time there was no thought of what had gone before. The tomahawk had been consigned to the back of Rachael's mind as a terrible memory but she refused to look at Henry, fearful of what he would do, even in this crowded place. She sat as motionless as a rock and listened to Mr Schrader as he began the case for a judicial separation.

Mr Schrader started by stating that the petitioner was a

member of the Roman Catholic Church and this had, indeed, been cause for some dispute between both parties right from the beginning of their twenty-six year marriage. The respondent was a Protestant. They had been married in June 1882 in Armidale, New South Wales, the marriage being conducted in the Wesleyan Methodist chapel, much to the displeasure of her mother, a devout member of the Roman faith. The petitioner herself was a Roman Catholic and as such, the religious upbringing of all seven surviving children into that church was of some importance to her.

'I have to let the court know, however, that the two parties have found it somewhat difficult to live together,' Mr Schrader continued. 'On many occasions, the respondent has deserted the petitioner and on one such time, he was found guilty of forging a cheque. This resulted in him being sentenced to a year's hard labour in Mudgee Gaol for embezzlement. Furthermore, on 28th November 1894, he disobeyed a Magisterial Order for the support of his wife. A warrant was issued for his arrest.'

Hearing this summation of his character in such a damaging way, Henry leaned back in his chair and glared at his wife. Rachael for her part still refused to look at him. Mr Schrader cleared his throat. There was enough in this case to warrant an immediate separation. At this stage, he had not gone into details about the grounds for separation due to cruelty deciding that if the Magistrate could be persuaded of the unsavoury aspects of the respondent's character first, the matter could be decided upon with some rapidity. He had been horrified to hear about the tomahawk from the respondent. In his mind, there was no justification for such behaviour. The man was a menace to society and if had his way, he would be incarcerated with the sentence of hard labour and the key to the man's prison door thrown away. The bigger problem at the moment, however, was the custody of the youngest children and the question of their religious upbringing. Neither the petitioner nor the respondent could come to any agreement. It looked as if no progress could be made until this unfortunate matter could be settled.

'At the present moment,' Mr Schrader continued, 'the three youngest children, a boy and two girls are with the petitioner. The respondent, however, insists that these children be brought up in the Church of England faith. In fact, these three children are receiving their religious education from the Roman Catholic Church.'

'What about the other children?' asked the magistrate. He was somewhat vexed with the whole case which looked as if it might drag on for some time given the intransigence of both parties.

'Two of the children are grown up and have left home. Two of the others are with the respondent and living in somewhat difficult circumstances, I believe, and the three youngest are with their mother, as discussed,' answered Mr Schrader.

'I see.'

The magistrate found the case troubling. He decided to hear further evidence about the cruelty inflicted upon the petitioner before he made a judgement as to who would have custody of the children. He asked that the petitioner be called to the witness stand. Rachael had no difficulty telling the court what she had been subjected to in her twenty-six years of marriage.

'It first started for no real reason,' she said. 'He threatened to cut me up with a razor once. Then another time he pulled my hair so hard that some of it came out. He laughed that time, I recall. But the final straw was when he came at me with a tomahawk after punching me in the face. He told me he would split me in two that time. It was then that I feared for my very life, I did; all in front of my three youngest that time, poor lambs.'

She wiped a tear from her eyes with a lace handkerchief and the magistrate coughed. Henry sat, stone faced and angry, at the opposite end of the court.

‘Thank you, Mrs Price,’ the magistrate said. ‘You may step down.’

When Henry was called to the stand, he did not deny any of the accusations. He answered the questions in a monosyllabic way and appeared to be indifferent. It was then that the magistrate decided that a legal separation should be granted immediately but there was still the question of the unfortunate children. An adjournment was decided upon with a view to a settlement being arrived at. Mr Schrader, and Mr Boyce who represented Henry, discussed the matter in private. Both Henry and Rachael refused to speak to each other. Both, it seemed, preferred that their lawyers sorted it out. Both Mr Schrader and Mr Boyce, after discussing with their clients, approached the bench.

The magistrate was somewhat relieved with the discussion that had taken place.

‘A judicial separation is granted,’ he said. ‘The respondent is required to pay for the petitioner’s court costs. Furthermore, he is required to pay the petitioner permanent alimony of £1 per week. Failure to provide this will mean a hefty fine or possible imprisonment.’

‘We now come to the question of custody of the children and their religious upbringing. After considering the matter, the three youngest children will remain in the custody of their mother with her undertaking that they will attend a Protestant school or if that is not available because of location, they will instead go to a public school. They should not attend a Roman Catholic school. The older children will be with their mother. The father is granted access to the youngest girls from Saturday afternoon to Monday morning each week. The other three boys will see their father on Sunday afternoon. Case dismissed.’

When she heard that the court had ruled in her favour, Rachael took hold of Mr Schrader’s hand and shook it somewhat enthusiastically.

'Thank you, Mr Schrader,' she said. 'What a relief this is. I must say I'm not pleased with not being able to send Bert, Linda and Gladys to a Roman Catholic school but I guess it's a small price to pay if I am now free of Henry. Between ourselves, I doubt very much if he will have much time to see the children. Whether he pays me the alimony is anyone's guess. I'll just have to make do the way I always have if he doesn't. Let the cops catch up with him in time, if they can, he's a slippery bugger, is Henry. But that's another story, ain't it now?'

****

Henry was the son of Thomas Price and Sarah Jarvis. He was born in England and sailed with his parents on board the Devonport. Rachael was the fourth daughter of Henry Fuller and Margaret Maher. She was born in Tenterfield, New South Wales. They married on 5th June 1882 and were divorced on 30th June 1908. Reports from the court with details of their divorce were reported in the Evening News 29th June 1908, page 5 and in the Daily Telegraph, Sydney, Tuesday 30th June 1908, page 10.

Sadly, cases of cruelty are not uncommon to this day. Married women, and women in general, had very few legal rights in the nineteenth century and it must have taken some courage for Rachael to take Henry to court.

Rachael lived to the ripe old age of eighty-seven and is buried in Brisbane.

Henry died alone in Sydney and was buried in a pauper's grave. Not one of his many children had anything to do with him.

Henry and Rachael Price
From a family collection

When Thomas and Sarah Price decided to immigrate to Australia in the year of 1868 with their three children and with another one on the way, it must have been a decision that they did not take lightly. We can only imagine the lengthy discussions that would have taken place between them before that final decision was made and they boarded the *Devonport* to set sail for New South Wales.

Thomas was a Welshman. Born in Llanwenarth, Monmouthshire, Wales in 1833, he was the son of Peter Price, a labourer and Ann Thomas. At some point in his life, Thomas moved to the London area. A tanner, he was to work in this trade all his life. It was here in London that he met Sarah Jarvis.

Sarah was born about 1831 in Lambeth, London. Thomas and Sarah married in 1855 at Southwark, London. Their first child, a daughter, Mary Ann was born followed by their sons, Robert and Henry. The possibility of finding a better life for them in Australia was realised when the family boarded the *Devonport* on 2nd May 1868 to sail to Sydney. The sea journey was horrific. Mary Ann died of mesenteric disease.[39] Sarah gave birth to a son, Frank Kennedy Price on board the ship.

When the *Devonport* arrived in Sydney on 31st July 1868, the passengers and crew were quarantined until 10th August. Foley states on pages 69 – 70:

The cause of the quarantine, during which three people died from 'fever' and one from erysipelas, was described as 'sickness of a febrile character'. It had been a singularly frightening voyage, since the bad distribution of a heavy load of iron and cement had caused the ship to roll 'frightfully', causing a 'great deal of discomfort and no small danger'.

[39] Ships Journal, Nominal List of Deaths on Board

Between-decks had been frequently swamped with water and the quarters of the 188 single women on board was almost continually awash to the detriment of their health."[40]

It must have been with some relief that Thomas and Sarah with their children and their newborn baby were finally able to set foot on Australian soil. Thomas was a tanner and *the tannery industry had been established in Sydney from 1803*[41] and demand for tanners was high. However, as the town of Sydney grew, it became necessary to remove some of the tanneries. *In 1848 legislation was enacted for the removal of noxious industries outside city limits.*[42]

Thomas no doubt was able to find employment without much difficulty and the family settled west of Sydney at Penrith, possibly at St Marys, where the Nepean River provided water for the industry. However, it is not known which tannery he worked in or for how long.

The insecurity of employment associated with the tanning industry during this period must have been a major factor in the development of St Marys. Frequent references were made in the Nepean Times to the difficulties associated with drought (insufficient water), wet weather (inability to dry the hides), the destruction of the tanneries by fire, and the vagaries of the market (i.e. the periodic conjunction of a high price for bark and/or hides and a low price for leather). Mismanagement was cited as a problem on at least one occasion.[43]

Two more children were born to Thomas and Sarah at Penrith, Emily and George Vere. Whatever the reasons Thomas and a partner decided to operate their own tannery and consequently the family relocated to Walcha, a small township some two hundred and sixty four miles north of Sydney on the

---

[40] Sydney Morning Herald 12th August 1868, page 8 (Manly Library Local Studies
[41] Birmingham, J et al, Australian Pioneer Technology,149
[42] Birmingham, J et al, Australian Pioneer Technology, 148
[43] Nepean Times May 1882 (Drought)

New England Tableland. It was here that Thomas sustained a terrible injury that caused his death in 1884.

Widowed Sarah found employment at a hotel in Armidale where she was to meet Scotsman John McAlister, a sailor turned farmer. The couple were married for twenty-four years until he was killed in an accident with a sulky. Widowed twice, she was to live on the farm at Daisy Hill for the rest of her life. Sarah died in 1913 at Armidale.

Daisy Hill, Wollomombi, New South Wales
From the McRae family collection

John and Sarah's farm at Daisy Hill, Wollombi, New South Wales
From a collection of Dorothy Griffey

Of all the children of Thomas and Sarah perhaps it is Henry, always known as Harry in the family, who would have caused them the most grief. Henry married Rachael Fuller when he was just twenty years of age. Their eldest son, William Henry died from diphtheria at the age of six. Then they lost their sixth child, William George from acute bronchitis in 1917.

The relationship between Henry and all his children must have totally broken down at that stage. William George named his mother a beneficiary in his will with no mention of his father.[44] Various letters from the Army to Rachael after the death of William George wishing to know the whereabouts of Henry were unsuccessful. Rachael had divorced Henry in 1908.

From the World War 1 Army file: *In March 1917, the*

[44] National Archives of Australia NAA:B2455 Price, William George Next of Kin: (Mother) Rachel Mary

pensioner states she was living apart from her husband, whom it was understood was then in America. It is not known whether or not her husband is still living... The Army could not trace him so agreed for medals to go to Rachael Mary.[45] A pension was granted to Rachael for her son's Army service on 11th August 1924.

Henry was to die in in 1933 in the Liverpool Hospital, Sydney and was buried in a pauper's grave at the Liverpool Cemetery and Crematorium.[46]

All the emigrant families the world over who made a new life for themselves left stories to pass on. The legacy that Thomas and Sarah Price leave to their descendants is one of strength through adversity for their own lives had much sorrow.

---

45 WW1 Army Records for William George Price 21 April 1923 Page 25

46 Liverpool Cemetery and Crematorium Pauper Burial Ground 10, Grave 054

ABOUT THE AUTHOR

Iona Carroll is the author of the Oisin Kelly novels about the life of an Irishman whose adventures take him from Ireland to Australia.

Her literary career started as a librarian and teacher. She has led creative writing workshops with the emphasis on short story writing. For many years she was joint editor of the Scottish Borders Council's literary magazine, *The Eildon Tree.*

An Australian, she now lives in the Scottish Borders with her husband and wire-haired dachshund, Millie.

http://www.ionacarroll.com

ABOUT SILVER QUILL

Silver Quill Publishing

Silver Quill Publishing is an established publishing group producing fabulous books for children, teens, young – and not so young – adults. Take a look at our website, meet our authors and browse through the titles we have to offer.
Every book is a thrill with Silver Quill.

www.silverquillpublishing.com

Printed in Great Britain
by Amazon

42946416R00182